THE BITTER TASTE OF TIME

Also by Béa Gonzalez

The Mapmaker's Opera

THE BITTER TASTE OF TIME

A NOVEL

BÉA GONZALEZ

THOMAS DUNNE BOOKS
ST. MARTIN'S PRESS NEW YORK

FOR MAMÁ & PAPÁ

This is a work of fiction. All of the characters, organizations, and events portrayed in this novel are either products of the author's imagination or are used fictitiously.

THOMAS DUNNE BOOKS.
An imprint of St. Martin's Press.

Library of Congress Cataloging-in-Publication Data

Gonzalez, Béa.
The bitter taste of time : a novel / Béa Gonzalez.—1st U.S. ed.
p. cm.
ISBN-13: 978-0-312-36467-0
ISBN-10: 0-312-36467-9
1. Women—Fiction. 2. Extended families—Fiction. 3. Boardinghouses—Fiction. 4. Spain, Northern—Fiction. 5. Spain—History—20th century—Fiction. I. Title.

PR9199.4.G668 B58 2008
813'.6—dc22

2008024934

First published in Canada by Harper Perennial Canada,
an imprint of HarperCollins Publishers Ltd.

First U.S. Edition: October 2008

10 9 8 7 6 5 4 3 2 1

Tell me a story.
In this century, and moment, of mania,
Tell me a story.

Make it a story of great distances, and starlight.

The name of the story will be Time,
But you must not pronounce its name.

Tell me a story of deep delight.

—Robert Penn Warren

THE BITTER TASTE OF TIME

PROLOGUE

Canteira, Spain, 1997

By early morning a throng had congregated to watch the scene unfold—the old women arriving first, dressed in their customary black, a speck of grey flickering in the odd blouse, a hint of green emerging from a shawl wrapped around an aged back, the young appearing later, excited, teasing each other in strident tones and insistent laughs, ignoring their mothers' admonitions to *be silent,* for this was no time for silence when look, *mamá*, *mira*, things are crumbling, the sky is closing in around us, the world as we know it is falling apart. Before them stood the demolition crew—tired-looking men dressed in blue jeans and dusty cotton shirts—smoking some of them, all of them amused by the expectation that was weaving its way through the crowd, the old lamenting already what they were about to witness, the young revelling in the excitement of what was to come.

The Encarna and Hope Hotel, once the most important building in Canteira back in the days of the Dictator—*the good old days* to some, the days of unbearable ignorance to most—would be the first to come crashing down. For the most part, abandoned buildings were left to wilt slowly, to fall apart bit by bit until they were nothing but carcasses, shells of concrete and granite that litter the outskirts of many a town and village of modern Spain.

This building stood on one of the prettiest spots in town, bordering the *balneario* that had once attracted so many people to its doors, *madrileños* and *sevillanos* dressed in impeccable white shirts, arriving here in search of a cure for all their diseases of the liver and the skin in the sulphuric waters of the *balneario*'s hot springs. But that was back in the old days, when people still believed in such things, when a spa provided the consolation that today arrived in tinctures and pills, in the days when people shied away from eating salad, convinced that it would worsen their arthritis and somehow darken their skins. In those days, the town bustled and boomed. Today, the town of Canteira boomed no more.

It had been the last of the great Encarnas—Gloria Encarna—who had bequeathed to the town the land on which the hotel stood. To be converted into a park, a glorious natural enclosure that would bear the name of her beloved son Artur. *Artur Encarna.* Gone over a decade ago now but remembered clearly still. Years after it had shattered the calm of a sleepy Tuesday night, his death remained the talk of the town, the story told as if it had happened just yesterday, the whys and the wherefores unclear even now, after so much time had passed.

Those in the town hall, responsible for approving such things, had been fiercely opposed to naming the park after him. Could imagine already the outcry that would arise from the townspeople at the prospect of seeing that name engraved in the regional colours of white and blue. For weeks, they had explored the ways they could avoid doing so, debated the merits, consulted the experts, wrestled and wrangled with the legalities of the affair. It had been Don Pastor, the town mayor, who had finally come up with the solution. *Name it after the other Arthur,* he had said. *Sí, hombre, he of the round table and the many splendid ideals.* A Celtic king for a Celtic corner of Spain—a poetic land lost inside the mist of its valleys, the lushness of its hills, the splendour of its ten thousand winding rivers and glorious streams.

That night, those in Canteira who could still remember would sit down to rattle off the names of the other Encarnas one by one. María *la Reina,* first of all. The matriarch, founder of the hotel back when the town still attracted people from across the region and beyond. Her sisters, Carmen the Holy One—a saint surely, one of the most religious women to have been born in this town—and Cecilia, fat as a bull, but what a storyteller, eh? A better one could not have been found. María's daughters, Matilde, her heart as pure as gold, and Asunción, lost forever in a world of her own. And finally, the last of the great Encarna women, Asunción's daughter Gloria, the most entrepreneurial of them all, smarter than a thousand scholars, but as harsh as the winds that battered the town during endless winter months.

Those who could still remember stood there now, watched in silence as the hotel came tumbling down in one resounding crash, the sight of it stinging their eyes, the sound jarring their senses, the taste of it searing the tips of their tongues.

The Encarna and Hope Hotel was gone forever now. That was how the great fell, how the old order tumbled and was no more. In mere moments all that was left was the rubble, the bits and pieces of the majestic building that had stood at the centre of this once vibrant town.

Amén, an old woman whispered. The last word in many a story. The last word to be said when all other words have been uttered and hands are clasped in prayer.

PART ONE

1920–1930

LATER, AFTER YEARS HAD PASSED AND THEY ALL HAD THE benefit of hindsight, they would comment on how truly strange Asunción Encarna had been from the start. A curious bird. As unpredictable as a goat. As peculiar as all those foreigners who arrived on the coasts of Spain dressed in gingham shorts and knee-high socks.

The roots of this peculiarity—the one that years later would have her collecting clocks in all shapes and sizes—they traced back to the events at the train station on a Friday in 1920. It was there that her husband of two short months, Manuel Pousada—*a lunatic himself*, one was quick to comment, *a criminal of the worst kind*, another added—aware that gossips loomed all around them and eager to avoid a scene during these, their final moments together, had tried in vain to stem her tears, silence her pleas, keep her from making a public spectacle of herself.

But then, he never loved her, they would say later. *No, not for one moment did he seem sad to leave her.*

Manuel Pousada and Asunción Encarna were at the station that day so that Manuel could take the train to the coast. From there, he would be boarding the ship to Brazil. *Brazil.* How long he had waited for this. The word rested sensuously on his tongue, the thought of it seemed like heaven. His wife's tears, her adolescent tantrums, jarred him now that the dream seemed so close at hand, now that his mind was already lost in the thought of much better things, on the stories he had heard from all those who had gone before him and had returned with gold and women and especially with the heat—*sí*, especially the heat, which they captured and brought back with them, and which glinted in their eyes and shone in their hair and glowed in their habit of walking with erect shoulders forever after.

And then one more kiss, one last backward look, a shake of the head, and he was gone, into the train and away from her life. And more tears and more anguish, and the promise—*Cariño,* he had said, *it is only a matter of time now.*

It would indeed be a matter of time before Asunción heard news of him, and then only after showering a mountain of abuse on the archaic and inefficient postal system of the region and the half-witted man in charge, who cried real tears of desperation because of it. When the letter finally arrived, she shared its contents with no one, stopping only to fold it neatly into its four parts once it had been read and announcing to all that her husband had now joined the ranks of the dearly departed.

Three months later, in August of 1920, after a long day and an even longer night, their daughter Gloria was born. In the room with Asunción, accompanying her through every heave and every push, were her mother María, her sister Matilde, and her aunts Carmen and Cecilia. There too was Doña Emilia, the town's midwife, and the two old women who accompanied all of the women in Canteira through the mysteries of labour, Doña Teresa and Doña Elena—greatly respected for having delivered eight healthy babies apiece, and eager to tell the story of each of those births as a way of reminding everyone that childbirth, fraught with so many dangers, could as often as not produce healthy, happy children.

Outside, the town of Canteira was as silent as the stars with only the occasional sound rising here and there to punctuate the night—the whelp of a dog, the gasping spasms of a donkey, the odd distant and disembodied voice emerging from the hills which appeared purple and bruised in the encroaching darkness. It was a hot night, one of the hottest of that year. The large windows in the bedroom had been left open, but the warm breeze that drifted in did little to alleviate the oppressive humidity. For months before the birth, Asunción had remained closeted in this room, grieving for her dead husband and praying for the health of her unborn child. There, at least, she was thought to be safe from the many dangers that lurked outside, like the moon—the source of inspiration to many a haunted poet, but which pregnant women avoided, believing that to look at it would be to risk giving birth to an idiot.

As the labour progressed, and Asunción's screams grew shriller, her discomfort greater, Doña Teresa and Doña Elena interrupted their stories to implore the midwife to take some extraordinary measures.

Bring us a pair of her husband's pants or one of his hats, Doña Teresa said between two particularly strong contractions. *There is no surer way to calm the pain than with some of the father's clothing. May he rest in peace*, she added quickly, crossing herself as she did so.

A prayer to San Ramón will do the trick, Doña Elena said. *The prayers I myself uttered can scarcely be counted.*

María, Asunción's mother, an imposing woman with little respect for the sayings of the people, for all the crazy ideas that circulated through town, the fears of the dead and the superstitions that held so many hostage, dismissed the suggestions of these women with an impatient wave of her hand.

She turned now to her sister Cecilia—a nervous, emotional woman, who would punctuate every contraction and accompanying scream with a furious *Dios mío*—ordering her to *boil some more water in the kitchen*—a command she issued more to rid the room of her sister than because any water was actually needed.

Later, it would be Cecilia who would tell the story of the birth, exaggerating and embellishing the details to such an extent that eventually no one who had been there could distinguish between what they could remember and the inventions of Cecilia's feverish mind. What was true, irrefutable because it had become a part of the history of the town itself, was that Gloria had been born into a world full of women. It was not only that her father had perished in an unimaginable and distant land before her birth, but that he had left his wife behind in the care of her mother, two aunts, and a younger sister. What was also true was that Asunción had almost perished from the effort, all the pushing and the pulling, all the tears, all the desperate screams. The screams had been heard, in fact, as far away as the region of Castile—this, again, according to Cecilia, who had held Asunción's hand through most of the ordeal, attempting to ease her pain by forcing almost two full glasses of *aguardiente* into her mouth, but carefully, one drop at a time, until Asunción had grown drunk and delusional from the devastating combination of liquor, longing and pain.

It is during childbirth that you discover love, Asunción would tell them all afterwards, once the child had been born and she was so overwhelmed with grief that she was sure she had caught a glimpse of Manuel, hovering over her like a dark, unforgiving angel. In her drunken stupor, she had slurred his name so many times and with such a deep feeling that the women had been reduced to a heap of tears and even Edelmiro, the barnyard help, who had never loved and never lost, even he had felt as if there were a hole inside his stomach too, created by the acidic vapours of such an intense and unfulfilled yearning.

At least it is a girl. The child's grandmother was the first to say it. Her two sisters, Cecilia and Carmen, and her daughter Matilde had thought this too but had refrained from uttering what could only have been said by a grandmother. María said this only after her daughter Asunción had ceased crying—only after three weeks of her sobbing did María say this, and then only to bring to the house a well-needed tone of order.

She had always mistrusted the child's father, Manuel Pousada. Insolent eyes; unspeakable desires. No better than a peasant traipsing into their lives, without thought or forewarning, seducing her daughter in one single furtive morning.

But now there was this newborn, his newborn, a girl of white marble. *Cabrón* she thought uncharitably. Another man lost to the other world where he could walk unencumbered by memory or obligation. Amidst her cursing, though, it occurred to María, not for the first time, that Manuel's death had perhaps not been an altogether bad thing.

Many days passed after the baby's birth before the rhythm of the house was restored to its proper order—before the women could return to the work that fed and clothed them in a world where money was always an uncertain prospect. For years the women had survived by providing room and board to the many travellers who passed through town on their way to the coast.

In those days Canteira bustled and boomed with the machinations of illegal commerce. Situated in the heart of the Spanish region of Galicia, between the Atlantic coast and the border with León, the town was the resting stop for the endless stream of *contrabandistas* who travelled through at first on horseback and later inside Renaults and Peugeots, on their way to the coast to retrieve the goods that would be peddled in the dark cities of the Spanish interior.

The country as a whole had by then fully declined into a slothful decay. One by one, the colonies that remained in the Americas had reclaimed their independence from the incompetent central government of Spain. After 1898, all that remained were bitter words scribbled by a generation of writers bleeding their shame into the gaping wound the colonies left in their wake. All Spain could boast of now were greedy landowners, fattened Jesuits, disgruntled miners biding their time till they could stand up against the owners of the fetid hellholes where they worked themselves into an early grave.

In Galicia things were worse. Long forgotten by the central powers of Spain, no easy path led people to this remote region of the country, no reason existed to travel to this poverty-ridden chunk of the world. In this northwest bit of the Iberian peninsula, the only constant visitor was the rain, which made lettuce flourish and pastures unbearably beautiful, but delivered interminable nights of darkness so that depression was more common here than in all of Spain. More green than Ireland, more melancholic than a thousand Romantic poets, the region was lauded for its otherworldly beauty. Her people, though, were more often than not dismissed as illiterate peasants by their fellow countrymen and by the odd visitor from other lands, who arrived brandishing Bibles and preaching conversion from the sins of popery—

only to find that it was not the Church of Rome that reigned supreme in the small towns and even smaller villages here, but superstitious beliefs of forest gods, black witches, and lascivious wolfmen, a legacy, like the bagpipes and stone hilltop forts, of the region's Celtic ancestry.

Canteira itself was a beautiful town even then—long before concrete and hotels had turned it into a vibrant, bustling affair, in the days before emigrant remittances, miniature cathedrals and five-day fiestas with virgins decked in gold and pearls—even then the town was an astounding sight, surrounded by the most beautiful natural scenery in all of the region, framed in summer by a night sky of infinite stars and a moon that gleamed like brittle porcelain.

It was María who had conceived of the idea of turning their house into a *pensión*. It was an enormous house, built by their uncle Ignacio who had left for Mexico when barely a boy and returned a decade later, a man straight and true, tall, handsome, and richer than he had ever imagined in his childhood dreams. He had built the house with the intention of marrying quickly and filling it with ten joyful children who would shower him with devotion and love. He was a happy man—perhaps the last happy man to be born to that family—and his infectious optimism blinded him to the climatic limitations of this corner of Spain, so that he built a house more appropriate to Andalucía, where the sun shines uninterrupted for months on end. The Galician workmen—ordinarily taciturn and sombre, suspicious of anyone who thought of the world as anything other than a vat of pain—were instantly seduced by Don Ignacio's enthusiasm, and grew to believe that the house he had designed in his head, complete with giant courtyard and a stone fountain decorated with cherubim carved in the south of Spain, would somehow defy the dreariness of Galicia's dark winter days. When the house was finally finished, Don Ignacio stood back and sighed in contentment. What he saw was a handsome rectangular mansion made from granite carved by the talented masons of the town, with eight bedrooms, four on the west wing of the house, four on the east, a sizable kitchen decorated with Portuguese blue and white tile, and at the front, the room he loved most of all, a parlour large enough to accommodate twenty people or more, heated in winter by a handsome wood-burning stove that radiated enough warmth to reach the many rooms that lay behind it on either side. Built on the outskirts of town, on a beautiful piece of land covered with apple, fig, and cherry trees, framed in the west by a bubbling creek and in the north by the splendour of Canteira's rolling hills, the house would soon become the envy of all who passed by on their way through town.

Sadly, Don Ignacio would not live long enough to fill the house with children, would not even live long enough to find a suitable wife, succumbing shortly afterwards to the typhus epidemic that took the lives of so many during the long winter of 1881. So it was that the house ended up in the hands of his younger brother, the father of María, Carmen, and Cecilia—a weak man who possessed none of the ebullience that had made Don Ignacio so loved in town, and who, despite all of his earnest efforts, was unable to produce a male heir who would survive the trauma of being brought into the world—a fact that he used to justify his wasted existence and the copious abuse he heaped on his wife. By the time he died, just months after María's marriage to Arturo Pérez Barreiro, the house had fallen into a state of pathetic disrepair, the paint on the walls eaten by the humidity, the wooden floors in various stages of decay.

It would take years of labour to set the house to rights again but María possessed all the determination that her own father had lacked and had a firm hand with her sisters besides. Carmen and Cecilia would remain unmarried, resigning themselves to assuming their respective places in the house, Cecilia taking charge of things in the kitchen and Carmen tending to the animals and managing the work in the fields. Two daughters were born in rapid succession to María—Asunción and then Matilde. Eight years later, her husband, not yet thirty years old, was dead. Faced with the uncertainty of a life without the income Arturo had derived as one of the town's schoolmasters, the sisters opened the house up to strangers a year later, offering beds made with sheets embroidered in Camariñas, wine from the Ribeiro Valley, and regional dishes cooked under the guidance of Cecilia—an enormous woman by then, driven to fat by a feverish, inexplicable hunger that she assuaged with *chorizo*, loaves of fresh bread, and, during the fall, pound upon pound of roasted chestnuts. Later, once Cecilia had passed away, Gloria made it a habit to take *chorizo* from the yearly slaughters to her great-aunt's grave where it disappeared shortly thereafter, eaten by the wolves or a graveyard loiterer—but really, Gloria believed, inhaled by Cecilia herself, who lay lonely and hungry inside her kitchenless coffin of black walnut and crushed velvet inlay.

Barely a week had passed after Gloria's birth when three guests arrived on horseback at the doors of the *pensión*.

Catalanes, Cecilia told the others in her best conspiratorial tone. *You can tell by their funny way of talking and because their shirt sleeves hang like curtains.*

The *Catalanes*, three men in their late twenties, perturbed to find themselves in a house full of so many women—*A newly arrived one too*, one of the men told the others, *though you can't tell yet; it's only when their eyes open up to swallow you whole that you can tell they've finally become women*—stayed there nonetheless, too tired to search for other accommodation. Later, once they had downed enough Ribeiro wine to cure themselves of their initial bashfulness, they sang songs, told stories, and hummed to the new baby in a futile attempt to rid her of her sadness.

The following morning, Jordí, the tall Catalan with the eagle eyes—the one whose singing voice they would recall for years after because it was a deep, lush baritone that reminded them of the processions of the dead at midnight—handed the women a bit of Belgian lace, telling them it was *for the child, señoras, for her baptismal robe.* María, unaccustomed to this sort of generosity from strangers, and especially strangers from a part of the country she disliked for no particular reason, took the lace, smiling for the first time since their arrival. Later, she would comment that it augured well to have these guests—three *Catalanes* no less—offering gifts to the newborn on this, the longest night of the year, because it was August, and August nights were good only for the tortures of memory.

Three months passed before the lace was attached to the linen that became the baptismal robe, three months too long for the parish priest, Don José, who warned the women of the torturous limbo that awaited the child were she to suffer the great misfortune of dying before receiving the touch of God upon her forehead.

That man is an animal in black robes, María told the others one night, as he approached her on his way to evening mass with yet another dire warning. María was still nursing the wounds inflicted by the death of her husband, Arturo Pérez Barreiro, a kind, gentle man who had descended slowly into an overwhelming unhappiness until the day he could take no more and, standing on a pine stool in the kitchen, hanged himself next to the salt-cured hams and cloves of garlic. He left a note, his words scribbled in the slanted way of those who know death is imminent, and the words engraved themselves on her heart until the day she died when she too, remembered to repeat them.

The flesh is willing, cariño, but the heart cannot go on.

It was her sister Cecilia who stumbled upon the body, swaying gently from the rafters, propelled by a soft summer breeze, the face grey and drawn from all the effort of a self-inflicted annihilation. The smell of Arturo's dead body would follow her everywhere thereafter, driving her into a fury of culinary experimentation with exotic herbs and spices that she used in copious amounts, hoping that their pungency would overwhelm the persistent and seductive odour of self-destruction.

Don José fought long and hard with María over the issue of a Christian burial for Arturo, arguing that God would not receive this unrepentant sinner into sacred ground, and depicting all manner of natural catastrophes that would be visited upon them should they try such a thing, until María, enraged with grief and longing, finally took the good priest by the collar, saying, *Don't think I don't know about those late night meetings with your political enamorados because I do, you bastard wretch.* Don José—scared more for his future in the tumultuous political climate of the time than of any dire retribution from the Lord—forgave Arturo Pérez Barreiro's sins on the spot, even going so far as to deliver an effusive eulogy at the funeral, never once taking his eyes off the widow, who looked at him fixedly and without emotion for the duration of the mass.

It was only after the baptism of Gloria, held on a cold

November day, that the house seemed fully restored to its normal order. That very night, Don Miguel, the Andalusian with the green eyes, long black hair, and the bearing of an aristocrat, arrived at their doors seeking accommodation. Dressed head to toe in black and tall—*as big as a Scandinavian,* Carmen told the others, though in truth she had never seen a Scandinavian—Don Miguel appeared to them in a haze of mystery. Instead of the usual collection of odds and ends carried by the *contrabandistas* on their way to the coast, the Andalusian carried books and vials and bottles filled with liquids that shone in the candlelight. Instead of the usual chatter of *I'm going to Vigo, señoras, and my wife's name is Teresa, just like the virgin of San Roca,* instead of the familiar talk of lonely men on the road, Don Miguel said little, issuing only the odd terse instruction to María about dietary preferences—*meat cooked rare, fish broiled always with onions. And, por favor, señora, more candles in the bedroom.*

The man looks like the devil incarnate, Cecilia commented to the others in a hushed whisper that very night, scared because of his height, the colour of his eyes, and his habit of wearing so much black, a privilege she had always believed belonged exclusively to unhappy women.

After a week had passed and Don Miguel continued to stay at the house, saying little and shunning all contact with anything but his books, which he read until the early hours of the morning, the women began to grow suspicious.

Look here, sisters, Carmen said one day to the others. *No one stays in this town longer than a day. After all, what is there to do here? What if this man is a criminal of some kind?*

Or worse, a violador—a rapist, Cecilia added, scaring herself so much that her chest heaved unnaturally for the rest of the day whenever the thought surfaced to torment her.

If you ask me, he is a lonely man, no more, said Asunción, who had been released partially from the depression of her husband's death by the distraction provided by Don Miguel, and who was feeling considerably more sympathetic towards him.

It was Cecilia though, tormented by the unhappy thought of an imminent and collective violation, who finally broke down and approached him.

And where is it that you are going, Don Miguel? she asked him, well into his second week at the house, as she served him a dinner of stewed pork and tomatoes.

Why do you assume I am going somewhere? Don Miguel said, not bothering to look at her.

Everybody is on their way to somewhere when they stop in this town, señor.

And I am not, he said, and buried his head in his meal, indicating thus that he would be saying no more.

But that very night, over a glass of *aguardiente*, as they all came together around the heat of the wood stove, the Andalusian finally broke his vow of silence and began telling them stories—of places he had been and people he had met, such stories that the women's imaginations blazed for weeks and months afterwards—travellers' tales and bits of poetry, recited softly by the light of white candles, words that enthralled the women into sleepless nights and days of endless rumination. Despite their many attempts to glean from these stories even the most minute detail of Don Miguel's own history, the women learned little about him except for a few of his favourite foods, his love for the poetry of Rosalía de Castro, and his strange habit of humming an unfamiliar tune to himself while he disposed of his breakfast in the morning.

For three weeks they repeated this routine, sitting around the heat of the wood stove, the women embroidering—all except for María, whose eyes had always been too weak to distinguish between tulips and camellias—and Don Miguel telling his tales. There, the women learned of faraway lands like Germany, inhabited, Don Miguel would tell them in his slow Andalusian drawl, by blond giants who spoke in grunts and barbaric growls.

But then Spanish, señoras, is the only language appropriate for the longings of the Lord.

Amén, the women would utter in unison, proud of their connection to such a holy tongue but unsure of what he really meant, because they had never heard another language except for Catalan and it was their distinct impression that Catalan was an invention of the people of the northeast to exclude them from their world and therefore not a language at all but a form of snobbery. There too, they learned of happenings in all the corners of Europe and stories of their own country, of Andalusian gypsies and Basque pastors and Madrid intellectuals who wrote poetry celebrated in countries they had never heard of.

On the dreariest nights, the nights when the winds blew most fiercely and the rain pelted the roof of the house with an insistence that seemed almost menacing, Don Miguel would take advantage of the women's incipient fear to tell the darkest, most disturbing stories in his repertoire. It was on a night like this that Don Miguel sat down to his customary glass of *aguardiente* and related one such tale, one they would remember for years, instilling such a fear of cats in the women, that they never allowed one in the house thereafter.

In the heart of Castile, he began, *in one of those towns that seem to have been abandoned by God, where even the dogs look like ghosts and where the only people to emerge in the dark are a legion of deformed, miserable beggars, lives Jacobo*

Ortega, a wealthy merchant, one of the wealthiest of the area though one whose wealth has always been rumoured to be founded on many a shady dealing. I always stay with him on my way through town, as did my own father in the days when he himself travelled through there doing his business.

It was my father who noticed their cat—a large, mangy thing with a vicious disposition and the ability to look right into your very soul. My father could remember seeing that cat on the first day he had stayed there, perched on a chair in the parlour, surveying his surroundings with careful attention. When I started travelling with him and we stayed in that house together for the first time, my father pointed the cat out to me. There, he told me, is an animal that has been around at least as long as I have.

I was curious about this creature; after all, it is strange that a cat should live so long, and he looked in excellent shape given what must have been his age. That night, at dinner, I asked the owner of the house about it. "Don Jacobo, how long has this cat been in the family?"

"This cat?" asked Don Jacobo, laughing and pointing to the animal, who seemed to be staring at me now with an even greater dose of his usual malice. "This cat, my dear friend, has been in this family since the days of my own grandfather."

That was impossible, of course! No cat could live so long—unless the strange creature was not a cat at all but something much more sinister. I could feel the hair on the back of my neck stand on end as I thought of the only one who could have been loitering in this house for so long now. The cat, as if sensing my suspicions, now attempted to intimidate me with an even fiercer gaze.

I asked that some holy water, kept at the front of the house, be brought to me. Don Jacobo laughed at my request, but humoured me nonetheless. "You're not thinking of conjuring up some of your Andalusian witchery in this house, are you, my dear man? Surely you know what we think of that nonsense in Castile, Don Miguel," he said to me, laughing still.

The people of the house had by now congregated in the parlour and were laughing with Don Jacobo, who handed me a glass of the holy water and introduced me to the company with a dramatic swing of his arms. "Señores and señoras, before you now is the newly appointed court magician."

I took the glass of holy water, ignoring their laughter. The cat seemed poised to strike at me, his body perched and taut, his eyes daring me to attack him. I dipped my fingers into the holy water and sprinkled some of it on the cat's head.

"Stop that!" the cat screamed immediately. "You're burning me!"

I sprinkled some more holy water on him. "I said stop that!" he screeched again, shuddering at the touch of God upon his neck.

"What are you doing here?" I asked him, my hands wrapped tightly around that glass of water. The people of the house were now silent, riveted by our exchange.

The cat laughed malevolently. "Waiting for those in the house to die," he spat out. "Those who have died here before have already joined me."

Satanás! The women dropped their embroidery at this point, their gasps punctuating the night. Only María remained impervious to the drama in this story, though it was she who ordered the women to be silent so that Don Miguel could go on with his tale.

Satanás, of course Satanás, dear ladies. His devious ways are too numerous to count. I took the rest of the holy water and poured it over the cat in one single dose, after which he evap-

orated in a billow of smoke but not before promising to return once more.

And then Don Miguel was laughing, telling lighter stories, a comic tale of infidelity from Barcelona, a tale of two thieves from Madrid. But it was the story of the cat that the women would remember, that would keep them awake that night, their eyes searching for signs of the devil in the dark. From then on, no cat would ever be viewed with anything but suspicion and even María would feel uncomfortable in the company of the many strays that roamed the fields around their house.

Every night brought a new story, a new reason to look forward to the after-dinner chats. Sometimes it was poetry he recited. From Bécquer, wondrous words of love—

What is poetry? you say
As you fix my eyes with your eyes of blue
What is poetry . . . you ask me that?
Poetry . . . it is you!

Words that scorched the hearts of the women, tantalized them with the thought that such feelings could emerge from the minds of men. Words that upset María, though, words that made her uncomfortable, that inevitably led her to complain—*Don Miguel*, she would ask, shaking her head reproachfully whenever he launched into a stanza or two, *are these the words for decent women?*

Ay, Doña María, he would respond, laughing, *these are the words that heal all wounds.*

Those were memorable days for the women, unaccustomed as they were to any excitement except the excitement of death, and they quickly grew used to these late night gatherings around the wood stove, Don Miguel's melodious voice silencing the howls of the wind outside, his stories thrilling them when they recalled them as they tended to their many chores in the morning.

It was with dismay, then, that they reacted to the news, a month later, that Don Miguel would finally be leaving. For a week after his departure, the women told and retold the stories, imitating his slow Andalusian drawl and his habits of inflection, until María finally put an end to such talk by screaming, *Basta ya! Enough of these stories,* worried that they were descending into a sort of communal madness from which they would never emerge.

But it was already too late for Matilde. Matilde of the huge heart and the gentle eyes inherited from her dead great-uncle Ignacio. Matilde, so plain of face, so pallid in the light of her sister's beauty. Matilde, who had been fading for some years now, relegated to the background with her mother's unmarried sisters. But she was now awakened—and emboldened, her mother thought. Where was the source of Matilde's new fervour? Only the devil could give birth to such things. The devil and cavorting with mysterious men in the darkness.

Matilde, what are you doing sitting there alone in the candlelight Matilde? her mother asked, worried to no end about her daughter's newly found radiance.

It was not Don Miguel's stories that had granted definition to the once shadowy Matilde, but the stomach pain he inspired, brought on by years of longing, first for a father and then for a purpose to her days, but now for him, for this man in black who had traipsed in for no other apparent reason than to awaken her to the power of the morning.

It was his hands that drew her to him at first—the way they held a glass of wine, the certainty with which they told a story; then, suddenly it was his eyes, so green, so full of mysteries that she thought she could read a thousand tales with a million different endings in those eyes, and she entertained herself with divining each and every one of them. At night, he appeared to her in dreams, a shadowy figure beckoning and then disappearing into the strange nooks and crannies of her feverish imagination.

One word, she thought. One word from you, Miguel, and I will find meaning in this small, relentless existence, in the pain of being cursed with a plain face, of having been abandoned by God in the middle of nowhere. One word, and I will see myself differently, climb mountains, write the words you whisper to us—*tristeza,* you say, *there is nothing as beautiful as sadness.* One word and I will finally be me, and not this empty thing that speaks to no one, that is afraid, that thinks of death during the unbearable hour between eleven and midnight—one word and I will be whole again and not half, the half which has been left by itself to wander.

Finally, when she thought she could bear it no longer and had exhausted herself with the intensity of her emotions, Matilde worked up the courage to approach him, but only after preparing herself to ask the innocent questions that would justify her intrusion: *Do you need a change of sheets, señor? How about some water?* And so on, mundane questions, the kind that would force him to turn around and distinguish her from the mass of women who surrounded him in that household.

In the end, though, the question that emerged was an altogether different one.

Do you want to see the prettiest spot in all of Canteira? she asked, fumbling immediately with the hem of her apron and fighting the overwhelming urge to burst into tears, for what could this man possibly want with the prettiest spot in Canteira when he had travelled the world and seen remarkable things, the things he described in his slow seductive Andalusian drawl: *Mujeres,* he had said, *there lies the world beckoning to you,* and there she stood, Matilde with her childish question, as outside the sun shone with the intensity of a thousand mornings.

But *sí*, he responded. *Sí*, he said, yes and yes, and then nothing else with his mouth but she was sure with his eyes he was saying other things. She was sure with his eyes he was saying, I know about you, about your loneliness, about your father's sadness on the occasion of your birth and your mother's emotional absence. I know it was your sister Asunción who shone the brightest. I know these things and others, the things that hide inside the crevices of your mind, the things that haunt you in the darkness. So give me your hand, Matilde, give me your hand and let me put you at the top of the world where you belong, and not here in the periphery of the night sky, dancing alone to the tune of a distant longing.

They walked there later that day, but only after Matilde had looked well behind her, making sure her mother was busy with tending to the animals, and her aunt Cecilia was labouring over the cooking for the household, and her sister Asunción, the sister with the alabaster skin and the eyes that hinted at a never-ending seduction, was occupied with the baby. The evening sky was red that night—she would remember the colour and the intensity for the rest of her life, would summon the memory during long days and nights of uncertainty—the squishing of their feet the only sound they made as they walked through the winding path to the edge of the forest.

Matilde had stumbled upon the spot when only eight years

old, at the time when she was losing her father to the profound sadness that would eventually kill him. She had stumbled upon the prettiest spot by accident, on a bright summer day, and it was the rock that had beckoned to her—a magical rock, a rock built by time, that jutted sharply from the ground to greet the sky. On the rock she traced with her fingers what someone had engraved there: a woman's head with hair made of coiling snakes and a six-pointed star and the mysterious words *anima mundi*. That very night, she had told her father of the rock as she had washed his feet and he had stared into the ceiling catatonic. She had told him about the woman with the serpent hair and the star, and she was sure that in the night of his lost stare, her father's eyes had registered something.

When Matilde and Don Miguel reached the spot, the prettiest spot in all of Canteira because from there the whole world was at their fingertips, the brook that lulled her to sleep in the afternoons, the ruminations of the animals and in the west, in the distance, the hills of Orense, hills that could be mistaken for mountains they were so majestic—when they reached the spot and Don Miguel had run his fingers along her magical rock and inspected every fleck and dot upon it, he had finally looked at her, not with the careless eyes of one who has seen everything, but with the eyes that appeared inside her dreams, eyes that beckoned and promised, eyes, above all, that recognized the living, breathing being inside of her, the genius who had found the mountain.

But then he was leaving and there was no special good-bye, no look, no furtive touch on a bare arm, no hidden message. Instead, he gave her one of his books, a leather-bound, ponderous tome full of so many words that she thought she would go mad just contemplating them. But nothing said, no explanation, no answer to the questions that had been tormenting her nightly.

After he had disappeared, leaving her devastated, she read each and every one of the words in that book over and over again in the slow, careful way she had been taught by Doña Gertrudes, reading forwards and backwards until she could recite entire passages from memory word for word, without even an inkling of their true meaning, reading the book over and over again in a futile attempt to glean the message she felt sure was hiding there. And then one day, finally, on page 159 there it was: *amor,* she read, the love of learning is the great answer. But it was only after a year of torturous rereadings that the word finally reached out to her, igniting a passion that would fill her days forever after.

From then on, she searched the town for every book she could find, and then paid *contrabandistas* to bring books from the coast, which arrived wrapped in foreign newsprint smelling of cod and ripe tomatoes—all of this she did to the utter chagrin of her mother, who warned her of the dangers that lay inside the pages of all the leather-bound volumes. *Books, Matilde, are the temptations of the devil himself,* María would tell her, worrying about what would happen to her household due to the obsessions of her ridiculous daughter, the one who looked the most like her husband, a resemblance that brought such pain to her heart that María had stopped looking at Matilde years ago.

Later, once Matilde had entered her sixth decade of life, holding enough words in her heart to circle the earth a thousand times, she would give talks to the young children in town about the beauty of metaphors, the music of poetry, the tranquillity of a world unsullied by smell, by the absence of touch, by the overwhelming pain of never being looked at by your own mother.

María knew she was not liked by the townspeople of Canteira. *Sí, hombre*, of course she knew it. The way they looked at her, the stories they told—of Arturo, especially, of how her husband had hanged himself on a Friday in July, and next to the hams no less. What dignity, they asked, could there possibly be in a man who chose death next to the hams and the garlic? In her rare moments of self-reflection, María would concede that she was not all that well liked by her family either. For the most part, though, these thoughts, when they surfaced, did not bother her unduly. It had been her lot in life to take care of things, to tend to the animals as her father lay on the floor of the local *taverna*, felled by too much wine, to care also for her mother after she had succumbed to the stroke that left her paralysed. And now it was the five women who needed tending to, her sisters Carmen and Cecilia (useless both of them), and her daughters: one, Matilde, a dreamer of the most illogical kind, and the other, Asunción, the one who looked the most like her, the one who had held some promise until the appearance of the wretched Manuel who had stolen her heart, left her with child, and disappeared into the Brazilian jungle to cavort with *el demonio* himself, for God, María was convinced, would surely have wanted nothing to do with that sinner.

In town, she was known as María *la Reina*—the Queen—because of her haughty way of walking and her habit of looking down at people, a relic, people thought, of her younger days when her beauty had been so great that it was almost legendary. *So who cares about her beauty?* the less beautiful women—the women who hated the thought that such power existed but did not belong to them—would ask. *With all her beauty, she still managed to drive her husband into an early grave, and that is what beauty does, eh? It drives men into the hands of death, and if you don't believe me, just think of her equally beautiful daughter Asunción and her equally dead husband Manuel. Sí, that is the power of beauty for you.*

Now older, still beautiful, still as forbidding as Italian marble, draped head to toe in the black she never managed to rid herself of because there was always someone dying, always someone to mourn—the black that only made María appear more outstanding, more dramatic, more regal than the ancient queens of Spain—with the passing of time, María had adopted an even haughtier air, inspiring even more criticism from the nastier tongues, some of whom had turned the thought of María into an obsession. If María knew of the commentaries—and everything in town was eventually known to everybody—she did not acknowledge them, mastering instead the dismissive look that drove both men and women crazy, the former with unspeakable desires, the latter with a suspicion that their husbands were feeling such things.

But now she felt old. Too many disappointments, too many nights reliving the pain of too many accumulated days. She thought then of Arturo's dead body, an image she had never been able to banish, and the thought of his hanging brought to mind the smell of her sister Cecilia's cooking, which had grown stranger with the passing of time. Cecilia was *loca*, had come undone due to the odour of death, and there she was at that very moment dumping so much turmeric into the rice that the house was sure to smell vaguely of a distant country for days and weeks after.

What to do? Once, as a child, in the fleeting moment before her mother's stroke and her father's descent into an alcoholic madness, María had dared to envision a totally different future for herself. Now, her life seemed burdened with dependent women everywhere, and complicated by the *contrabandistas* and their loneliness and darkened by her memories of death, yes, especially her memories of death, of her father and her unhappy mother and, above all, her inconsolable husband, Arturo—

Arturo, where are you, Arturo? Are you hiding again? Don't scare me.

Arturo. Why had it been Cecilia who had bumped into his dead body in the kitchen when surely the initial shock of his death belonged to her, the first encounter with the lifeless body, the first knowledge that he had hanged himself, just to flee from her? *Why Cecilia dear God,* who was never anything more than an appendage in the household, the unmarried sister given to fat and to endless melodrama, *why her, Señor, when that moment was mine, as sure as the night it was mine?* No matter, she would think of it no longer.

Outside, the morning light mixed with the interminable rain, rolling off the window panes like Cecilia's laughter. On a day like this María had married Arturo against her parents' wishes and to the surprise of all the townspeople, who had expected a grander choice from *la Reina,* because even if her inheritance amounted to a pittance, her beauty promised her more—one of the Nogueira brothers, for example, who owned vast expanses of land and who dressed in linen suits of the highest quality, or Joaquin Rodríguez, the mayor's son, a man who still harboured a deep and unrequited love for her.

But Arturo Pérez Barreiro? Not only was Arturo from an ordinary family but he was a known weakling, a man given to tears at the most inopportune moments, at fiestas when inspired by the brilliance of the night sky, and at public ceremonies where he often took to reciting stanzas from his nebulous poetry—poetry that so befuddled the townspeople that he was known as *el poeta confuso*, because they thought that only someone labouring under a terminal case of confusion could possibly have dreamed up such cumbersome lines, such cryptic allusions. *But that is what an education does to you, eh?* That was the comment—an education was good only for the useless outpourings of poets, and as one of the town *maestros,* Arturo had nothing if not an education. And when he died, so young and so violently, the people of Canteira held the poetry responsible for his madness, the poetry and María—who, according to the more sinister minds, had driven him to poetry in the first place, depriving him of his senses with the promises she had surely never delivered.

In the morning
your face takes on the contours of the moon,
prolonging the night
prolonging the unbearable, beautiful darkness

So he had said, so he had written in his schoolboy's hand, words, seductive words she would never trust again. Now it looked as though Matilde had inherited the lunatic seed, the love of words that had driven her husband to an undignified death and had thrown María into a ceaseless mourning because she was never to rid herself of the burning pain inside her heart and in the pit of her stomach which is where real feeling ends.

After a day of these dark thoughts, the kind that kept her awake during the night (and which she would blame on her rheumatism the following morning), after a day of these thoughts and the anguish that arose from them, María unleashed her frustration on the women, a habit she had developed even before the death of her husband, and one that was sure to guarantee her at least one night of sleep—even if it kept all the others awake for much more than just one night afterwards. As usual, she directed her anger towards Matilde first and launched her attack even before the first course of chestnut soup was served, signaling to all that this would be an unhappy dinner.

No more books Matilde, do you hear me?

Sí, Mamá, don't worry.

Don't worry? How can I not worry when the town is on fire with talk about you. Some even say you pay men money to bring you books and let me not find out that you are paying men, because that would be the end of me, do you hear me, Matilde?

Bueno, María, leave the child alone now. This was Cecilia speaking in her calm, dulcet tone, hoping to put an end to María's tirade before the dinner was ruined and the night turned mad and they were all at each other's throats, cursing and furious. Cecilia hated these dark moods of her sister's, the infernal moods that made eating tense, and Cecilia wanted nothing interfering with her dinner. But her sister's intrusion only worsened María's turbulent mood, and she now unleashed her ire on Cecilia, accusing her of trying to kill the household with a combination of spices that could only rot the stomach and pervert the mind, reminding her of that day when, as a child of only eight, Cecilia had poisoned—that was the word she used, poisoned—the entire family with the half cup of *pimienta picante* she had dumped on the octopus, and look, it had nearly killed the *abuelo* already seventy-six and ailing. *Sí, even then you were up to something.* Cecilia had heard this attack before, but it never failed to reduce her to a crumbling heap of self-pitying sobs, for after all, there she was, a slave to the stove, cooking her inventive dishes—*hermana*, she would say between hiccups and nose blowing, *this type of cooking does not come easy*—and suddenly the whole kitchen was in an uproar, with one consoling the other, the other berating another, and so on, until there was nothing to do but walk away from the table and take refuge in the barn, in a bedroom, in the hall, anywhere where one could be alone. All except for Cecilia who would remain in the kitchen eating, but only between hiccups and sobs, and without any enjoyment whatsoever.

On those nights, Cecilia would finally crawl up to bed at midnight, after eating her portion and everyone else's and, full of food, creep into the bed she shared with her sister Carmen—a woman a third her size due to a disorder of the bowels that made the easy digestion of food an impossibility, but which made sharing a bed so much more comfortable—and Carmen liked sharing a bed with Cecilia, the heat of all her sister's flesh warming her in the winter, the sound of her breath reminding her that she was not alone in the world, a world she had never understood or even cared for. There she calmed her fat sister, reminding Cecilia of all the fiestas of their childhood. *Shshsh, hermana, it is almost daylight.* And soon they were both asleep, dreaming of the stars, the moon, and the planet Mars—the planet, an old *meiga* had once assured them, that was the architect of all misunderstanding.

The month of March in Canteira was cold; the kind of cold that seeped through bones, invaded the heart, and then spread slowly to all other organs below. The kind of cold that years later, would make a mockery of advertisements lauding the sultry heat of Spain, the countless operas where sensuous Spanish women are forever seducing hapless *señoritos* in the shade. And the sunshine—this was the land of sunshine, was it not? The place the Germans and the British would invade in droves decades later, hoping thus to escape the misery of their cold countries up north.

But this was Galicia, the north of Spain. The green, Celtic, rain-infested, so-beautiful misty north, so misty that if you looked hard enough, you could see God traipsing about on distant hillocks, angels dancing on treetops. But so cold that few thought of coming this way, not even later when isolation became a thing of the past, gone the way of chaperones and faith healers with the arrival of three-lane highways, financed by European subsidies and twenty years of unparalleled growth.

In 1926, the month of March was an especially bitter one. Cutting winds penetrated unabated through doors and windows, and there never seemed to be enough blankets to burrow under. Black shadows appeared beneath eyes. Phlegm formed in lungs. Blistering coughs punctuated the light of the early morning. At nights, cold and coughs merged, sleep escaped through window cracks, rain fell on rooftops, and eyes remained open searching for consolation in the darkness. In Canteira, that month would be remembered for years to come—not because of the unbearable cold however, but because that was the time when the virgin lost her head at the patronal feast and Carmen became known as Carmen the Holy One forever after.

At the *pensión* of María *la Reina* the fiesta preparations had begun in the early morning with the arrival of the fresh oysters, barnacles, and the lamprey, with María's ill mood and with Cecilia's creative exertions in the kitchen. Twenty guests had been invited from as far away as Santiago de Compostela, many whose names were preceded with *estimado* this and *estimada* that, a group that included at least three wealthy merchants and two prominent priests, and the excitement had been building in the household for weeks now. By then the reputation of María *la Reina*'s *pensión* had grown—*Stay there, señor, in that house on the outskirts of town, the one that belongs to the Encarnas.*

No better meals can be found in the whole of the country, no talk better than there, in their parlour by the candlelight, people would tell each other excitedly. As more guests had arrived over the years, more money had been made, and now, finally, María announced it was time to celebrate their success so that others in the town would realize the extent of it.

That year, the colour in fashion was forest green. Dresses were made princess style, embroidered with rose petals, and hats were worn by even the poorest farmers. All through the year, there had been an unusual number of marriages in Canteira, precipitated by a spate of unplanned pregnancies and an equal number of enraged future fathers-in-law. That year, the winter cold was followed by the intense heat of an unusually long summer. *Contrabandistas* arrived bearing strange contraptions from the coasts of Galicia, inventions from the eccentric and often perverted minds of the French and the English.

Inside the *pensión,* new dishes had been bought and fashionable dresses had been ordered for the women from Isabel *la sorda*, the renowned seamstress from the nearby town of Tres Luces, who could weave miracles with linen and disarm the devil himself with her expansive collection of imported buttons. That was the year María *la Reina* sacrificed a bit of her mourner's black to wear a dress in grey and green, colours which accentuated her stunning cat-like eyes and inflamed the jealous tongues of the women of Canteira even more. They whispered to each other furiously throughout the fiesta mass, for *How could she? Sí, mujer, it is much too soon after her husband's death and that of her son-in-law also, and anyway, that is a dress more appropriate for a very young girl than for a grandmother.*

María had used her grey-green eyes only to observe every deficiency in the household from the quality of the fish that had arrived that morning, fresh from the coasts of Vigo, to the culinary concoctions of her sister Cecilia, so excited by the prospect of feeding the distinguished guests on that day that she had outdone herself, creating dishes bearing names of local luminaries made with ingredients no one had ever heard of.

In the church, a new virgin shone by the altar. Made by the craftsmen of Canteira and decorated with freshwater pearls, a gown of white brocade, and eyes painted with drops of gold and silver, this was to be her official debut after endless collections from the townspeople and a final donation from María *la Reina* herself, which drew a nod of approval from Don José and a thunder of disgruntled criticism from others in town even more envious of her newly fattened purse than of her legendary beauty.

At half-past eleven, six men in black appeared at the church and placed the virgin on their shoulders. A hush filled the cold air as people waited for the mass to begin dressed in their fiesta finery, huddling behind the virgin in preparation for the customary procession around the church's perimeter. Rain fell outside, littering the earth, granting an air of solemnity to the proceedings. Inside, the air bristled with excitement. The virgin's face, luminous, as splendid as one of the statues described by the town's most learned man, Emilio Larra, upon his return from a visit to El Prado, beamed at the congregation from beneath her golden canopy.

Soon after the ringing of the church bells, the men commenced their walk around the church behind Don José, who was singing the *Gloria* in a voice that cracked and irritated, with the congregation dressed in their forest green and high-heeled shoes following closely after them. Among them was Carmen Encarna, who was thinking not of God, nor of the beauty of the newly decorated virgin, but of the strange heat that had begun invading her body well over a month ago now and that was keeping her awake at night with painful desires, the product of a million indecent thoughts and as many furious longings.

She could speak to no one about the heat, not even to her sister Cecilia, her sole confidante throughout her quiet lifetime. Not to María. *Dios mío,* not María—who knew what María would make of her new-found preoccupation? Not to friends, she had few friends in any respect because her time was fully occupied with toiling at the *pensión.* In any case, these were indecent longings, the kind they had been warned about since they were young children, the kind Don José was forever railing about on Sundays and on other holy days.

As the people chanted and the men rocked back and forth with the weight of the freshly decorated virgin and Don José's voice continued to crack and meander, Carmen's thoughts grew increasingly more intense, the heat more unbearable. Thoughts of indecent caresses and kisses in the moonlight—no, by the church, here, amidst the graves of Canteira's forefathers, a kiss, a caress, the hot lingering touch of a mysterious man dressed in a suit of English wool and a stunning black fedora. Yes, *Ave María* and all that. Yes, *sin pecado concebido* also. The virgin, God, Jesus Christ, and all the saints, Popes too, *sí the Popes if you like,* but a hand slipped sensuously down her back, the passionate kiss of an unknown stranger—*sí, señor, as well to all that too, God almighty, our Father who is most certainly in heaven, for where else would he be?*

Just as thoughts grew hotter, and rain mingled with sweat making Carmen's discomfort all the greater, Antonio Fernández, the baker with the limp who had been entrusted with one of the corners of the virgin's canopy, tripped on a jutting stone, lost his balance and sent her flying backwards where she landed on the ground with a crashing thud, losing her newly painted head, which rolled furiously backwards until it came to rest at Carmen's feet, whose own head was lost at that moment inside her many indecent thoughts and who started to scream deliriously at the sight, associating the impurity of her desires with the tragedy of the virgin's face that lay before her, and who continued screaming until well after the ceremony had ended and the fiesta meal had been ruined and María *la Reina* had threatened her with a whole range of reprisals—which failed to diminish Carmen's tears or to scare her into a more private contrition, however, for she felt secretly that she deserved these punishments and fervently longed for each and every one of them.

In Canteira, the talk of the day's events filled the town for weeks and months after. Despite the most earnest attempts to reattach the virgin's head to her spectacular baldachin robe, the crack in her neck remained visible, so that she was condemned to wear a white gossamer scarf at each successive fiesta for years after. Of Carmen's strange behaviour—behaviour that grew stranger in the days that followed as she took to her catechism with a passion that seemed more appropriate to the pious nuns of the nearby Convent of Santa Clara—much had been said with no conclusions reached. After that day, Carmen Encarna came to be known as Carmen the Holy One, baptized by the events at that year's fiesta by words from God himself, a God she would tell one and all, who had spoken to her from inside the pearly head of the decapitated virgin.

It would be Asunción's fate that, born already with a delicate mind, she would fall in love with the one man in town who had the power to unhinge her completely.

She met him at the Fiesta of San Andrés, at her first dance, when she was just sixteen—too young to know the ways of the world, yet old enough to fall madly in love with Canteira's most notorious fiend. Already Asunción was known for being beautiful—not as beautiful as María maybe, but certainly sweeter, because she had inherited her father's weepy disposition and had none of that haughtiness of her mother's that so disturbed the busy tongues of Canteira.

The object of Asunción's obsession was one Manuel Pousada, the son of a local farmer with little land and even less sense, who was adored by the women in town, the *señoritas*, who watched him behind their fans, whispered things to him from their verandahs. At twenty-five, Manuel could already boast of an abysmal reputation—especially among the fathers and mothers of Canteira's young women, who fretted endlessly about the state of their daughters' virginities and the disgrace that the loss of that state would bring to their families and entire generations of their descendants. His reputation was so dark, the rumours of his conquests so exaggerated, in fact, that merely to be seen with him would sully a girl's reputation. No matter. Manuel Pousada cared little for the talk, or for the stains he brought upon the names of the women he spoke to. He had fallen so in love with the stories of his conquests that he had begun inventing women and situations, blending fact and fiction to such an extent that even he himself grew incapable of distinguishing between them.

In any case, it was not the women Manuel lived for but the thought of Brazil—a name he had heard first in the mouth of his father's brother José, and one that seemed to him replete with unlimited possibilities. At night, it was the scent of the heat that came to him, the feel of the feverish dancing and the sound of the songs uncle José had learned when he worked at the Hotel *Boa Esperança*—songs that spoke of streets paved with gold and of glorious, redeeming sunshine.

His uncle was not the only one to have succumbed to the lure of emigration. For decades now, the men of Canteira and the surrounding villages had been leaving—one by one at first, in droves later—for Brazil, Uruguay, Argentina, and the tiny nations of the Caribbean. They left for these countries in search of work, dignity and, above all, an opportunity to return to their small towns and even smaller villages, their pockets bulging with the wealth that would buy them the respect they had always dreamed of. In their countries of choice—in the Brazils, the Cubas and the Argentinas—these emigrants worked arduously, constructing bridges and houses for the ostentatious new-world rich, cleaning up in restaurants and hotels, making unheard-of sums of money running prostitution rings and peddling contraband liquor. In all cases, as they cleaned, peddled, and bribed, they pined for their homeland, waxing so nostalgic in bars and in restaurants that jokes soon surfaced about these foreigners, these peasants lost in the dream of the return. *What is there to return to,* they would be asked, *when you came here to escape the misery, the poverty, the dirt, even the green hills and the chestnut groves of your glorious Galicia*?

Back home in the desolate green hills and valleys of Galicia, the women tended to their families, fed the animals, and laboured in the fields, waiting for news from their men, many of whom succumbed in these exotic countries to yellow fever—which was rumoured to devour the liver and turn the eyeballs yellow with sadness—and other diseases, even more frightening and evil, convincing those back home that their men had departed to a hell on earth, from which only the very lucky few could hope to return.

Those who did return—after having cleaned interminable bedrooms and bribed a bevy of faceless officials—would arrive bearing puzzling gifts and carrying with them the smell of their new countries, a smell that lingered for days, sometimes weeks on their clothes and on their breaths, reminding all that the men's stay would be a short one. But it was the ground they would kiss upon landing, the earth bathed in the perennial mist of their homeland, the mist they had longed for during the endless sun-filled days when the world seemed too bright, imbued with too much laughter, laden with sweltering sunshine. They knew—instinctively and with certainty—that it is the rain that holds the real promise of eternity, the rain, the mist, and the impenetrable darkness.

The more successful of the emigrants—the Pérez and the Rodríguez families, for example, who had accumulated what seemed to those back home to be suspiciously large amounts of money—had returned to build houses that were not houses, but ponderous jagged things, fashioned from granite and marble and built into the nooks and crannies of the region's more desolate hills and valleys. Some, like Ramón Camacho, who had made his fortune in furniture—though no one, it was true, could figure out just how he could have made so much money with tables and chairs and things of the like—had even decorated his windows and doors with what were believed to be diamonds, because they glittered beautifully in the sunlight and beckoned to his door in the night all manner of forest animals and *contrabandistas*, seduced by the beauty and majesty of this house.

For the most part, though, the people who returned—those who had survived the arduous work and the plethora of deadly and largely unpronounceable infections—found, to their horror, that things had changed irreparably in their absence. Now Andrés the mason was dead, and Jaime, the owner of the local taverna was nearly blind, and even their families had grown older, more weary, had dared to go on, altering forever the sacred memories of childhood. And their children, babies when they had left, transformed now into total strangers, shrinking visibly from the men they could not remember, who stood before them now, claiming to be their fathers.

Then the tears began in earnest, not for a land or a people, but for the dreams the men had carried in their heads for too long, the nebulous, beautiful memories of a time and a place now utterly transformed, a place forever denied to them.

But Manuel Pousada would never miss this land. Had never been obsessed with a land wet with rain and tears when the land denied them the dignity of work, when she failed to offer a way to survive the interminable nights, a way to assuage the pain of all the frozen mornings. Manuel's only dream was of the heat, of the sunshine that rolled off backs and rested on top of heads, the kind of sunshine he would only find in America—Europe was too old now to offer anything but the same tired darkness.

When he caught a glimpse of Asunción at the Fiesta de San Andrés, holding awkwardly to her woollen skirt, her huge black eyes looking at him in the way he had come to recognize long ago as the longing of a smitten woman, he had experienced no great lurch of the heart, no great moment of recognition.

Instead. *That niña has eyes for me, Juan*, Manuel told his friend, laughing at her under his breath because he had grown bored with the attention paid to him by all the women long ago.

That niña, idiota, is the very daughter of your beloved María, Juan responded, eyeing Asunción as he did so, surprised to see her staring so boldly at his friend, a man Juan resented deeply, judging him to be wholly undeserving of such exaggerated female attention.

María? María la Reina? That is María's daughter? Manuel's cynical smile now disappeared because if there was one woman in the world guaranteed to perturb Manuel, it was María, the woman who dismissed him with an empty look every time he contrived to bump into her at church—which he attended only to catch a glimpse of her—or to brush by her in the market near Carmiña's stall, where María stopped to purchase fresh sardines, silver hake, and salted cod on Fridays. Instead, all he had succeeded in doing with his bumps and brushes was to annoy María thoroughly, *for who was this clod?* she would ask herself after he had bumped into her yet again, and what was he doing brushing up against her, a woman who could be his much older sister? For the most part, though, she ignored him completely, managing thus to aggravate the flames of Manuel's ardour, because for Manuel the thought of María was as powerful as the thought of Brazil, her gaze as seductive as the heat he so longed for. *Caray,* and now here before him was the daughter—pretty too, no doubt, but nothing like the haughty María.

Leave her alone, Manuel, Juan warned him now, worried about the look in his friend's eyes, a look that Juan had seen all too often and that warned of a whole series of impending improprieties.

If her mother knew the girl was looking at you like that she'd lock her up for the rest of eternity.

If her mother knew.

Juan had no idea why Manuel obsessed over María the way

he did, when she was almost a decade older, when she was as imposing as a French aristocrat and as difficult to read as the dolmens in Lauredo. María was beautiful, but shrewish and proud and altogether impossible. No one, in Juan's estimation, was worthy of the kind of attention his friend devoted to her, an obsession that had lasted for years now, this mad, relentless love—when all around him the most beautiful women of Canteira sighed and fainted at the mere mention of Manuel, offered themselves up to him. And here he stood, the *idiota,* besotted by this dark, unapproachable woman.

In Asunción's lovesick stare Manuel saw an opportunity, the one he had been praying for since first setting eyes on María, and no amount of cajoling from his friend, no lengthy enumeration of dire consequences, would stop him. Before long and with minimal effort, Manuel was at Asunción's side, catapulting her into a frenzy of love in just one hour and invading her mind to such an extent that even years and years later, after all the tears he had caused her to shed, it was his face that she saw before succumbing to the disease that killed her.

After the fiesta, they met secretly in the forest and by the church, Asunción crazy with love, Manuel biding his time until he could get to her mother. It would be the only time in her life that Asunción would outsmart María, finding clever excuse upon clever excuse to run an errand in town just so that she could spend precious moments with the beautiful Manuel, the man who looked like an angel, the man whose passion surprised and overwhelmed her. The consequences of this passion she was quite ignorant of, believing as many young women did then—sheltered and protected as they were from the realities of life—that babies came from Paris and things of the like, and she was thus earnestly perplexed by the range of symptoms that eventually afflicted her and that the older women quickly surmised could add up to nothing other than a pregnancy.

Later, when María sat down to try to make sense of it all, when she paused to determine how she had been deceived so easily when her instincts were usually so sharp, when she had lived all of her life to avoid such things, the only answer that came to her was that it was Matilde's fault, that if María hadn't spent so much time worrying about her younger daughter, she would have been watching out more closely for Asunción, would have saved her from a fate worse than death, the fate of having to spend the rest of her life with a man undeserving of her.

It was with a shock then, matched only by the shock she had suffered from the death of her husband Arturo, that she received the news that her beautiful daughter Asunción, barely more than a girl and as innocent as the sun, had managed to get herself pregnant and by that clod Manuel—and where had she seen him before? María asked herself.

They were married a week later, quietly, with few in attendance apart from the aunts, who sniffed into their handkerchiefs, and shook their heads at the virgin, and *oohed* and *aahed* underneath their breaths at the glorious man who was about to join their household. That very day, after the marriage ceremony—and after Asunción had vomited almost without respite for an hour, trying with all her might to defeat wave upon wave of morning sickness—Manuel moved into the granite house and began taunting the women with his often disrespectful behaviour.

At first it was his appetite, so voracious that it scared even Cecilia, who had thought no one desired food more than she, and who stared at him dumbfounded as he inhaled the *chorizo* and the salted ham and the plates of Galician *cocido*, washing it all down with bowls and bowls of the best *vino tinto*. Then it was Manuel's habit of grabbing his new wife in the presence of the virginal and shocked aunts, who hummed and hawed and looked at the floor and out the window in an effort to avoid embarrassment, but who managed, nevertheless, to observe every grab and every pinch out of the corner of their eyes, mesmerized by the sort of behaviour they had always fantasized about, and by a man like that! *Imagine, hermana*, Carmen told Cecilia one day in bed, *just imagine it*, making it clear with the tone of her voice that she was spending a good deal of time doing just such imagining herself.

But it was María he outraged the most, making her skin crawl with the intensity of his stare—*What is he saying Good Lord, what are those insolent eyes telling me?*—with his habit of brushing up against her in the parlour—*Oh so sorry, Doña María, I didn't see you there*—outside by the barn as they tended to the pigs and, worse, in the hallway between their respective bedrooms, as María prepared for bed and Manuel ran to catch up with her, coming so close she thought she could feel his hand slide impertinently down her back, his breath heavy on her frightened earlobe. Soon María was wandering the house in a state of complete and utter terror, fearing another encounter, another brush with her son-in-law.

The naked insolence in Manuel's gaze spoke to María of the things she dared not acknowledge, because *Dios mío*, no, how could she have driven her husband to his death and now this, be intruding upon the happiness of her daughter? It was her face again, her treacherous face, for it could not be her demeanour. She was as cold as stone to Manuel, as foreboding as a thousand widows in mourning. No, she would not accept what his eyes told her during those furtive moments when he caught her gaze, eyes that said the things his mouth never dared utter. That was how to keep the insanity of a man's desire at bay, that was the trick to sleep undisturbed at night and awake calmly in the morning she told herself. But the torment remained, the knowledge that this despicable man lurked in the shadows of her house like a rabid rodent.

One night, after Asunción had retired to her bed early complaining of fatigue and the other women were busy tending to the guests at the *pensión*, Manuel's ardour turned into abject carelessness. He found María alone in the kitchen, peeling the potatoes for the morning *tortilla,* lost in the darkness of her thoughts, in the fear that things would never be right again. She was thinking that Manuel Pousada was no better than vermin, just like each one of his sorry ancestors—especially his lazy father and the madwoman who had been his mother, dead now, worn down by years of abuse and the depression brought on by their wretched poverty. How had this happened, *Good Lord what is it I have done to be paying for my daughter's mistakes? How long must I weather the insults of this impossible animal?*

Lost in her thoughts, she failed to hear Manuel approach her from behind, failed to stop him before he had placed his hand on the small of her back. And then—the line had been crossed.

First though, there was confusion.

What? What are you doing? How dare you.

So sorry, señora, thought you had called. Thought you had need of my services.

And then his laughter. Ringing in her ear, the one final insult.

And you will leave, she screamed, knife in hand, liver in throat, enraged beyond her wildest imagining. *You will leave this house now, not tomorrow, nor the day after, but now, do you hear me?*

You will leave, I say, leave before the morning, she told him again when he continued laughing, the smell of liquor enveloping her, aggravating the insult. A contemptuous peasant, that's what he was. As rough as those pigs they slaughtered in winter. Ay, that would be a fine destiny for this man, on his back, neck slashed from ear to ear, his blood staining the dried grass beneath him.

I don't understand, Doña María, why? Why do you want me to leave the house? Manuel asked knowing full well why and daring her to voice the words he himself dared not utter.

My reasons are my reasons, Manuel. At that very moment, she wished fervently for a lightning rod to descend from the sky and fry him thoroughly and completely. He was like an infection—a pervasive, insidious infection. Where had he come from? Why was he here? Away with him, away from this house, from her life, from the debris he had made of her most beautiful daughter! She was so incensed her whole body was shaking, a fact duly noted by the infection in question.

And my pregnant wife? You do remember Asunción, don't you, Doña María?

Cállate, animal! Don't you even dare speak the name of my child. I will secure a passage to Brazil for the both of you. I want you to take your wife and start a new life there, do you understand?

His dreams of Brazil finally realized, and by her, María, María *la Reina,* no less. He could hardly believe it.

Yes, I understand. But if I go to Brazil, I go on my own, just so you understand, Doña María, he told her coldly, sacrificing his wife and his unborn child in a breath. He cared little for Asunción and her childish tantrums when right there, in the same house, in the next room at night, lay his true love, María, a woman who so beguiled him that it took all of his willpower not to grab her again now and put an end to his waiting. *It is all right though;* he told himself. *A little waiting is a good thing. All good things require a long period of wanting. So much better the having later.*

As you wish, she answered him gravely. *But if you leave alone, it is better that you think of never returning.*

And then it was over, the agreement reached that he would depart for Brazil the following month, leaving his wife and unborn child in the care of the women. That very night he told his wife the news, lying about where he had found the money for the passage and promising that he would return for her when she started crying loudly and inconsolably. He was careful, though, to instil the right amount of fear in Asunción's heart so that she continued sobbing well into the night, keeping the entire household, and especially María, awake for the duration of it—a fact that made Manuel's rest all the more peaceful.

With the passing of time the popularity of the *pensión* of María *la Reina* had grown so dramatically that new furniture had been bought and the parlour had been expanded in fits and starts to accommodate the nightly reunions that took place around the large wood-burning stove. It would be Cecilia's fervent storytelling and her astounding creativity with fish and veal croquettes that would contribute most to the growing popularity of the *pensión*. It was her dramatic re-enactments of tales of death and destruction, love affairs conducted in secret hideaways, that would bring them all to her door—the expectation they had of hearing a new story or even of hearing an old favourite, told with the same flourish as if for the first time and all were ignorant of what was to come. Every night brought a different traveller to the *pensión—contrabandistas* from Lérida, students from Santiago, labourers on their way to find work in the streets of Madrid—eager for the warmth of the Encarna parlour, the delicious tales told by a dramatic Cecilia to whittle away the darkest winter nights.

Every evening, the townspeople of Canteira also began arriving at the *pensión* once dark descended, eager themselves for the talk that transpired around the giant wood-burning stove. There women would embroider and men smoke, listening enraptured as travellers related their own fantastic tales from their wanderings through Spain. Few newspapers existed then; there were few ways of finding out what was happening beyond Canteira except by way of these men, who offered not only goods for sale, but their own village gossip, news from Madrid, the fashions, the theories, and all the other bits and pieces that made up the larger, more interesting world. Still, despite all the news that arrived with the strangers, it was Cecilia's tales that drew the people most of all. Sordid stories of their very own, gossip that had travelled into Cecilia's ears and mingled magically with other information, with her dreams, and with the mysteries she claimed she could read in all manner of inanimate things.

Witness. *Just down the way*, she told the packed parlour on a particularly vicious winter night, when winds and rain howled furiously outside, *just down the way there lived a woman years and years ago whose parents never tired of claiming was virtuous as a thousand nuns. White frilly woman with canary yellow ribbons in her hair. Virtuous, they said. So virtuous that on her marriage night she refused even her husband, told him that she was saving herself for the Lord. Days passed like this, with him begging, her refusing, until one night, standing it no longer, he forced her onto the floor. And then, guess what, good people?* Cecilia would raise her hands, signalling to all that the drama was about to unfold. *The woman, as the husband found out to his dismay, was no woman at all!*

Screams greeted this revelation. Laughter and glee. Women ceased embroidering as Cecilia embarked on a yarn of her own. Visits to Madrid awaited the virtuous woman, exorcisms at the hands of the Bishop of Salamanca, rituals enacted by local *meigas*, who advised the parents to carry an empty casket across the Río Avellana in the dead of night and to feed their unhappy daughter chestnuts boiled in milk. Finally, just as mysteriously as the very ailment she suffered from, the woman was cured—but not before Cecilia had squeezed the last drop of blood from the story, described Satan down to his pointy red shoes, luxuriated in telling how that same woman, poor soul, went on to give birth to twelve children, only two of whom made it past the age of three.

Story followed upon story, retellings of events that happened, concocted tales more often than not. Tales of the supernatural, of the dreaded *Santa Compaña,* the procession of the dead, who emerged at the stroke of midnight, candles in their long, bony hands, announcing with their chanting who in town would be next to join them on the other side.

Winter nights passed like these. Women embroidering, men smoking, *aguardiente* plentiful, Cecilia's famous *empanada* passed from guest to guest. From the corner of the parlour, María watched and listened, unamused. She enjoyed Cecilia's tales as well as the next but had long learned to cloak any happiness she felt with a look of barely concealed distaste, and she was bothered by this congregation made up mostly of non-paying guests. Yet despite her discomfort, María knew it was Cecilia's gossip, her habit of lacing every tale with an offer of a bit of food, her dramatic rolling of the eyes, the heaving of her chest, that brought the paying guests there, that had allowed the *pensión* to expand since its establishment all those years ago.

So let her tell another story, another farcical tale told for the third night in a row. What mattered were the pesetas, the wealth that would stave off the uncertainty of winter, calm the sharp winds that tore through town and made cold nights even more so. By the wood-burning stove in the parlour, with men smoking and women embroidering the sheets for their daughters' trousseaus, at least no mention was made of the Encarnas' own lives—the tales that amused so many in town who congregated by the heat of other wood-burning stoves. Inside the warm parlour of the *pensión*, María could not hear those loud whispers, the titters that emerged here and there, the biting words spoken by gossips who, like Cecilia, found much to enjoy in the miseries of others, in the bad luck that at one time or another visits us all.

Of her early days, Gloria remembered the feel of embroidered sheets, the colour of mourning donned in honour of her dead father, the endless hours of bickering over neighbours, and an ocean of dreams full of indecipherable omens. In their house of Galician granite and silver-grey balconies, she spent her youth listening to the whistling of the wind, seeping through the cracks of doors and windows, delivering promises that never quite managed to materialize.

Her most potent memories were laced with the tangy smell of the sea. It was to the sea that she travelled every year with the great-aunts, her mother, and her aunt Matilde. Cecilia arranged these sojourns to the coast, obsessed by a fervently held belief that an annual dip in the waters of the Atlantic was the only way to ward off the debilitating menstrual pains that had plagued all of the women in the family since time immemorial. Every July, the women would travel to the coast—all except for María, who dismissed Cecilia's belief in the curative powers of the ocean as horse manure, and who insisted in her best high-handed way that the other women suffer their monthly inconvenience as she did, with dignity. But she encouraged them to go anyway, savouring the thought of a month on her own without the crying of a child, the worries brought on by the platoon of women, and, above all, a month thank God, without the smell of Cecilia's strange and pungent cooking. Once at the coast, the women would walk up and down the sandy beaches near La Coruña, pausing only to dip their fully clothed bodies into the warm salty waters of the Atlantic and relishing the air that was a heaven-sent respite from the terse, foreboding mountain winds of Canteira.

It wasn't until she turned seven and joined Doña Gertrudes' small class of ten other girls that Gloria realized she was fatherless, and then only because of Carmelita Pereira, the mayor's daughter—who informed her of the fact with considerable relish during morning recess. *You, Gloria, are the only one in all of Canteira without a papá*, she had said. It wasn't really true. Many of the children in town had lost their fathers to emigration, had seen their fathers once, maybe twice in their lives, but the men were spoken of at home, were remembered by those they had left behind. Gloria could not remember ever seeing or hearing about a father, not from her mother, not from the great-aunts and certainly not from her Nana María, who was, in any case, too busy to talk and too intimidating to question.

That afternoon as she walked home, after being strapped

into her coat and berated by her great-aunt Carmen over the milk stain on her navy blue uniform, she noticed the existence of fathers for the first time. They were everywhere. They dressed in pants and smelled of tobacco and had whiskers and big hands, just like those of her great-aunt Cecilia. They said things differently, more gruffly, a bit like Nana María, actually, when she was angry, when she was screaming at the great-aunts, or lamenting her luck, or telling Edelmiro that he was a useless ass and a brazen sinner. Where had the fathers been until now? And, more important, where was hers hiding?

Once at home, she ran to her mother, tears streaming down her face, for she wanted the whiskers and the big hands, and felt suddenly deprived in the deep, devastating way felt only by children.

What have you done to my father? she asked her mother, her unhappy, distant mother. Her mother who seemed like stone, who forever failed to exude the comforting, warm breath of her aunts, though not, it was true, of her grandmother.

For years after, Gloria would fantasize about her father, imagining him tall and handsome one moment, warm and loving the next. For a long time, she even fantasized that her father was Angel Rodríguez, the richest man in Canteira and the owner of the very first car in the region—a black, regal machine with gleaming white interior, inside of which Gloria imagined herself seated next to him. *Papá,* she would say to him, and then not much else, for it was the name on her lips that she savoured, the thought that this absent, unknowable man was the answer to all of the questions in the universe.

Years later, when Angel Rodríguez was butchered by communist sympathizers during the final days of the Civil War—stabbed fourteen times and left to die like a dog on the side of the road—Gloria cried real tears for this man, for although she had never really known him, he was the only man she could ever call by the name of Papá, though she knew there was no foundation whatsoever to this wish.

Her real father, it seemed, was dead. Her mother told her so, on the very same day Gloria discovered that she was fatherless. Brazil and a train and an accident—*kaboom*, her mother told her, reenacting things—*kaboom* and *adiós* forever. It would be years before she stopped telling people that her father had been killed by Brazil—years before she realized that Brazil was a happy land full of people, and not an accident that had left her lost inside this murky world of women.

At eight, she was ushered into a new world by her aunt Matilde, the kindest woman of them all, no heart was as large as Matilde's, no eyes could determine more astutely the things that amused children best. It was then that Matilde took her to the magical spot, the prettiest spot in all of Canteira because from there the world seemed larger, the sun brighter, the possibilities endless. There, in the afternoons, as they tended to the cows, Gloria learned for the very first time of the existence of magical things, of things known only to her aunt because they spoke from within the covers of her secret books, the books Matilde hid from Nana María and shared only with Gloria, and only here in the prettiest spot, hidden next to the rock decorated with medusas and circles and other mysterious and impenetrable symbols. It was her aunt Matilde she liked best, Matilde and great-aunt Cecilia, with her cooking smells and her never-ending theories about saltwater cures and the meaning of signs that could be read in the cloud formations, about the need to cross a bridge seven times to ward off illness, about witches and demons and the wolfman who lived in the forest at the back of the house, waiting patiently for the chance to devour girls like her, girls on the threshold of becoming women.

Ay, hermana, Carmen would say, whenever she caught Cecilia telling Gloria such tales, *if you continue with these stories, you know what awaits you. The infierno, hermana, the infierno.*

Carmen could certainly never forget hell, could imagine the terrors to be found there ever since that fateful day with the decapitated virgin, terrors that strengthened her resolve to give her life up to God, just like one of those famous mystics, Santa Teresa de Jesús or San Juan de la Cruz.

I have become a bride of Christ, she had announced to the surprised women of the household one day.

The only brides of Christ are those nuns in the convent, said her sister María, who had no time for Carmen's religious fervour—nor come to think of it, for the ponderous sputters of the nuns of Canteira. But Carmen dismissed this statement as she dismissed most things that did not accord with her new-found worldview, reserving her strength for the task of memorizing all the saints and their deeds: Cecilia, the patron saint of musicians (why was her sister so afflicted by odours? she would wonder); Santa Monica, mother of her favourite saint, Saint Augustine; and especially Saint Benedict, whom she invoked on the darkest nights to ward off evil temptations—like the temptation to scream at María, to abandon the cows in the pasture, and, worst of all, those temptations she dared not articulate that focused, *Ave María Purísima,* on her niece's beautiful and now dearly departed husband.

Ridiculous, you are ridiculous! María would scream at her, whenever she caught Carmen praying into her rosary or pondering the dimensions of hell by the wash basins. *You'd be wiser to concentrate on tending to the animals, Carmen.*

María was forever fretting about the animals, worrying that

the cows weren't getting enough sun, that the quality of the hay was inferior because it was a leap year, that the colour of the milk pointed to an insidious infection, that the chickens looked constipated and unhappy. Carmen knew that the insults were María's way of expressing her love, of telling Carmen that she was appreciated in the household, even though she was as skinny as a rake and was forever disappearing inside the folds of Cecilia's large grey and white aprons. Carmen knew that María's love came enshrouded in insult, tried to convince Cecilia of this fact, when she was wounded by María's words, left in pieces inside the kitchen to assuage her injured feelings with stewed rabbit *a la Carmiña* and sardine *empanada*.

It was Carmen who taught Gloria all the lessons of the catechism, Carmen who taught her each and every prayer, Carmen who prepared her for Holy Communion, for confirmation, and, years later, revealed to her what hell could really be like, destroying her faith and catapulting her into a life of questioning. But it was not the catechism she liked best, it was the stories told by Matilde and Cecilia of half-human, half-animal beings who preyed on young virgins, of witches and magical rocks, and of mysterious men dressed in black who arrived bearing silver trinkets, promising things that were never fully revealed to her.

It was to these two women that she retreated because her own mother was a silent, wounded mystery. Her aunt Matilde told her it was due to her father's death, that no sane woman can survive such a senseless and utter tragedy.

Your mamá is busy thinking about the patterns of life. Remember, Gloria, things happen always in circles.

Gloria remembered, would remember all of Matilde's theories with respect to her mother, without for a moment understanding even one of them. In Gloria's mind, her mother was forever floating away from her—a nebulous, unfathomable being, as beautiful and as unreachable as marble. Her real mamá was a big lump of Encarna women; the cooking odours of Cecilia rolled into the religious fervour of Carmen, blessed and embellished by Matilde's imaginative stories and framed by the two unfathomable bookends—her grandmother who rarely smiled, rarely emerged from her state of black, and of course her mamá, floating atop them all like a distant, unanswered question.

The resurrection of Gloria's father, Manuel Pousada, happened on a Friday as the bells tolled in honour of Santa Teresa, the patron saint of Canteira, whose lifelike effigy—constructed long ago by a local mason in a drunken stupor—stood at the border of town, welcoming all with a smile that seemed both lewd and cynical. It was Pedro Ruiz who saw him first, ambling along the main square, dressed in a white linen suit and a multicoloured cravat of silk and phosphorescence. On his arm, Manuel Pousada had one Gabriela Costa, a beautiful Brazilian, taller than any woman ever seen in those parts, and dressed so sparingly that the widows of the town—women in black outraged at the slightest indiscretion—began crossing themselves immediately at the sight, chanting *Ave Marías, Padre Nuestros,* and *Holy Mother of God, what have we come tos?*

Manuel Pousada, thought dead for more than nine years now, seemed oblivious to the commotion that had erupted all around him. After all, the sun was bright, this was the town of his birth, *what are you looking at?* he said with his eyes to the widows, to the shopkeepers, to those who remembered him and to those who didn't because they had been too young, had been away, were burdened with imperfect memories.

Pedro Ruíz, who could remember, and who stood there staring, stupefied as Gabriela Costa strutted her perfect golden body in front of them, was the first to finally say something.

Señores, he said with studied care, *if this is death, let her come for me any time.*

That night, the town came together in the tavern of Roberto Madriñán to discuss the extraordinary sight of the dead Manuel and the otherworldly woman who had walked by his side. There they reminded each other of the day when he had left, over nine years ago, of the ungodly rain that had fallen—*torrential* was the way one put it, *a warning from the Lord himself,* added Don José, the town priest, a dramatist of the best kind and well known for his habit of introducing God into every story told, every memory unearthed.

What they recalled above all else was the memory of his disconsolate wife telling the town of her husband's death in distant Brasilia. *So devastated she was,* said one. *And so pregnant,* added another, relishing the memory because this was no ordinary wife but one of the Encarna women— Asunción Encarna, *a strange creature, that one, a bit loose around the head.* But an Encarna nonetheless, and no other family had given the town so much to talk about, so many vivid disasters to share on winter nights. No lives seemed as exciting, as shocking. And now this, one of their men had returned from the dead—oh, hands were rubbed in expectation of what was coming, the smiles beamed outwards as far as Madrid.

And did you see that woman on his arm? No, señor, that was no woman. That was a goddess, a goddess has come to town. So it was true. Manuel had indeed died, gone to heaven, and returned with a sample of what awaited them once they too were forced to face the music and *what music, eh, señores?* An Argentinian tango could not compare with this. All of this was said amidst great peals of laughter and loud snorts, as they celebrated this momentary respite from the harshness of their everyday lives, content in the knowledge that this event would surely unfold into a story of legendary dimensions, a tale to be passed on from generation to generation till the end of time.

The news of Manuel Pousada's resurrection did not take long to reach the ears of Juana de Castro, Canteira's most notorious gossip—a large woman with a moustache who, years before, in a tragic twist of fate, was one of the last to learn of her own son's death in Cuba of the cholera. Don José had received the news first, then told the butcher, who in turn told every farmer tending to every cow in the district until word reached Juana herself, who cried out in pain, fell to her knees, and was revived only by a good shaking delivered by Don Roberto de las Aguas, Canteira's only doctor. Even after the irony of this, after seeing her own tragedy bartered and traded among the townspeople, after experiencing the effects of sordid gossip firsthand, after all of these things, Juana continued as the town's most incorrigible talker, remained addicted to the telling of a story—the greater the tragedy, the better—and oh, how she relished the sight of the resurrected Manuel, how her heart beat madly in the anticipation of the telling.

It was Cecilia, in turn, who heard the news first from Juana—news she received with screams of shock and repeated mumblings of *mamaciña, mamaciña* as she held onto her expansive stomach, and then, in a final dramatic flourish, she fell to her knees, pointing her arms up in a mad supplication towards the heavens. Her loud and garbled shrieks soon brought Carmen outside to see about the commotion, and then Matilde, and finally María, who quickly dispersed the group that had gathered by the drinking fountain with her loud demand of *What in the demonios is going on here?*

It was up to Cecilia to relate the news. Juana had retreated into the background, too afraid of *la Reina* to do the telling, but too much of a gossip to leave before she could see the look on María's face when she found out that her dead son-in-law not only had returned from the dead very much alive, but had returned in the arms of a tall, spectacular foreign woman.

As expected, the news of Manuel's return came as a shock to María, who responded by immediately ordering Juana to *get off my property*—even though they were, in fact, standing in front of the communal well and nowhere near her property, but who was Juana de Castro to argue? María then turned to her sisters and her daughter Matilde, huddling together horrified by the news and more nervous now that María had learned of it.

And what do you think you're doing, wasting your time with gossips like Juana? María barked at them. *Get back to work! This is not a circus, nor is it a mass for the dead, and there are things to be done, animals to take care of.*

Later, once the women had sat down to a meal of five courses—it was Cecilia's long-established habit to cook excessive amounts of food whenever a crisis loomed—it was María who divulged the news to an unsuspecting Asunción, who had wondered, it was true, just what was going on with all the food and the silent faces of the usually loud and irrepressible Encarna women.

It seems that lout of a husband of yours is back from the dead, María told her between bites of *salpicón* and Cea's famous corn bread, and without revealing any emotion whatsoever.

While Asunción stared at her mother dumbfounded, the other

women stuffed huge bites of food into their mouths, trying with all their might and powers of concentration to assuage the tension of the moment with their determined and exaggerated mastication.

How strange this visit from the dead, don't you think, Asunción? But then it seems that only the louts of the world ever do make it back.

More chewing from the women and then loud and inconsolable wailing from Asunción, who tried to get up from the table but was stopped by her mother's furious order to stay right where she was and tell the women, finally, what news had arrived in that letter so long ago, a letter, come to think of it, that no one but Asunción had ever read.

Don't make me talk Mamá, she told María, who continued to eat calmly as if nothing were amiss, as if this were just one more night like the rest and a dead relative wasn't roaming the streets of the town giving the people plenty to talk about

But of course you must talk, Asunción, of course you must talk, María said, finally dropping her fork and with it the composure she had managed to maintain since early that afternoon. All around her, the women shook with emotion, with fear, with an overwhelming sense of trepidation.

How is it that a man who has perished in Brazil can show up, nine years later, dressed in a damned cravat and holding onto a godforsaken woman?

Mamá, you do not want me to talk, I promise you, Asunción told her between enormous sobs, so loud and dejected that they completely discouraged the women from their determined chewing.

Sí, I do, I do. I want to hear what was in that letter, Asunción! I want to hear it, I tell you.

María was on her feet now, pounding at the table with a

ferocity that shook the room and frightened the women who were already terrified by all that had happened and heartbroken to see Asunción—the tragic, no longer widowed but most certainly abandoned, Asunción—weeping inconsolably into the tableware.

But suddenly it was Asunción herself who was standing up and shaking a fork into the amazed face of her mother, screaming unbelievable and horrifying things. *It was you, wasn't it Mamá, it was you who sent him away in the first place, you who paid for his ticket, you who seduced him, took him from your own daughter!* And then other accusations, and more screams and gasps from the women at the table, who had no idea, could not believe, *what a revelation!,* while María, sombre, unflappable María who, good God, should deny such things, said nothing, sat down, stared silently and without emotion into the face of her enraged daughter.

Later, after Asunción had run from the table and into her bedroom where she continued to sob madly for hours, after the stone-faced María had forced the rest of the women to eat all of the food of all of the courses until they were bursting with unbearable nausea, after they had finally retired quietly and in terror to their bedrooms where they could not sleep, where they could not possibly talk, where they prayed silently and fervently that the day would disappear and with it the nightmare of Manuel and his Brazilian lover—after all of this had transpired, María, donning a black cape and wrapping a handkerchief on her head, set out into the cold early December night to have a word with the man whose sudden and unforeseen resurrection would alter her life forever.

Inside his room at the *Pensión Nogueira*, Manuel Pousada shuffled the playing cards he had purchased in Río one day, not long after his arrival in the land of his dreams, the ones he had kept close to his breast ever since—an amulet of sorts to ward off the evil spirits. And there were many according to the crazy Brazilians—the suspicious, magical Brazilians, the happy, beautiful people who had had the good graces to live up to all of his youthful expectations.

By now, he reasoned, María *la Reina* would know all about his return, would know about Gabriela, would be seething in her cold-blooded, arrogant way. He wished with all his might that he could have seen her face when she received the news, delivered gleefully, no doubt, by one or another of the town's many gossips.

In a chair next to him, Gabriela gazed into his face defiantly. *This country of yours, meu amor, is a dark, unpleasant toilet.* By her side, Natalia Costa, Gabriela's mother, snorted in agreement. She had accompanied them here not out of any desire to protect the virtue of her daughter, nor, for that matter, to stave off any talk that was sure to arise from Gabriela's transatlantic cavort with a married dead man. She had come with them because she felt it was her due to travel, to reap the benefits from her daughter's beauty for the few years that she could lay claim to them. And back home, in any case, there was nothing waiting for her.

Manuel had grown tired of the two women long ago, had come to regret bringing them here just so they could shock the town and drive María to the brink of madness, just so he could humiliate her daughter and the entire family so publicly and loudly that she would have no other choice but to see him. Gabriela and Natalia were impossible women, both of them forever whining, the daughter no better than the mother when all he could contemplate, the only thing that mattered to him, was the thought of his reunion with María. *María.*

After he had settled in Brazil almost nine years ago, after the novelty of the experience had worn off in the country that had promised so much, that had dazzled him in his dreams during the dark nights of Canteira's impossible winters, after he had grown accustomed to the heat, surprising himself with how fast he had done so, he had woken one day with the sun streaming in through the window of one of the innumerable houses he had inhabited during the years, and had decided there and then that Brazil, just like one of the lovers from his turbid past, was nothing but a hollow shell of what he had imagined.

He grew depressed. He changed cities, still looking, taking on small jobs in restaurants where he was harassed by customers who pulled at his apron strings and made fun of his surliness, taking on work in countless hotels afterwards, until he was thrown out, inevitably, because of his laziness. Then he tried his hand selling furniture in one of the small shops of Brasilia, run by a Portuguese expatriate who complained about his carelessness, about Manuel's habit of accosting the women, and finally, in a fit of exasperation, drove him away as well. Manuel didn't care, he continued to be bored, continued to search the streets for that elusive something. Later, after years of aimless wandering, he would finally find his niche in construction—in laying down lines for the railway that was to connect remote regions of the country to other remote regions and in paving roads side by side with countless young children, enjoying the noise of the hammering and the soldering, the sound of endless building, the only racket that could silence his ruthless and punishing mind for even a moment.

Still, he could not stop thinking about María. Despite the

ongoing love affairs, despite the beauty of the women, despite the heat of Brazil, so seductive it could dissolve even the most potent obsession, still he could not stop thinking of her. In place of his youthful fantasies of Brazil—of the scent of the heat and the promise of the long days—there was now, exclusively, the image of the beautiful and haughty María. He was sure—could not live without the thought that deep inside the part of her that remained hidden from the world—María loved him as deeply and as passionately as he loved her.

I will tear the heart from your body, María, if it should be otherwise.

At that very moment, the object of his fervent desire was navigating through the back streets of Canteira, noticing nothing but the road ahead and the treacherous sky that hovered above her. It was a beautiful night, cold and dry, but thankfully—because it was December, the month of long nights when the famous depressions that afflicted the residents of Canteira were more pronounced and even more desperate—she bumped into no one. Most people were safely ensconced inside their kitchens, warming their feet by the wood stove, waiting for the long night to end and summer to arrive and with it some semblance of happiness.

Among the news disseminated by the gossiping Juana de Castro had been Manuel's whereabouts in Canteira. The owner of the *Pensión* Nogueira, a quiet and dignified man and one of the few people in town to see no value whatsoever in the peddling of a story, received María at the door that night without commentary or question. *The first room on the right,* he told her, disappearing so quickly and so quietly that she had no chance to thank him for his discretion.

It was Gabriela who answered the door, dressed in a white

robe of silk and lace, her hair slicked back with *brillantina.*

What do you want, señora? She asked her, in her singsong way, in the tone of a woman bored and tired and exasperated by the circumstances of her life but incapable of dreaming of anything more pleasing at the moment.

María. Finally. Manuel appeared suddenly behind Gabriela, breathless and nervous, stopping only to order the two women to the adjoining room using a tight, controlled voice intended to discourage any discussion.

María, this is María? Gabriela screamed, between guffaws of disbelief, and motioned to her mother, who ran to catch a glimpse of Manuel's great love and saw, standing before her, a woman not much younger than herself—*sí,* beautiful in a jutting, aggressive way, but this was an old woman, not the young, spectacular creature she and her daughter had envisioned.

Old sí. But also decent never forget it was María's reply to the women, issued without even a glance in their direction and spoken in the language of the region, which so resembled Portuguese that the women understood not only the words but all of their hidden meanings.

Before they could utter a response and exacerbate the already unbearable tension, Manuel ordered them once more to Natalia's room, this time allowing for no discussion, and off they went resentfully, casting backward glances at María and, once in the room, immediately plastering their ears to the wall, intent on hearing every single word that transpired between them.

Manuel did not see an old woman. Yes, she had aged, he had been away almost a decade, after all. But time had passed for him too and many dreams had died, felled by force of circumstance, by the pressure of too much sunshine upon his skin. Before him stood not an old woman but the only dream left to him in this unfathomable world, and he would do nothing to forsake it.

You were not supposed to return, Manuel, María said in a quiet voice, looking straight into his eyes so that he would know she was not afraid and would not concede defeat, though she felt it—deep in her heart and in the pit of her stomach, she felt it.

Have you heard? You have a daughter. To say nothing of a wife.

I have heard of the daughter, Manuel responded still breathless. *As for the wife, it was you who drove me from her or don't you remember?*

María shook her head. She was tired. Back home, her daughter was crying, was desperate, had suffered more today than she would perhaps suffer ever afterwards. María wanted this over with.

Now that you're back, I suppose it is better that you return to the house and assume your role as husband and father, Manuel. Though, as you must know, the thought of this is completely distasteful to me.

There it was again—the disdain. Perhaps what had inflamed his ardour all this time was this disdain, the ease with which she could dismiss him. This was *la Reina*, after all. María *la Reina*, tormentor of his nights, the inspiration at the heart of his miserable days and nights of longing. Could she not see how much he loved her? Did she not know how long he had waited for this moment?

Had you left this miserable town for even a week, Doña María, you would have learned something about the fine art of negotiation. Insults, he told her, his breathlessness now replaced by wounded anger, *are not a part of this art.*

You have not changed in the least, Manuel. You are still as disrespectful as an Andalusian peasant.

At least I live truthfully.

He could not believe his ears. All his dreams of this reunion, of hearing María admit that she had thought every day and every night of him during his absence, dissolved into thin air, eliminated by her disdain—her very real disdain, it appeared, though even now he could not fully admit it. How could he have misjudged things so? She must be lying, he decided, lying to him as she had always done, unable to acknowledge her own feelings because of her fierce, ridiculous pride, the pride that would one day explode, leaving her wasted and withered.

I will return to the house if it is to be with you, he said now, exhausted by years and years of waiting for this moment, only to see it crumble into a thousand pieces before him.

How can you ask such a thing? How can your mind think such thoughts, your mouth utter such words of insanity? It was useless, she saw that now. She saw that her long walk in the night had served for nothing, that her daughter would never forgive her, that maybe her granddaughter, once she was older and was told of it, wouldn't forgive her either. Even though he had never touched even a single hair on her head, had never stood close enough to inhale her breath, people would always think otherwise. That was the way of the world, the manner in which all things unfolded. The situation was such that she would be damned with him in the house and damned without him. There was no God, there could not be a heaven, when the sacred love of a child could be threatened by the kind of man who stood before her.

She was wrapping her head in her black scarf when Manuel took a step towards her, a desperate man, seeing his dream disappear yet again, this time forever, and—*Wait*, he shouted at her. *Don't go. Maybe I could learn to live in the house, in a world without sun, with a woman I do not love. Yes, maybe it can be done. At least it would mean being next to you, María*—all of these thoughts, mumbled-jumbled in desperation, came tumbling nonsensically from his heart in a final frantic plea, uttered so loudly that the women in the adjoining room heard them clearly, and by then they had had enough. Out came Gabriela, screaming at him, *You bastard wretch, bringing us to this horrible town just so we can listen to you humble yourself before this witch!*

And to María, *Leave now, leave before you live to regret it!* Then she stopped suddenly because her mother had materialized behind them all and, grabbing the candelabra given to Señor Nogueira by a traveller from Almería, stabbed it into the shocked face of María, gouging out her left eyeball, and there was blood everywhere, and the cries that emerged from Manuel, Gabriela, and especially María filled the night, ceasing only after she had crumpled to a heap on the ground, defeated, silent, nearly blinded.

Can you believe the things that happen to those Encarna women? the gossips will ask each other gleefully in the days that follow. *Husbands hanging by the hams, others resurrected with Brazilian whores by their sides. And María? What was she doing there that night? God knows how long the love affair between Manuel and María had been going on! Poor Asunción! Stabbed in the back by that arrogant mother of hers. See? That is what beauty does. That is what beauty brings. Thank God for María la Reina! Saving us from another season of despair and in the end only an eye paid for the privilege señores. A single, perfect eye.*

PART TWO

1930–1947

BY THE MID-1930S THE STREAM OF *CONTRABANDISTAS* that had been pouring through Canteira for decades now had begun singing a different tell-a-tale tune. Where once their stories, their lives, the accounts they told the women over dinner and *café* were of the *my-wife-is-Teresa-of-las-Montes-and-I-live-on-the-Rua-Pilar*-variety—now their talk was of darker matters, of upheaval and revolution and the *peligro amigos*, of the dangers that were looming all around them. It was a flurry of words, of strange and heady ideas that were all the rage in the neighbouring region of Asturias and in Madrid—a place that appeared increasingly dangerous inside the stories told by José from Toledo and Ramón from La Línea. Anarchism was on their mouths, anarchism and socialism and even darker things, abortion and votes for women and *who needs the vote,* Carmen would ask Cecilia, shocked and shaken by such talk, *when all that matters are the words of the Lord? And the Lord, eh—the Lord has no need for votes or other crazy ideas.*

Gloria, no longer a child but still unendingly curious just like her aunt Matilde, relished the new political climate, loved hearing the stories told by the men who stopped at their *pensión,* who told of events that were happening in the rest of the country, a place that seemed as far away from Canteira, and as foreign, as *la India*. Despite Gloria's many desperate pleas to be allowed to study beyond the confines of Doña Gertrudes' small classroom—despite her entreaties and even her threats when all the begging had failed—despite all Gloria's efforts, María stood firmly by her belief that women were better off at home tending to the animals and the household, enjoying the slow rhythm of the quiet town life and not running around in the big cities, with their noses stuck inside books, learning all manner of strange and unchristian ideas. *Your life is here, Gloria, here with your mother, your aunts, and the decency of Canteira.* And she would allow no opposition, not from Gloria, not from her daughter Matilde, and not even from Asunción, who had no opinion on the matter, but who had felt it her duty to oppose her mother on everything in life since her husband's strange and violent resurrection long ago.

In the intervening years—María, her face disfigured, her sight now almost gone, with one eye gouged out, the other clouded by cataracts—since that violent day María had become, if anything, more intransigent, more intractable, haughtier than before, though no one would have thought it possible, not after what she had been through, not after the humiliation of that night, left to wrestle with the candelabra-wielding mamá of her son-in-law's lover, and to endure the talk that ran through the town. And the theories, *señor*, in all of the town's history there had never been such theories.

It was Don Nogueira who had come to her rescue that night, Don Nogueira who had called Canteira's aging doctor to his *pensión* and had tried, in vain, to have Manuel and his Brazilian accomplices apprehended—but the three had disappeared in the ensuing commotion without leaving a shred of evidence as to their intended destination. It was Don Nogueira who had travelled in the night to relate what had happened at the *pensión* to the Encarna women—who had screamed, gasped and, in the case of the impressionable Cecilia, fainted upon hearing the horror of it. But not Asunción. Asunción had listened quietly, demonstrating little emotion and then, disappearing upstairs almost immediately to see about her daughter, had never mentioned the incident again, had banished the affair to that part of the mind fashioned exclusively for forgetting, had proceeded with the business of life much as if her husband had never returned, and his Brazilian hotter-than-hell lover and her sidekick, *la mamá loca,* had not been wandering the streets of Canteira waiting to strike at the heart of the Encarnas' hard-fought-for decency.

After spending a number of days in the ill-lit room of Santiago de Compostela's famed sanatorium, and after resigning herself to the loss of an eye with a rapidity that bordered on the suspicious, María had returned to the house full of nervous women, issuing her orders much like before. Even in her weak and uncertain state, she was still yelling. *What have you been feeding the animals—they have the starved gaze of condemned prisoners. And the house looks as if it hasn't been cleaned for weeks, hermanas, look at the floors in the parlour, and the kitchen, Cecilia, the kitchen reeks, as usual, of your indecent cooking. And no questions, do you hear me?* she would tell them, whenever a curious eye was turned her way. *Not one single question.*

Between her daughter Asunción and her, it was, from then on, a continuing war of looks with few if any words spoken between them. In the initial aftermath of María's return, Cecilia, eager to set things to rights once more, had attempted to throw the two women together on every occasion she could muster, asking endless questions of Asunción—*And what does your mother want me to serve for dinner?* and *Niña, go ask María if we should varnish the floors in the bedrooms*—but she found that nothing, neither her begging nor her tears (which came later, when Cecilia had nothing left but the weight of her emotions) would bring Asunción to look at her mother, to forgive her with a kind act or a single word. There would be no room for forgiving.

The years had passed. Gloria was left to the care of the Encarna women, who doted on her and spoiled her silly, trying to compensate her for the humiliation of being saddled with Manuel for a father. There, inside the *pensión* of María *la Reina,* she had grown up, thriving above all on the tales from the *contrabandistas* who passed through her home and welcomed the attention of the young Encarna girl, *the one*, they would whisper to each other, *with the bastard of a father whose lust resulted in the blinding of the once beautiful María.*

Around town, worse things were said, as that terrible night was relegated to the annals of most-often-told stories. Nothing of the kind had ever happened in those parts, not in recent memory, and this being the age before movies and the magazines of the heart that would become all the rage decades later, the happenings of that night soon adopted all the trappings of a legend, the thing you told the odd visitor who appeared in town. *Amigo,* you would say, *let me tell you the tale of Manuel and the once beautiful María.* The story had been told so many times, in fact, and in so many different ways that it soon became unclear what had really occurred on that night, and eventually, it was rumoured that money had been involved, and then prostitution and that

Manuel Pousada had perished in Argentina during a revolution. Later, the story was changed again—no, he had died of syphilis somewhere in Chile—but in truth no one really knew if he was dead or alive, despite the arduous and often ridiculous efforts of many in town to determine such things.

Gloria learned of the event as soon as she was old enough to make sense of it, the women reasoning that the story would have been impossible to keep quiet in Canteira—*a town of hens and roosters clucking away at people's miseries,* Cecilia said, though she herself was surely one of the town's greatest gossips. Gloria never told the women that she had seen her father on that fated day, had run to the *Pensión* Nogueira on a tip from Carmelita Pereira—*Oye, look, your papá is here in town, has come to life again*—and off she had gone, not understanding why or how but needing to catch a single glimpse of him, which she did, in the Calle del Príncipe, his arm in that of a tall, imposing woman. The sight had so confused her that she had almost run to him, only to be stopped by her mother, who had appeared magically out of nowhere, and who had grabbed Gloria's hand and walked her back home in silence. After that, the events of the day remained forever unspoken between them, much as if they had never happened at all and Manuel's resurrection had been a confusion, a mix-up, a bad dream like the kind that plagued Gloria during the nights when the winds were particularly strong and the rain came down relentlessly, in wave upon wave of melancholy.

And then, one day, fifteen years after his first and fateful visit, Don Miguel, the mysterious Andalusian with the green eyes and the sonorous way of speaking, appeared at the *pensión* of María *la Reina* once more—older, less regal than they remembered him, but unmistakably their Don Miguel, a man whose stories had so enchanted and entertained the women once that even now, after all those long and absent years, they had never forgotten him.

It was Carmen who saw him first and off she went, running to tell Cecilia, who shrieked in delight and ran from the kitchen to the parlour, then back to the kitchen again, to stoke the embers of the fire and pour more paprika into the *caldo gallego,* and then off she went into the fields announcing the news, between gasps and wheezes, to María, Asunción, and a perplexed Gloria, who had been a baby when Don Miguel last visited, and could not fathom why the women were in such an uproar.

By the time Matilde arrived from giving her morning lecture to the students at the school, after strolling through the Tuesday market chatting with the farmers from the nearby villages who peddled their hams, eggs, and chickens there, by the time she entered the house her mind fixed on the news of all the unrest plaguing the region of Catalonia, by the time she had been greeted by the excited women in the household, who tormented her with their incessant entreaties to *Guess who has appeared at our door! Guess, Matilde, though you'll never get it*, Don Miguel had installed himself comfortably in the *pensión*, had bathed in cold water and run a comb through his long, now sparse, white hair. Although older and more weathered than during his previous visit so long ago, he appeared before Matilde in all of his past glory, the sight of him propelling her into a frenzy of buried memories and almost forgotten desires, desires that had changed over time, adapting slowly to the circumstances of her life until they had become so nebulous and distant that she could hardly remember their original meaning. But now he was here, back again before her, his face exactly as she remembered, the eyes that had beckoned to her once inside her dreams, as green and as full of promise as ever.

You have not changed one bit, Matilde, Don Miguel told her gallantly, for, like him, she had of course changed infinitely more than one bit since their last meeting. Her hair had turned grey and her features, large and unbecoming then, were more pronounced and even less becoming now, so many years later, but the sincerity in his eyes and the fact of his remembering her after all those years and after his endless roaming over the unknowable earth, after all the people he had surely met there—his remembering her so astounded and pleased her that she could not doubt for one second that he was being anything less than honest, despite the arch of María's right eyebrow at his words and the sarcastic grunt from Asunción, seated as usual by the window.

He too did not bring good news. Where once his stories had been full of extraordinary beings and the long dark night of the soul that opened up the heart to the workings of God's infinite wisdom, now his talk was of more frightening things, of government mishap and unrest in the region of Andalucía, of the lynching of priests and nuns in Barcelona.

Our world is a ball wound tight with anger, he told the women that first night, as he drank his customary glass of iced *aguardiente* by the heat of the wood stove in the kitchen. *More anger than could ever have been imagined.*

Matilde, now older, less given to romantic fancy and wiser from all her years of reading and contemplation, soon dispensed with her habitual shyness and engaged Don Miguel in a spirited debate on the state of the nation and the ideas of the communists and the consequences that could be expected from all the strikes being waged by the miners in Asturias. The other women—

except for Gloria, who listened to every word with a focus that María would later declare to have been *unbecoming in a woman*—yawned and stirred at this talk, interjecting every so often to implore Don Miguel to tell one of his stories from the past, *por favor*, *you know, of that two-headed man*, *remember*? and his German mistress and the tragedy that befell them inside one of the sleepy towns of Castile. Finally, smiling at Matilde, Don Miguel had abandoned the talk of politics to retell some of the tales that had enthralled them once, that had made the women famous in Canteira when they recounted them again and again, imitating Don Miguel's Andalusian accent and adding new details at every telling.

The following morning, Don Miguel walked with Matilde to the prettiest spot in Canteira, still spectacular, unchanged, the chestnut trees as vibrant, the hills as striking as they had once been, the endless shades of green overlapping like the waves of the Pacific—the ocean, he had told her once, that held the key to life's ultimate meaning. There, sitting on the rock engraved with the alchemical symbols, they soon turned their talk to the subjects discussed in the black books that had arrived regularly for Matilde, hidden inside crates of fresh fish and American tobacco. They stayed there until the day darkened and the sky, particularly clear on that night, hovered over their comfortable and peaceful silence.

One afternoon, a week after his arrival, Don Miguel accompanied Matilde to town and there, by the steps of the ancient stone church—the church that many years later would be sandblasted and cleaned on the orders of the new parish priest from the city of Burgos, a cleaning that would reveal a plethora of mysterious pagan symbols hidden behind the crucifix and the virgin, symbols that scared the priest, a man who, despite his staunch religious training, believed in black magic and the witches the locals referred to as *meigas*—on the stairs of that ancient church, Don Miguel took her hands in his, and confessed that *during these last blissful days, Matilde, I have fallen in love with you.*

Matilde had fantasized about Don Miguel for years after his departure, had dreamed of a moment like this—though perhaps not by the church, a church she had long given up for more esoteric learnings—had thought once that only he could bring her the happiness she asked from God, the God who had always failed to answer. And now here, look, Matilde, can your eyes ever believe such a thing, your ears take in the music of his yearning. Here stood Don Miguel professing his love and she was at a loss how to respond to him.

The time has come for me to settle down, he told her. For years now, he had been wandering, looking for things he could not name all across the wide earth, and the time had not been right before for settling down to a quiet life inside the small town of Aguas Verdes near his native Granada. *But now, Matilde—the distances I've travelled, the things I long to tell you.*

Matilde, older now, and past the reasonable age for a marriage, she thought, now that her habits had become obdurately entrenched after years of living almost exclusively in the company of women, now that the circumstances were so different, with her mother nearly blind and her sister fatally embittered—now, she knew, she was needed right where she was, right where she'd always been.

Miguel, she told him, *it is, of course, now an impossibility.*

Don Miguel, feeling older at that moment than he had ever felt before, with the weight of his ridiculous belated dream dispersing with her smile, the smile that spoke of so much love for the world that it was almost intoxicating, accepted her words without comment. He also had lived too many years on his own, straddling the world here and there, searching endlessly for the string that had led him inevitably back to her, and things always happened for a reason, and he knew that her words had a greater meaning. It must be so, her refusal was a predetermined certainty. But his heart hurt from the weight of the moment, from having glimpsed the promise of immortality in her smile only to see it forever denied to him, from being left with the unbearable thought, that in the end, his life had been a complete and utter failure, for he had travelled the world, seen outstanding things, only to be rejected—late in life, when each and every desire is a truth—by this plain, spectacular woman, whose heart was so large, its extensions so deep, that only with her did he feel he could find peace after all the fruitless years searching for it.

He left the very next day, leaving the women once again at odds with themselves. Cecilia, with no one to tell her the secrets of French and Russian cuisine, no one to taste her heavily adulterated versions of these foreign dishes. Gloria, with no one to tell her the goings-on in the vibrant and heady world of politics, the turmoil and the waves of revolution that were occurring all around her while she lived here, at the ends of the earth, an unbearably quiet life inside a town of barbarous ignorance. María, who cared little for Don Miguel and had sensed long ago that he had been the one to lead her daughter Matilde down the path of bookish perdition. And finally, Matilde herself, who smiled at Don Miguel as he climbed upon his horse, communicating with her eyes her sense of loss at the wretched machinations of time, time that brought feelings to one person while forgetting the other, relegating then her, now him, to the realms of unrequited love and unrealized dreams, to the torment of what never was, yet surely should have been.

The tensions that Don Miguel had spoken of did not take long to materialize into something infinitely more sinister. A year later, on a warm night in July of 1936, the quiet world the people of Canteira had known began to unravel furiously. Later, those who survived with bodies and minds intact would tell their grandchildren of it—they would talk of the hardships they had endured, the hunger, the unending fears for the future. For three years, shots rang out and fires burned and the country fell, bit by bit, into the hands of one and then another and then another still. This war was, truth be told, a very complicated thing. Ideas had taken over the land, ideas dressed in army gear of red and green and even more complicated colours and guises. For the next three years, families would be ripped asunder, nuns raped, priests crucified. And in the end, there would be no songs sung in triumph, no flags waved about in glee. In the end, sadness, death, prisoners shot and poets exiled, and the arrival only of a violent, wretched misery.

As always, it was a small tale, a tale of troubled love and sibling rivalry, that signalled to everyone that life would no longer be the same. Later, when the people of Canteira told the story inside the tavern of Roberto Madriñán, they said that this had been the first fatal shot to be fired in the war, though no shot was actually fired. That this was the first breath of the winds to come which would, during the years that followed, raze the country, leaving families unhinged, houses burnt, and a million love affairs unrealized, so that more broken hearts were left than eucalyptus trees, planted on the order of businessmen, eager for cheap lumber to sell to men in lands faraway.

It was Cecilia who told this story best, who held onto her heaving heart with the most emotion, even after she had told it a thousand times and the whole town had memorized each and every word and each and every accompanying heave of her ponderous chest—even then, she would continue to emote with all the intensity of an earnest soprano. It was Cecilia who paused at the right moments, adding colour and suspense to every passing detail. It was Cecilia who whipped out her handkerchief, brushing away the tears at the sad bits, and it was Cecilia, finally, who would pepper the most dramatic moments with her incessant and inappropriate exhortations to José—*You must try this year's ham, the things I've done to it*—or to Juan—*Eat the soup, hombre, how else is that big body going to survive in the winter's cold?*—returning to the story without missing a beat, taking a breath, or forgetting at what point she had left off to order a neighbour to eat something please, or to drink at least some of the year's excellent *aguardiente*.

The story of the beginning of the great war she told like this. *Around these parts everybody knew of Roberto's great love for Pilar. The poor boy followed her around like a stray dog, do you remember, Javier?—Pant, pant, panting after her like she held the secret to the universe inside that rather big head of hers. They were supposed to be married that year, in June, I believe*—here Cecilia would stop to roll her eyes, a signal to all that she was thinking, was it June or was it July? No, maybe it was May, because May had been the month for weddings that year, since the stars were forecasting an impossibly hot summer . . . At this point someone, almost always the drunkest in the group, would scream, *It was June, damn it, Cecilia, of course it was June*, to which she would reply, *Ah, sí, of course, claro, José, Juan, Florentino* (whoever it happened to be) *and by the way, José, Juan, Florentino* (whoever), *have you tried the fried chorizo? It has never tasted better. It's the quality of the pigs, better pigs I have not yet seen* and before she could continue raving about the incomparable quality of that year's pork, she would be shouted down by a wave of entreaties to *tell the story, Cecilia, por favor!*

Ah, of course, claro. Bueno, as I was saying, Pilar and Roberto were to be married that very year, the year of the beginning of the war, and all the misery that came with it and all the pain we had to suffer because of it—and there had never in all of the time of our remembering been such a love affair, such passion, Jesús, you would think it was something out of one of those fairy tales or Matilde's Shakespeare. Here a pregnant pause, a hand to the chest, and an opportunity for everyone to remember the greatest love story of all, that of Manuel's lust for her sister María, the sister who lacked a left eye now, but still possessed the sharpest tongue in the vicinity, the one María would use at this moment to order Cecilia on with her tired story before she threw everyone out into the street, starting with Cecilia, and excepting only the paying guests.

Well, Cecilia would say, picking the story up again unfazed in the least by her sister's ill humour, *despite their love and their passion and all the fairy tales and the stories of an entire kingdom, there was an obstacle. The great lover Roberto had an even greater rival, his older brother Cándido, who was going to inherit all their father's lands, who had been promised that inheritance since his youth, even though, we all know what tragedies these promises have caused in the past, what poxes visit the houses of those who distinguish between their own children. Why, do you all remember the story of Jaime Mata? . . . Cecilia!* her audience would all shout at this point, knowing that she was heading down the path of another story, one they were not in the mood for, when what they really wanted was this, the telling of the first story of the war, of the town tragedy that foreshadowed the conflagration months before its very arrival.

Perdón, you know the mind wanders. So Roberto's rival was none other than his own brother Cándido, who loved this runt of a girl, this Pilar, who was no beauty, even in her younger years she was nothing to look at, but there it is, those are men for you—Juan, eat some more of the stewed kidney, I soaked it in vinegar.

Pilar knew of Cándido's love for her, of course, and how could she not know, the fool spent his time sending her trinkets, trying with all his might to buy her affection, reminding her that he was going to inherit his father's lands and not his as-equally-lovesick brother. But Pilar was adamant—it was Roberto she loved, Roberto she would be marrying.

Now sometime before, the two brothers had declared themselves to be of different political leanings—politics, politics, the headache and the bane of our existence. Who cares about all these ideas, I ask you, when there are mouths to feed, deaths to mourn over? I have always . . .

Cecilia! came the cry again from her audience.

Bueno, in the name of God—you'd think I'd just threatened to bed the priest of Canteira!

Roberto was a confirmed socialist, a red flag-waving socialist and a writer of socialist tracts though no one, it is true, ever read them—come on, Florentino, one more pimiento, I stuffed them with mushrooms and liver this time.

The other brother, Cándido, the man who would be inheriting, had, of course, little time for socialism, for any idea that would be taking his land and dividing it among the already disinherited—can you believe that father of theirs, disinheriting the younger son just because he was born later, can you believe it? Here her hand would go to her chest and she would inhale sharply in outrage.

Once the troubles started, the stories that came to us by our good friends the contrabandistas . . . .

At this point María would interject angrily, afraid for herself and her family in those later years, given the charged political climate. *There were no contrabandistas, who told you such things, you ignorante? They were merely salesmen—salesmen, sister. Whoever told you they were contrabandistas? Where do you see one around here I ask you?*

Sí, of course sister, the mind, you know, the mind forgets, I am old—

—and as fat as a cow, María would add immediately, in an ill humour that would last for the rest of the evening as she envisioned the three-cornered hats of the *Guardia Civil* marching into the house and arresting all of them. Her words would catapult the always-sensitive Cecilia into big, heaving sobs—*If I am as fat as a cow, it is because of all of the cooking, all the taking care of things in the kitchen, that is why I am as fat as a cow, sister, and don't you forget it, eh?*—and then the parlour would erupt in commotion as people tried to bring the story back to its proper place, tried to calm Cecilia down who would not be calmed, but would remember to tell Antonio the stone mason to *eat more sardines, they are as fresh as the rain in November and delicious,* and soon enough, after more tears, more accusations, more entreaties to *quiet down, you're waking the animals,* Cecilia would finally return to telling the story.

Now, all the rage in the country was the talk about ideas—socialism and anarchism and who knew what other isms, for who can remember? This country was a country of fools then, a country abandoned by God, and in the middle of it the two lovesick brothers, Roberto the disinherited and Cándido the spurned, and of course, Pilar, their loved one. One day, and citing their different ideas as the issue, Cándido challenged his younger brother Roberto to a fight to the death on the bridge over the Avellana River. There, on one of those dark days you see only here because we have been born in the land of the never-ending darkness, a darkness darker than dark, or so the contraband—quick look at María—*er, the salesmen tell us. Juan, you're not eating Juan. Try some of my tortilla, I added ham this time. There on that dark day, they met, the two brothers, fighting over politics, but we all knew it was about her, about Pilar, that woman, who had somehow brought these two men, these two brothers, to the edge of that bridge to fight it out like a pair of misbegotten Castilians. In the end it was Cándido, a larger man by far, who pushed his brother over the edge. Roberto lay hanging onto the railing of the bridge with one hand, his body swinging from it like a frightened scarecrow.* Here, Cecilia would stop to bring her hands together as if in prayer, but really to point to the despair of that poor man, hanging by a thread from the bridge with his brother looking on and doing nothing to help him.

Roberto pleaded for help, for compassion—who wouldn't? There he was, hanging on for sheer life, in the rain, in the cold knowledge that his own brother was ready to kill him over an idea, though they both knew this fight was about Pilar, because no idea in the world could have inspired such madness. Cándido did not heed his brother's desperate pleas for help—of course not, he had Roberto exactly where he wanted him. Instead, he took his axe from his belt, the kind of axe men carry with them to clear paths and cut wood for the kitchen stove, and without any remorse whatsoever, he cut his brother's arm off in one fell swoop, one clear severing of a limb, sending Roberto to his death. Later, Cándido denied the whole thing, of course, denied that he had cut his brother's arm off, had sent him to a certain death, but no one believed him.

Of course, who could? grunts of disbelief and shakes of heads usually followed this sentence.

Although they never found Roberto's body, they did find the severed arm and much was made of burying that instead, although it didn't please our old parish priest, that Don José, who was always harsh and unforgiving and had his own politics, his own ideas. But it was Pilar who insisted on the burial, who begged, implored, tear-ridden and desperate, that there must be a funeral for her dear Roberto, and soon enough her wish was granted—just to shut her up I always thought—and there we all were, lining up behind the casket that held the severed arm, walking behind as Pilar led us with the rhythm of her wailing. At this point, for some reason, Cecilia would break into great peals of laughter, stopping only when she caught the look in her sister Carmen's eyes, the look that warned her that she was entering religious territory with this talk of death, this reference to a Christian burial, and that her laughter was entirely inappropriate here.

Ah well, time passed as it generally does, but not much time before we learned that the heartbroken Pilar was suddenly betrothed to the brother Cándido, the brother who was to inherit his father's lands, even though he had murdered his own brother in cold blood, on a bridge, in weather so dark it was like hell itself. There she was, our innocent and God-fearing Pilar, about to enter into wedded bliss with that animal—here Cecilia gasped, opening her mouth wide in astonishment for even at the thousandth telling and after decades had passed, she still gasped in astonishment—*and sure enough, without a proper period of mourning having passed, she married that little murderer.*

Years later, many, many years later, after the war had ended and the memories had faded of its worst crimes, its worst transgressions—look, mira, they murdered priests and nuns don't you forget it, and they lined up peasants against walls to shoot them for minor crimes, killed they were, in cold blood, by those seeking a different future for the land, that's the kind of war it was, that was the kind of insanity that ailed us—years after it had passed, and we finally awoke to find the sun shining again, years after the incident on the bridge and the marriage, years after Cándido had sold his father's land and squandered the earnings on cognac and endless nights of gambling, years after he had been forced by sheer necessity to become just one more of our town's tailors—and not a very good one, eh? Not like you, *Javier, ah, he only wished such things—years later, a man showed up at his shop one evening, dressed in that strange way of the Andalusians—ah perdón, Don Pascual, I did not see you there—* Cecilia would say, suddenly noticing one of the paying guests, an Andalusian. *Years after, this strange man showed up at Cándido and Pilar's house, looking to have a suit made of grey wool for an "occasion."*

Cándido thought there was something familiar about him, about his voice, although not the Andalusian singsong accent. "Do I know you?" he asked the man, perturbed by an indescribable feeling. He could not see the stranger's face well because it was an early evening in winter and almost dark, and the man wore a large black hat, the kind that was fashionable back then.

"Maybe you do know me," the strange Andalusian told Cándido, "but maybe it is best that I help you remember."

Cándido was still confused, for there was something, something vaguely familiar about this mysterious man, but he could not put his finger on it. As luck would have it, he was joined at that point by his wife, Pilar. The man then took off his jacket and revealed a stump where his right arm should have been.

"Now do you remember me, you son of a bitch, you perverted monster? Now do you remember?" he asked, taking off his hat to reveal his face. It was Roberto, Roberto who had survived the murder attempt or maybe it was his ghost coming back to get them both, now that they no longer loved each other because too much time had passed, and desire had abandoned them like the leaves of a birch tree in winter.

They never saw Roberto again, but they never slept another night peacefully after that. One always stayed up to watch the windows, watch the doors, to watch for the brother who had been killed, or maybe not, for an idea, for a woman totally undeserving, to watch so that he didn't return to hack them into a thousand tiny bits, to make them repent for that time when the first shot rang out—except it was the blow from a brother's axe that signalled the misery we were to endure for three long years afterwards.

And now you must all try my flan à la Cecilia, made with a touch of anisette and a dollop of chocolate sauce.

In the town of Canteira, that's how the war arrived, on the backs of two brothers bickering over a woman as plain as a dark winter's day, in a story told a thousand times, always in the same way, so that those who retold it, in towns far away, found themselves adding culinary references—a drop of cream here, a pinch of paprika atop the sardines—found themselves drifting naturally into the story of the beautiful María and the evil Manuel, found themselves throwing their arms up into the air and asking, *Señor, Señor, how could you have abandoned us to the nightmare of those days?* They would weep at this story so as not to weep for their own loved ones, their own tragedies, the memories that ate away at their hearts, so that years and years later, their own stories remained untold, lay safely trapped inside, because the telling, they knew, would bring it all back—the fear, the torment, the pain that could only be silenced by Cecilia's food-laced, emotion-laden civil war tale.

During those long nights, as war raged in the country during the three years that followed the first shot in 1936, once the other women had fallen asleep, Matilde and Gloria would get up at quarter past ten and meet downstairs to make their own sense of things. Every night, they crept to the parlour with spoons and cups and coloured handkerchiefs ironed to perfection by Carmen the Holy One after morning prayers. The white handkerchief they would place at the northwest corner of their makeshift map of Spain. A flag of surrender. A sign that Galicia had fallen already, had succumbed to the axe of Franco's insurrectionist troops, bolstered by Moroccan lancers dressed in their pristine white cloaks. In the hidden pockets of Galicia, in the nooks and crannies (and there were many nooks and crannies in Galicia, many spots from where to plot and plan) those who still fought for the Republic—socialists, communists, anarchists and some who belonged to no party, had no ideology, but hated the army generals with passionate spite—hidden from all but the very few, these dissidents met throughout the war, hoping, plotting to rid Galicia of the fascist oppressors before the fight was lost in every corner of the land. In honour of these fighting spirits, Matilde would sprinkle some paprika, red and hot, over the white flag that occupied their glorious bit of the world.

There, she would say, *lies the only hope left to us at this time.*

It was a war of colours. On one side, the colours of Spanish fascism—the blue shirts of army generals and of the Falange, the red berets of the Carlists—all of them seeking to bring an end to the unwashed rabble who made up the democratically elected government of Spain. On the other, the democratically elected government of Spain: the Republicans—a messy hodgepodge of anarchists in black, socialists and communists in red, and a multitude of other parties, other colours—holding on for dear life to the power the people had granted them. In July of 1936, it was the Republic, this hodgepodge, that toppled, attacked from the shores of Morocco by a group of army generals, a group of dispirited warmongers, seeking to bring order to this unruly piece of the world.

And then the colours rose, mingled and exploded into one. Coloured shirts, colourful ideas, the colour of mourning as people died, shot by the fascists and the socialists and the anarchists and anyone who happened to reign supreme at any given time—the point was to kill, *eh*, *señor*? The point was to make those bastards—whoever they were—disappear.

The socialists wore red scarves. They listened to fiery slogans, chanted songs of liberation, spoke of the glorious future that was about to unfold. The anarchists sported black scarves, black as the night. In Barcelona, during their all-too-fleeting moment of glory, they levelled differences and, for the first time in history, made the world a fair playing field. All the *señoritos* and the *señoritas* gone in one fell swoop, eliminated with the dawn of that glorious age, where no one ruled, no one led, no one ordered anyone else about. Instead of guns and knives, the anarchists carried guitars, fighting the war with furious flamencos, with the engorged strumming from their energetic hearts. Women wore trousers, smoked publicly, received free birth control, were warned to protect themselves against the dangers of venereal disease.

Atrocities were occurring everywhere. They learned of them from the *contrabandistas* who still travelled through town. They heard about them, Matilde and Gloria, once the other women had retired for the night. *In Andalucía*, said one, *the fascists are killing the peasants. In some places they are butchering them in droves, in others, one by one*. Their crimes? Failing to attend weekly mass, preaching their admiration for President Roosevelt, daring to read those godless ruffians Rousseau and Kant. Their fate? The Falangist signature of a shot between the eyes.

In Barcelona, the anarchists are lynching nuns and priests—*sí, I tell you, señoritas, they are, with lances and axes. So much for the anarchists and their harmless guitars. Their crimes? Believing in God, believing in God and the Lord Jesus Christ. Oh, yes, anarchism is a dangerous blight.*

And have you heard of the atrocities being committed by the communists in Asturias? *Sí, señoritas, just east of here, imagine the havoc that would descend should they ever triumph! Decent men and women tortured and shot. Decent men and women deprived of their lives without reason or rhyme.*

But the *contrabandistas* wore their own invisible scarves, had their own secret reasons for supporting one side or the other or the other one still. Each had a tale of woe to tell, a father killed by the fascists, a brother butchered by the communists, an aunt, a most sainted and innocent nun, tortured by the anti-religious zeal of the anarchists. And because of this, in the parlour of the *pensión*, when dark descended and Matilde and Gloria reunited for their re-enactments of the conflict with whatever traveller happened to have arrived for the night, they saw the same story from a different prism, heard the same tragedy in a different voice.

They have bombed Guernica. The fascists have bombed it to bits.

It was the communists, I tell you. It was the communists who have blown the whole town into the wind.

Time would tell. History would measure the final toll. The world would one day get to the bottom of this.

For now, the news arrived and they received it the way they had all other news before. No different from any of the other countless atrocities being committed across the land. Yes, the Germans were involved. The Condor Legion with their Junker planes had bombed the Basque town into smithereens, finishing it off by flying down close so they could machine-gun those who had somehow survived the bombing from above. Of course, the Germans were involved. Spain was nothing but a laboratory to those people, the country nothing but a pit of squalor and despair to the rest of the world. No matter, great art will come of this. A great work will emerge from the gifted hands of an exiled artist, a giant canvas will one day grace the cover of history books in countries too numerous to count.

In the meantime, the Republican government begged for help from the rest of the world. The Americans closed their eyes. The British curled their stiff upper lips. The French waffled—*oui* then *non,* then *oui* again, and then finally *non, it cannot be done.*

As the doors closed on the legitimate, the elected, government of Spain, quietly, clandestinely, the Germans and the Italians sent their support to Franco's forces, lending troops, weapons, and songs to the fascist cause. Only the Russians were willing to help the Republic. Only the Russians were willing to send fighter planes, guns, and troops to this part of the world. *But at a price, eh?* Only in exchange for all the gold in Spain. All the gold in Republican coffers, all the wealth in the land.

And then suddenly, just when it looked as though Matilde and Gloria's makeshift map of Spain would be overwhelmed by white flags of surrender, happily, amazingly, the international brigades with their three-pointed stars, their canvas shoes and their Lucky Strikes finally arrived.

For it is better to die on your feet than to live
on your knees.
For the Republic must be saved.
For it is only in Spain that ideas have triumphed.
Who would have thought it possible in this backward corner of the world.
For the world must be saved from fascism. The
Germans and the Italians must be stopped.

And happily, happily, this fight for the history of the world is being fought in a land of sunshine, in a land of smashing *señoritas,* good food, and abundant wine! So off we go merrily, off we go singing revolutionary songs until we reach the glorious South.

And so it was that the international brigades arrived in Spain to fight the good fight. To die in droves on the plains of Castile, to be remembered as *that idealistic lot,* those radicals who suffered and died for the good of a questionable country down south. To be rejected by respectable people back home. To survive the fight, some of them, and return to their countries—Britain, France, Canada, and the U.S. of A.—with their stories and their memories of the good old fighting days in beautiful, sunny Spain.

For it is for ideas that we live.
For it is the world that is at stake.

For never, never in the history of the world has
there been such a fight as this. A twentieth-
century fight. A fight till the bitter end.

For Franco's forces may win, but they will never,
ever convince.

Neither Gloria nor Matilde ever met any of these men. They never saw one of their earnest foreign faces. On their makeshift map, they sprinkled a smattering of sugar to honour these young recruits. A smattering of sugar that sparkled briefly and then blew away.

Outside, at the back of the church, on the shallow banks of the Avellana River, inside the forests and by the side of the roads, the bodies kept appearing. The region had fallen to Franco's troops, but pockets of resistance remained. The nooks and crannies. The hidden places. Socialists, Galician nationalists, anarchists trying with all their might to regain the upper hand. And the falangists, dressed in blue shirts, fervent supporters of the Francoist fight, struck back. Killed the intellectuals—doctors, lawyers, teachers and the like. They would have killed Matilde had they realized that women too could aspire to intellectual heights.

One day in 1939 the handkerchief folded. The war ended, colours collapsed. Sugar and paprika mixed, slid and drifted defeated to the ground. The disjointed pieces of the Republic—socialists, anarchists, communists, and the remains of the idealistic foreigners—routed soundly by the fascist fiends. And suddenly Spain had a new leader. Spain had its own special king. And then the world shut its eyes even more firmly. The world forgot all about this depressing piece of itself.

But not before a toll had been exacted at the *pensión* of

María *la Reina.* Something which would be remembered long after the final shot had been fired, the last bomb dropped on a battered Spain.

Inside the *pensión* of María *la Reina* there lies a secret. *Shush*, one sister tells another, an aunt tells a niece, a mother tells a daughter. Inside the *pensión* of María *la Reina,* the war arrives by way of five young men, drunk on anisette and red Ribeiro wine, and determined to enjoy themselves, even if for just one night. Later, once the war is over and they are all told to forgive and forget, the women, forced to pass by these men during the Sunday afternoon stroll, bite back the despair that has eaten away at their hearts until, inevitably, one of them cracks—usually María. For look here, *mira,* she simply cannot forget, has no God to help her forgive, and so she stops one of them, intent on his Sunday strut, and she stares right into his eyes, only to find *nada* there—no apology, no remorse, because it was war, *señora,* and those things happened then.

The things that happened then happened long before the war ended, on a Friday in 1938. By this time, the women had become accustomed to Friday happenings. After all, Asunción's husband Manuel had left for Brazil on a Friday, and on a Friday he had returned in the arms of another. On a Friday, also, María's husband Arturo had stood on that stool in the kitchen and hanged himself next to the smoked hams and the cloves of garlic. *And don't forget Jesús*, Carmen the Holy One would be sure to add. *No greater happening has ever occurred than on THE Friday, eh, señoras*? she would say, fingering her crucifix, to which María and Asunción were sure to mumble their *Améns,* but with little conviction because their own tragedies seemed greater, the kind that kept you awake at nights for years, decades even, and no crucifixion could possibly hope to compare with them.

By 1938, the region was firmly secured in the hands of the fascists—the ones who would triumph in the end—although, of course, no one knew it then. At that point, no one could even envision a future without war, they had all grown so accustomed to it, the uncertainty, the fear, but most of all, and strangely enough, the scarcity of sugar to make sweet things with. There seemed to be no young men left in Canteira. They had all departed, at gun point more often than not, drafted to shoot prisoners—poets and anarchists from Catalonia, the Basque region, and from farther afield, from little-known, distant countries. The only young men to be had in Canteira nobody wanted. They were the Pacos and the Ricardos and the José Marías who strutted about, guns strapped to their backs, luxuriating in their new-found wartime importance.

The *contrabandistas* continued to stay at the *pensión* of María *la Reina,* in smaller numbers now, cloaked in the shadows of the night and carrying more flammable goods, the wolfram that would be used by one side and then another and then another still—there were many sides and no one could really distinguish among them all. The *contrabandistas* had no time for ideas, had no need of them. They were businessmen and businessmen had no use for such things—only for pesetas, *señor*—even as the world around them came apart at the seams, even then what counted were the pesetas.

A few were caught, their wolfram and tobacco confiscated, the men shot as examples to others contemplating such things. But many more remained alive, relying on their usefulness during those barren days—*Señor, I know just where to find this or that,* they would tell a soldier who would spare their lives in an instant in exchange for the promise of the Cuban cigar or the bottle of whiskey that was sure to arrive inside the next shipment of cod to be picked up at the harbour of La Mariñar.

On a Friday in 1938, five young soldiers, dressed in their falangist garb, had appeared at the *pensión* of María *la Reina* looking for just such contraband. They had arrived near midnight on a hot night—that the women would always remember, because it was August, and August was always the hottest month in Canteira, a month of night-time tosses and turns in beds and daytime searches for shade beneath oak trees.

The women had been in bed for almost an hour when they were awoken by the insistent knocking at the front gates.

This cannot be one of ours, María tells the others, for the *contrabandistas* arrive discreetly, carefully, wary of arousing the suspicions of patrolling soldiers or the keen eyes of nosy neighbours.

No, María says, *this is the knocking of crazy men.*

In the moments it takes to put on robes and assure the men that they will be let in shortly—for they continue to pound on the door and the windows like madmen—the younger women, Matilde, Asunción and Gloria, crawl through the back and hide themselves in the barn with the animals, leaving the three older women to answer the door, the near-blind María, fat Cecilia and Carmen the Holy One, who will not stop her incessant chants of the *Padre Nuestro,* even after María has told her to *be quiet sister.* Even then she will not cease, *for it is moments like these,* she tells them, she reasons, *moments like these for which prayers were invented in the first place.*

By the time they open the door, the men are in an uproar. They storm through the hall smashing the Galician vases and the

Andalusian crockery, and they topple the bowl of holy water to the floor, ridding the house forever of God's blessings and intensifying Carmen's prayers—for this is the last straw, and surely now havoc will descend upon all their lives, even upon the lives of their offspring, she managed to tell herself, between the endless *thou art in heavens* and *hallowed be thy names.*

What is your business with us, señores? María asks the men in her strident tone, because yes, she is nearly blind, but she is still María *la Reina*, and a none too happy *reina* at this point. She will simply not succumb to this type of intimidation.

Who are you to ask questions, vieja? Don't forget where the guns lie, one of the men says in an alcoholic snarl, the air around him immediately assuming his angry young man's smell of sweat and iced *aguardiente.*

María squints her eyes. Her half-blindness is no impediment here. Anger has overtaken her and she thinks she knows this small gun-toting weasel, thinks she recognizes his offensive silly-boy snarl.

Hombre, I believe it is José Juan, the son of Emilia of Lazar. Is it you?

Be quiet, witch, José Juan screams at her, because yes, it is him and he is extremely bothered by the sound of his mother's name on this foreboding woman's lips, this woman who he grew up hearing so much about but who is today, alas, only one more old person in a young man's playground.

Ah, José Juan. If your mother could see you now, José Juan, the tears she would shed, María says in her sarcastic tone, the kind she has used to intimidate everyone since the very beginning. But it does not work now—it serves only to further enrage the young man who has had enough. He did not enter the house to be reminded of his dearly departed *mamá*. Slowly, he raises his arm and strikes María hard with the butt of his rifle and she falls, is reduced to a black heap that contrasts starkly with the white trim of the windows and the green of the walls.

And then the panic begins. Cecilia in hysterics, trying in her fat, awkward way—*must shed some skin mañana, must lose some skin*—wiggling like *crème caramel* as she huffs and puffs and tries to pull María up again, only to be stopped by the men, who slap her as well and then add insult to pain by laughing at her fat—*you are as big as a farmer's bull, ha, ha!* Carmen keeps praying, her chants growing louder with the passing of time as the men continue to shout and plunder in their search for contraband, because they know this is where the *contrabandistas* stay and that there must be some tobacco, some sugar, some whiskey, *sí*, they are sure of this, have conceived of this plan for days and will not leave until they have found at least one of these things. And then one of them, Paco, the men refer to him as Paco *el pollo*—the women don't know why, but they will remember his name for days and months and years after, will be reminded of it every time they are forced to eat chicken, regardless of how much sweet paprika and how many wild mushrooms Cecilia hides it under—it is Paco *el pollo* who raises the question now that the women have been dreading from the very beginning.

And where are the others, Doña María? Where are you hiding your granddaughter, the beautiful Gloria?

María, half lying on the floor, half upright, answers in a daze. *In La Coruña,* she says, not sounding anything like herself. *We have sent the others to La Coruña.* And because she utters these words in a half-conscious state, her head bursting from the pain of the beating, a trickle of blood running down her face, because she says these words so naturally, they believe her and do not go searching in the barn where the three women lie huddled, fearfully awaiting their fates.

But the men are not through. They have ransacked the house, turned it upside down only to find *nada,* a few coins, which they take, a bottle of *café liquor* and some bread, but nothing of their imaginings—not the silver of their dreams, nor the American tobacco, nor the fine Scotch whiskey, nor, especially, the beautiful Gloria with her eyes of gold, who the men have spent nights envisioning here, traipsing around in flimsy garments of white lace. Nothing. And so they grab Carmen, her eyes still closed, her mind focused on her endless *Our Fathers,* and they rape her instead, one after the other, all except for the tall, bearded man, too drunk to even remember his own name, who stands nearby, cheering the others on with repeated slurs of *Olé* as Cecilia, held back by one of them, continues to cry and María lies silent in the corner, the trickle of blood now pasty and hardened, marking her outrage across a once beautiful face.

Later, after the men have left and the others have been summoned from their hiding places; much later, once Carmen has repeated a thousand *Padre Nuestros,* a thousand *Ave Marías,* has begged God to forgive her for soiling the body she had been saving to offer up to him and María has attempted to stem Carmen's tears by washing her bit by bit, trying furiously to erase the traces of the men that still remained; later, once Carmen has told the others of her fears, of crosses hanging upside down and Jesús speaking to her through the crevices of doors and windows; later, after she has recited endless other prayers, the *Credo*, the whatsitmacallit, all the odds and ends of the catechism; and later still, after the damage has been swept from the floor and the war has finally ended, the women take their Sunday stroll in town and find themselves in front of José Juan or Paco Vilar, both now Civil

Guards—so lucky, rewarded for having the foresight to align themselves from the first with the victorious side—and see no remorse whatsoever in their eyes, for *it was war, señoras, guerra pura,* and there is nothing more to say. Except that María does not accept it, will not accept it at all. She stops in front of them at every opportunity, immobile, half-blind, but not so blind that she can't recognize them, and she stares into their eyes, and as sure as night becomes day and the reverse is true also, she rips her eyes right through them until, one by one, they cease with their *it was war, señoras* excuses and drop their gaze.

Among the women, the night is never discussed. Cecilia continues to cook her cream and saffron dishes, continues to huff and puff. María busies herself with the running of the *pensión*, ordering the women about as she has always done. Nearby, Matilde stares into the courtyard, trying to make sense of the events that will leave the country irreparably transformed. Asunción and Gloria sit, one on the bench in the courtyard, the other on the chair in the kitchen, attempting to come to terms with the events of that night. And Carmen—Carmen continues to fill the day with the endless *Padre Nuestros,* the countless *Ave Marías,* the thousand *Améns.*

And when the stories of the Civil War are told, they, like everyone else in Canteira, listen carefully to the *it-happened-to-someone-else* tales, aahing and oohing at all the right places so that they don't get up one day, in the middle of a ponderous winter's night, on a night when the winds blow with special ferocity, so they don't get up and, grabbing a butcher's knife or their farmer's axe, go in search of Señorito Paco or Señor José Juan—lately of the famed Civil Guard—and cut their fingers off one by one, and then their arms and their legs, until they arrive there, at the very heart of things, and grab that too, pickle it to bits, and heave it into the fire, over which Cecilia's famed *caldo gallego* simmers and brews, a brothy, barely contained Spanish stew.

The end of the war did not, of course, mark the end of the nation's misery. If anything, the misery only increased as foodstuffs continued to be rationed and the world punished Spain for the small, funny-looking man who had emerged victorious, and who now held the reigns of the country in his tightly wound, mason-hating, Santa Teresa de Jesús–loving hands.

Honestly, Cecilia would tell Matilde as she was left to concoct her sophisticated dishes with fewer and fewer ingredients, until there was nothing left but some cabbage and the occasional pepper from Padrón, *that man looks like a soaked rat. I tell you Matilde, we have been abandoned to the mercy of a wet rat.* These words she said quietly and directed exclusively towards family ears, for these were dangerous times, these days of war aftermath, and stories abounded of people still being shot in makeshift prisons deep inside the Catalan interior and on the outskirts of Madrid.

All around them, they saw the ravages of this insane war, this war that had pitted lover against lover and brought entire families to their ruin, that had murdered the very poetic heart of Spain—shot it in the bottom against a blood-splattered Andalusian wall—and banished all other hearts forever, the Pablos and the Luíses and the Juans, who were left, *Dios mío,* to create their art in foreign lands where they failed, each and every one of them, no matter the poultices and bland diets of their old ages, to outlive the regime—or more precisely, to outlive the rat-like man who would rule the country of their childhoods until he went stark, raving mad—and (by outliving them) would deny them the pleasure of returning to inhale the air that had left its imprint on their sullen, exiled hearts. After the war, all that remained, all that could be seen by peeking outside on those rainy, interminable days when clocks and the world stop—all that remained were the maimed men and women carrying about their chopped-off stumps, their bits of legs and arms, looking for a peseta or a warm drink, which, sipped slowly and deeply, helped to keep at bay the cold, dark night.

For María, the post-war period was a godsend. *Be quiet, hermana*, she would tell Cecilia whenever she caught her referring to their new dictator in unflattering terms. For the new dictator, the sullen wet rat of Cecilia's estimation, was bringing order back to the nation, returning discipline to the people and dignity to the land and *He is one of us, don't you forget it, women, born not more than two hours from here on that coast you so like to dip your feet in during summertime. Salt of the earth, dust of the sky, he is.*

At night she counted the money. Because besides being a godsend, a discipline-wielding, salt-of-the-earth, dust-of-the-sky man—the little dictator and his three-cornered hat regime had lost control of this black market land, and there were suddenly fortunes to be had from hidden flour, American tobacco, Colombian coffee, and a million other types of contraband. María, half-blind, long past her beauty's prime, long past remembering her disgorged left eye and those who took it with them on that distant December night, focused her strength on peddling her own contraband, secretly and in private of course (she was a decent woman after all) but peddling it until she had money hidden everywhere, inside mattresses, in between floorboards, in the backs of cheap furniture, and in the cellar with the wine.

As all around them people dreamed of long-lost days full of

anisette *roscas* and other barely remembered sweet things, Cecilia, still mumbling about rats and the new regime, would be handed a sack of flour or a bag of precious sugar, which she kissed, she simply had to kiss, and used to make her towering desserts, her dream-of-night creations, her flan and her fried milk peppered with a dash of contraband cinnamon and a wave of her experienced hand. So it came to pass that the *contrabandistas* who stayed at the *pensión* began arriving in even greater numbers, although many had to be turned away for lack of room, and the place soon became, much to the chagrin of María, Canteira's unofficial meeting ground, the locus of town gossip and laughter that lasted well into the night until María could take it no longer. She announced to the women, *The day has arrived, señoras, to build ourselves a proper fifty-bed hotel and café-bar.*

As luck would have it—and there seemed to be luck available for only a very few, the few who must have sold their hearts to the *demonio* himself, because how could these women, while all around them people starved with their ration of old bread and rancid olive oil, how else could these women be prospering, without previous known wealth and a well-known lack of men, if they had not sold themselves to the devil?—sure enough, as luck would have it, in the midst of all the misery, a government official declared that the magical waters of Canteira were very magical indeed and conducive to curing all sorts of diseases of the liver and the skin, and within months of this striking discovery, the rich and the not-so-rich began arriving in groups of five and six to take the waters at the new Canteira *balneario* and cure-all spa.

It was on the edge of the *balneario* that the new hotel was erected, the Encarna and Hope Hotel, so named on the insistence of Matilde, who argued that the addition of Hope would remind the poorer Canteria dwellers, those who hobbled about dressed in ragamuffin garments, worn and torn at the seams, held together here and there by giant safety pins—to remind them and all those with stumps and other missing bits, that the future had arrived and what lay before them was hope and the possibility, *sí, hombre, I tell you sí, of better days, better garments, and an end to the seemingly never-ending misery.*

María did not like the name, not one bit—*We are not the nation's keepers nor are we its priests*—but she was busy-busy, hiring the men and children who banged and painted every day from dusk till dawn, long days of labour interrupted by months of inactivity that even today is the gaping, festering wound that plagues construction in the land, so that there is always a half-built, forlorn-looking skeleton waiting for flesh of mortar and brick, waiting for the accrual of more pesetas which happens slowly, eh? because money does not fall from trees. So it was with María, who was forced to stop the work from time to time, leaving her workers to scrounge and beg for months while she wheeled and dealt and peddled her contraband until there was more money, and a new flurry of activity could begin. More calluses and sore limbs, but food too, and shelter, and the odd new dress or jacket to honour the virgin at the yearly town fiesta.

The hotel took three years to build, all in all, piece by piece, an ugly grey concrete mass full of new beds and sparkling white bidets, the kind that would outrage the odd arriving Brit—*Look here,* the Englishman tells his equally-English bride, *evidence of the sexual perversity of the Mediterranean mind*—but the Spaniards loved them, all that hot running water in the white basins to rid the feet of soil and remove the grime from other, more private, body parts.

They open on a Friday—*to cure ourselves of our Friday fears,* María tells the other women, each of whom objects strenuously and no one louder than Carmen, who will not appear on a Friday, she simply refuses to, and who belts out her *Ave Marías* with greater force and determination on that day as the cheap three-member band plays its happy off-tune tunes and the ribbon is cut, and *empananda à la Cecilia* is served in the cavernous yellow dining room—*And did I tell you, señor, that it seats one hundred and we specialize in weddings, baptisms, and other days of joy?*—and young men dressed uncomfortably in stiff black slacks, their dark hair slicked back, hand out glasses of anisette, *aguardiente* and black market cognac, and María watches from beneath her half-blind hooded eyes, and Cecilia runs to and fro, cooking up a hake and goose barnacle storm, and Matilde smiles, remembering other days and other guests, and Asunción grunts her usual grunts, and Gloria runs about, flirting with the young waiters, making them all blush and shake with every bat of her beautiful catlike eyes, every accompanying wiggle of her behind. And in the background, Carmen gradually reaches a thunderous crescendo, ending on a high-C of a *Padre Nuestro, que estás en los cielos, hallowed be thy name-o.*

The Encarna and Hope Hotel had officially arrived.

There, during all those years, of building hotels and enjoying the good luck that had suddenly made them rich, years of languishing in the tepid springs and the summers of sometimes oppressive heat; there, as her daughter travelled through adolescence, making her way into womanhood with nary an indentation or a sign—no unseemly facial eruptions, no unbecoming facial hair atop the lip, and, *por supuesto,* none of the debilitating menstrual pains that had plagued the Encarna women since the very beginning of the line—there before Asunción she stands, this very serious young woman in her mid-twenties, no man in sight. But it is only on the odd day, after a day of wandering through the rough Canteira moors or sitting too long in the punishing mid-winter rain, that Asunción even notices her own daughter, Gloria, who is more a stranger to her than the ground she lies on when tending to the cows in the green pastures of Canteira's common land.

For over ten years now, Asunción's only interest, her one obsession, has been the machinations of time. Ever since the day when Don Hermisindo Carré, the strange three-fingered man who wandered through town on the way to the coast, not to fetch American tobacco or whiskey, but clocks, in all shapes and sizes, from as far as Argentina and as close as the town of Lalín; ever since that day when, staying at the old *pensión*, Don Hermisindo engages the usually vacant Asunción with talk of these glorious, mechanical things—of how the ticktock tick tocks, how the clang announces the passing of time, and with this talk of springs and astrolabes, finds a way to finally penetrate Asunción's darkness, to fill her days with the rhythm of the ticktock, the passing of the minutes, the arrival of each loud, beautiful hour.

In the parlour of the house, now renovated, walls painted, floors shellacked, Asunción has placed the seven clocks she has obtained from Don Hermisindo during each of his stops through town—a small, weathered man he is, aged by the strenuous efforts of selling time.

There lie clocks with pendulums, a lantern clock of iron, and one surrounded by yellow and purple porcelain flowers—*uglier than a bare rock,* María tells the others privately—a wood dial clock from England, and a mahogany encased tall clock from the Americas, the showpiece, Asunción's pride and joy. At night, they gong and clang their way through the hours keeping the entire household awake until somehow, unbelievably, they all grow accustomed to the noise.

It is Matilde who finally raises the spectre of madness that María had wished forever to deny. It is Matilde who draws the comparison between her wretched sister and her clocks and the Holy Roman Emperor himself, Charles V, *the very Charles, Mamá, who retired after a life of glory, who abdicated, and you know what havoc ensued from that. The Charles who handed over his kingdom to his son. And do you know why? So that he could spend the rest of his days locked up in a castle with his clocks, that's why. He had dozens of them, just like our poor Asunción. And for the rest of his life his one obsession, Mamá, was getting all of the clocks to clang and tick on time.*

María refuses to see it. *You know,* she tells Matilde, *she is no different from you with your books, everywhere I look there are books. Clocks are bigger and louder; no difference otherwise.*

But inside she knows, knows that in Asunción's vacant stare, in her shocking lack of concern for both her daughter and herself, in her odd behaviour—why just yesterday María caught her trying to lift one of the clocks up, caught her telling Cecilia that this was the only way to hasten the passing of time—in all of these things, there is the imprint of her father, *el poeta confuso* himself, Arturo Pérez Barreiro. Good God, all those years, thinking Matilde had inherited that lunatic seed, the love of cryptic words, the dreamy disposition, the inability to live happily inside the rudeness of the world—and now, at long last, María sees. Sees that it is Asunción and not Matilde who has inherited Arturo's madness, who is the victim of the same illness that led her husband to the path of self-destruction so long ago.

So let her have clocks, let her purchase all the ticktocks in the world if they will make her happier, if they will keep her from death's door. María places money in Don Hermisindo's hands, sends him straight to the coast where another fine specimen awaits a home: a wagon spring clock, a steeple clock, the mantle clock of cast iron that Asunción places on the table in the hall. If we cannot talk like mother and child, María thinks, let her find happiness in the tolling of the hour, in the passing of each infinite minute as measured by the movement of hands inside dials.

But seven is enough eh sister? Matilde tells Asunción one day, when she finds her speaking quietly to Don Hermisindo during his last pass through town—for not two months later he is trampled to death in an accident somewhere down south, and then no more clocks, no more peddling of time. Asunción contents herself with her seven, one or two of which—maybe more—are valuable antiques, maybe even the one with the porcelain flowers, but *God what a horrendous piece* is the comment from all those who visit the house, and who say this only to Cecilia, and quietly, lest they should be overheard.

Those who visit, who stop by for a *café con leche* after the siesta hour, to share the latest gossip with a willing Cecilia, who bribes them with a whole range of sweet delicacies, those who come into the kitchen, where all talk generally takes place because that is where Cecilia passes the time, those who find themselves inundated with the cacophony coming from the parlour next door never fail to bring the subject up. *Hombre,* they tell Cecilia, *this is a house for madmen. All this ticking, all this clanging. How can you sleep with all this barullo? With all this racket, how can you shut your eyes at night?*

Bueno, Cecilia answers, shaking her head in resignation. *Bueno*, she says and then says no more. For what can be said? Her niece is a broken thing, a piece of cracked porcelain, that's for sure. And it is no use complaining about it, when outside the sun is shining for the very first time in weeks, when the intense green of the pastures, the blue of the sky, foreshadows the coming summer and with it, endless days of fiestas, of dancing in the town square in new dresses and patent leather shoes. And the food—Lord, the endless courses of food, the appetizers, the enormous crab, the squid in its own ink, and of course the other six courses, three types of meat, two types of fish, and the desserts, well . . . we won't even speak of the sweets. And the guests sit in the parlour, the only room large enough for sixteen family members and two priests, where they eat course after course for hours until they are bursting at the seams, and amidst the loud talk and the laughter is the ticktock, of course, the endless gongs and clangs of Asunción's cherished clocks from as far as Argentina and as close as the town of Lalín.

Because there can be no such thing as an interminable rash of good luck, not even for those apparently brimming over with it, the families wading up to their eyelids in pesetas—because luck is a teetering-tottering thing, a thing that comes and goes without rhyme or reason, the seven-year rash enjoyed by the Encarnas, seven years of hotel building and silk blouses bought with the profits, seven years of four-course meals at the patronal feast where the town pays tribute to these enterprising women, these *survivors*, as the mayor puts it, knowing nothing of the rape but plenty about the bad luck that has befallen them in other ways—as luck will have it, luck ends one morning, and the world grows suddenly still. Carmen the Holy One has suddenly stopped praying. Carmen the Holy One suddenly refuses to eat a thing.

What is wrong with our Carmen? María asks the others because like the town itself and those who visit the town and stay at the hotel, she has grown accustomed to Carmen's endless prayers, her endless religious pilgrimages to church and cemetery alike, all the complicated sermons delivered on Sundays from her pulpit atop the kitchen chair. This new silence is an oppressive, frightening thing.

Sister, she urges Carmen, *one more Ave María, please. One more Padre Nuestro, por favor.*

The doctor is called. It is not Don Roberto de las Aguas, the doctor of old, now retired, caught with his pants undone as he checked on the condition of a patient's liver, not yet fifteen years old, caught pressing too hard and salivating too much, and banished summarily, of course, this is the Dictator's Spain, and there will be no perversity, no kissing in public or up on the black and white screen. Kisses are cut, scenes rewritten, and salivating doctors banished to small towns where they pray for the salvation of their skins. Instead, a young doctor arrives, a Don Gerardo, straight from the famed hospitals of Madrid, sporting a waxed, upturned moustache and a grey hat, who peruses the beautiful Gloria from the corner of one eye, but not too obviously, eh, because Doña María is about, half-blind but well known for her ability to see right through to the heart of things, to sense, especially, all acts of perversity. So the young doctor reminds himself to stick to the task at hand—the examination of Carmen the Holy One, lying prostrate, eyes closed, hands clasped over heart, suddenly unable to deliver even a tepid *Amén.*

It is a gastro-intestinal disease, no one can name it, but the very one that has kept her rail-thin, no matter how much pressure Cecilia puts on her to *Eat, hermana, eat!* Because Cecilia fears just this, her sister's illness from lack of food, fears being left on her own with no one to calm her fears, no one to share her bed and gossip with. Oh yes, Carmen's sudden turn of health is a disaster for Cecilia, and she assuages her terror, calms her erratic fat-encrusted heart, by eating everything in sight, eating so much that María—afraid she is on the verge of losing not one but two sisters—starts berating her at every opportunity. *Look here, Cecilia, must you eat Carmen's share too? Is nothing enough for you? Basta, please. Enough.*

Carmen's illness has mixed up her words, words once relegated to celebrations of the Lord, chants and songs and meditations under brilliant Canteira skies. Now Carmen, ill and delirious as a rabid dog, has become obsessed with just one thought.

My body soiled, my innocence gone. What do I give to Jesús, what do I give to God?

The women try to talk some sense into her—in between spoons of cabbage stew and chicken broth, in between the tiny amounts of food that manage to keep her alive, the women dole out consolation. *God loves you, Carmen, God has always loved the holy ones.* And as the others soothe Carmen's nights with shushes and carefully delivered assurances, fill her days with rotations of food and embraces, María resorts to the only thing she knows, the only thing available in her own catalogue of care—while the others shush and feed, María *la Reina* issues her usual words of intimidation. *You must eat, sister, and that is that. Now is simply not the time to die with our newfound wealth and all the praying still needed for the Virgin Pilar. And didn't you hear the church bells toll last night? They called out for you, to remind you of the beauty of life. No, you must not die, no, now is not the time.*

No one suffers through those days more than María, left once more to assume her well-worn mantle of unending guilt, all the peddling of contraband goods, all the money stored in boxes and vases—*banks are uncertain places, full of all those eager-to-please greedy clerks*—all the luck of these peaceful years, all the work they did, polishing and cooking for so many sick and tired faces and *now here, the rewards finally arrived, our house newly painted, the memories fading, no more the dark face of Arturo as he swings by the hams, no more the nightmare of Manuel and his lust, and no more the shadows of the five young men, no more José Juan, no more Paco Vilar*. But no, this is a lie. She has failed her sister—failed her the way she failed her husband and daughter alike. She has left the criminal elements to wander the town, their heads erect, their gaits unperturbed, when she could have denounced them publicly. With all her power and wealth, she could have deprived them of their dignity at the very least, but she chose silence instead. Anything to avoid another scandal, eh? Anything to stave off another family disgrace.

And soon María can think of nothing but the faces that visited them on that hot August night, leaving a broken Carmen behind, leaving her to spew out the endless chants and prayers—the chants and prayers that she will mumble silently in her sleep until the moment of her death, when, rhyming willy-nilly, they will consign her into God's hands, dizzy from all the repetition, all the effort of uttering the words right.

Finally, one morning, after Carmen has deteriorated into a thread, María announces that she has found the way to ward off death. *Look*, she tells the other women, the nearly hysterical Cecilia, who cannot make Carmen eat, no matter how much she cries, and Matilde who wanders through her world of words trying desperately to glean what remedies exist—not Asunción, *por supuesto,* not her, look, she still sits by the window, lost in her own world, in her own dreams, and not Gloria who has been left to manage the hotel and the waiters as the others attempt to make Carmen well again. *Look,* María tells the others, *there is only one way to stop this death from arriving. We must, of course, make those men pay.*

And how do we make them pay? Matilde asks, confused by the urgency in her usually unflappable mother's voice—but then, it is true, tough times make lunatics of us all.

We must kill them, of course, is María's exceedingly calm response.

Pandemonium. *No talk of death, por favor. There is already enough talk of death, I can't believe you, sister,* sobs Cecilia, upset beyond repair. That's all we need, she tells herself, more death, more violence, and surely there is nothing left to do but eat. And so she does, her own cream *cañas*—a dozen of them—a delicacy unequalled in all corners of the land, perhaps the world.

Matilde sighs. *How can you talk of murder with your own sister at death's door? What kind of crazy solution is this, Mamá—what kind of madness are you swimming in?*

But no stronger reaction arrives than the one delivered by Asunción—Asunción, who has long ago ceased speaking to her mother altogether, who has lacked the strength to forgive and forget even after almost twenty years have passed. *Here you are,* she screams, her face contorted with rage, *ready to kill for your sister when for your daughter you gave nothing but an eye! After all that you stole from her, you gave only an eye.*

And after these words she says no more, recedes back into the world where *Mamá* is an absent black thing, a place where trees and birds and the night speak in soothing tones, hinting at the return of an unending, unimaginable love, and where she is a child still, running to find *Papá*, who is hanging from the ceiling, swinging to and fro, promising an end to all her misery.

That very night Carmen dies at a quarter-past twelve. A new

day in 1946, eight years after the debacle—a thousand *Ave Marías,* a million *Padre Nuestros,* countless other prayers ago.

It is Friday, Cecilia tells the others, exhausted.

Of course, Matilde says, María thinks. *It is a Friday, of course.*

At the funeral, a line of mourners emerged from the Encarna house and wrapped itself along the winding road, became a long, silky dark thread out of which only whispers and the odd bobbing head could be discerned.

The mourners had been arriving since the bells tolled for the very first time announcing Carmen's death. They had been arriving dressed in dark colours and wearing dark faces, faces that grew darker as María *la Reina* issued her sharp admonitions that this was not to be the usual wake. *Not the usual feasting, do you hear? Not on Carmen's skinny, lifeless body will we gossip and tell jokes, not as she lies there, extending one hand out to God while keeping one foot still on the ground. No marriage proposals by the kitchen, no flirting of young men and women with downcast eyes, and no cognac, no anisette, no wine of any kind. No food will be offered, though many have come expecting it, no food can be offered when she herself died from a lack of it. With her intestines revolting she died, and what would she feel, our Carmen, watching us enjoying a bit of food and wine? Nada, do you hear me, people? Nada. Those of you who come here must come here to pray, to remember, to recite the Ave Marías she herself can no longer mumble. Those of you here must limit yourself to tears, to prayer, to silence.*

This announcement was received with little enthusiasm by the veritable army of mourners who had arrived at their door. The people had come from far and wide, mourners who had never seen Carmen the Holy One but who knew plenty of other tales, the stories of Manuel and María, of Arturo's suicide, and, above all, of the Encarnas' spectacular newfound wealth at a time when few pesetas were for the having—when the black dress worn by Doña Sofia and the dark suit sported by Don Julio Anduriñas were the only dress and suit available in such barren times. Yet these women could boast of a fifty-bed hotel, a renovated house jutting here and there unexpectedly due to the addition of new wings, and floors and the clocks, *Dios mío,* how many clocks do these women need, how many ways to count the passing of time?

So it was that many of those who had come from far and wide did not come to honour the dead Carmen—though *sí*, they say she was a saint, so throw an *Ave María* or a *Padre Nuestro* her way. Those who arrived at their door came to inspect the wealth that they themselves did not possess. They came to peruse the Encarna house from beneath heavy lids and out of the corners of hooded eyes, to assess the worth of the newly varnished hardwood floors, to examine all the furniture in mahogany, walnut, and oak, to imprint inside their heads the smallest of details—*Did you see all the porcelain, Lladró for sure, and the crystal goblets . . . Tell me, what could they possibly use all that glass and silver for*—to steal a look at María *la Reina* and once more recall the sordid tale of her forever disfigured face, and to gawk at Cecilia—*Did you take a good look at her? A bull, I tell you, she looks just like a Segovian bull.* And no food offered did you hear? No small piece of bread, certainly no famous Cecilia creations, no sugar coated rum balls, no *crème caramel.* Such wealth, such beautiful spoons, glasses, and porcelain saucers and cups and not even a drop of *aguardiente*, not a spot of bread, a fried *chorizo,* or a bowl of chicken broth.

Matilde had taken care of the details, the ordering of the walnut coffin from Florentino, Canteira's coffin maker, so renowned for his artistry in making these drawers of death that he was constantly inundated with orders from as far away as Madrid. Walnut brown and shiny like a newborn child, Carmen's coffin was large and imposing, much larger than Carmen herself, who had withered away like a broken reed, left with only bones and diseased intestines to her name.

Less for the termites to dispose of was all María could think to say.

The day before the mass the five women sat solemnly in the parlour, keeping watch over Carmen's body throughout the day and into the long dark night, a night when the rain came down with such intensity and the winds blew with such ferocity that it seemed that the weather was in concert with their grief, that Mother Earth understood, down to her very winding, encrusted roots that this woman who had achieved nothing in life but to become a conduit for God's words, needed to be mourned just like every paterfamilias, every mother, every artist worth his name.

On the morning of the funeral, some of the mourners in the interminable black line wailed like banshees though they had hardly known Carmen (but death comes to us all, death is a democratic thing at least, and when their turn arrived, as it surely would, they too would appreciate some grief, so they gave their tears in the expectation of the ones that would one day be shed for them)—on that morning, a morning that dawned as grey and rainy as the night before, with nary a luminary in sight, no remnants of moon, no hint of sun—on that morning, Carmen would receive in death what she had never been given in life, for a scant hour before the funeral mass, the opportunity for justice finally arrived.

It was José Juan, the son of the long-deceased Emilia of Lazar, dressed in a rather well-turned suit, a dark, sombre woollen jacket and matching dark slacks—no green Civil Guard uniform for him today, today he is not a working man—with his arm lying proudly inside the arm of his wife, Marinita Fernández, a very plain woman with whom he shares two rambunctious children and a quiet, decent family life.

It is Cecilia who spots him first, who clutches onto her heart and then runs to the coffin covering it with her enormous expanses of fat, who cries into the mahogany, screaming, *hermana, don't look, hermana, for surely it will break your heart.* The mourners in the parlour at that moment are not unduly surprised. Death is a hard thing and the only way to confront it, to pry its tyrannical fingers from your eyes, is to cry and scream a little, to mourn out loud—there is no dignity, they believe, in locking the pain of loss inside the well-cushioned confines of the mind.

It does not take María long to spot the sombre-looking José Juan, the same José Juan who made an indentation on the side of her face, left her like a lump of coal to bleed by a green wall, who urged on the other men to take the glory from Carmen's name. Mother of God, what in the *demonios* was this lecherous thug doing here on this day?

She takes Matilde aside, Matilde who has been busy calming Cecilia, who has been repeating words of comfort, *ala, tía, ala, tía, shushh*, who has been trying, it is true, to determine what has brought about her aunt's new bout of grief, attributing it finally to the fact that they are moments away from taking Carmen to her final resting place. She cannot believe her ears when her mother tells her who waits in the mourners' line, making his way slowly once more into their lives.

Matilde leaves Cecilia in Gloria's hands and is soon at José

Juan's side. *You must leave,* she tells him in no uncertain terms. *You must leave now.* The other mourners, lined up silently and respectfully, are shocked by Matilde's words. Can you believe these Encarna women, with all their pesetas, their fancy hotel, and their sweets, can you believe that one of them is screaming at a Civil Guard no less, on a day of family sorrow such as this? But then it is true—God does not grant heads to those in whose hands he places so much money. That, *señores*, is a well-known truth.

Before José Juan has a chance to respond to Matilde's strident demand, before he can answer his wife's perplexed look of *what is this about*? María *la Reina* herself has arrived, limping slightly, her sight a damned, cursed blight, but she can still see, eh? Can still smell and feel all the anguish of that hot August night, and she plants herself in front of him, yelling and waving her new shiny walking stick about. *You little murderer—no, worse, you rapist, get away from this house,* screaming so loudly that the mourners are aghast with shock and expectation—shock because this is the normally unruffled María screaming on such a sombre day, shouting unbelievable things (oh, how the town gossips love this scene, how they rub their hands in glee), and expectation because a long, winding story will surely emerge from this, a tale to be passed on from generation to generation until the last Encarna woman is gone. No, the town gossips simply cannot believe their luck.

José Juan tries to calm María down, defends himself from the onslaught of her ire. *I was young then, Doña María, seventeen and barely a man, and it was war. It was war, I tell you. I have paid for it over and over again.*

You have paid for it, you bastard wretch? No, *Carmen paid for it, I paid for it. You have not paid for anything just yet,* María says.

Matilde attempts to calm her mother, worrying suddenly about the effect this confrontation is having on María's already burdened heart. She calls to Gloria for help—Asunción, as always, is too lost in her own grief, in her own world, standing in her corner, mourning other times, to be any use at all. Still screaming, María *la Reina*—the once beautiful, regal María, the townspeople tell each other by the heat of the wood stove that very night as the winds blow fiercely through forests of oak and pine, the one who seduced her own daughter's husband and paid for it with an eye (God, these Encarna women live such incredible lives), is led away from the nervous José Juan, who takes his wife and departs hurriedly from the scene of his Civil War crime.

The funeral mass is beautiful, the Latin chants of the priests floating through Canteira's cold stone church like a haunting, angelic hum, punctuated and embellished by the bitter winds that blow on the hundreds of mourners, by the misery of the Encarna women who cry and cry, by the whispering of the young people, who attend the funeral just to catch each other's eye, and by the sound of the rain as it continues to fall in sheets, making the rolling hills that surround church and town a greener than green mantle of unbearable bliss.

It was around that time that Carlos Ferreira came calling for Gloria, kept appearing at the doors of the hotel, black hat on head, flowers in hand, timorous eyes pasted to the floor. For years, he had admired the Encarna girl, for years he had watched her from afar, waiting, hoping, desiring her with a fervour equalled only by his obsession with the life of insects, an obsession that had brought him some fame in Canteira, a town that boasted few luminaries, had little expertise to offer the world. As Carlos Ferreira—Don Carlos to most in town, respectful of his powerful father, descendant of a venerable family, a family that had become even more venerable after the war—as Carlos waited and pined for the beautiful Gloria, a scion in her own right, beautiful, *sí*, of course beautiful, but smart also, never forget how smart—as Carlos pined, Gloria occupied herself with ensuring that the hotel would be a spectacular success, worked to ensure that its fame would extend past the wretched confines of the region.

As other young women paced the streets of Canteira, peering from downcast eyes at the *señoritos* available to them, the possibilities for a husband in this town, Gloria was busy investigating other possibilities, reading newspapers, questioning the guests who arrived from afar. What was happening in other cities, what were people interested in, occupying themselves with, in more exciting places than here? *Ay, señor,* to be stuck in the middle of nowhere like this, surrounded by *ignorantes* on all sides, how could she survive? It would have been impossible were it not for the news that arrived regularly from more interesting parts of the world. Even Matilde could no longer console her. Even Matilde could no longer convince Gloria that she had not missed the boat she had been destined for at birth. Matilde, with her tired assurances that what lies inside is all you need. How could she know, Matilde? How could she know when she had lived all her life here, had ventured no farther than to the edge of the Atlantic Ocean for a quick dip of the feet?

So she doused herself with ambition, bathed herself in elaborate plots to expand the business, swathe the family name in glory, amass the fortune so that no other family could hope to compete with theirs. But as the success of the hotel grew greater, her disposition, already haughty and impossible, grew even haughtier than before. *Go figure it*, the townspeople whispered to each other, Gloria had gone and inherited *la Reina*'s conceit, her damned arrogance, her habit of looking down at all of them. But just think of what happened to *her*, they told each other gleefully. That girl's downfall was as predestined as her grandmother's was. *Sí, I tell you*, one would say to another over *café con leche, churros con chocolate,* or a simple *agua mineral* in the local bar, *her downfall will arrive soon, just wait, Clara, Rosa, Mari Flor—her day is coming, for that is the way of the world.*

In the meantime, every Tuesday, Carlos Ferreira, dressed in his splendid wool suit and matching grey scarf, would appear at their doors. Every Tuesday it was Cecilia who greeted him there, making excuses for the lovely Gloria, busy, too busy to stop for poetry and uninterested, in any case, in all of the attention Carlos wished so fervently to shower upon her.

At night, Cecilia argued with her great-niece. *He is a lovely man, that Carlos. As respectful and elegant as I have ever seen. And intelligent too! You should hear what the people say about him.*

Gloria had little interest in what the people thought of him. Saw only a country boy, attempting to masquerade as a glorious prince, sporting clothes that seemed ill-suited to the peasant she saw lurking within.

Sí, a peasant, Cecilia, she would tell her, when Cecilia tried to plead with Gloria to receive him, to accept his invitation at the town fiesta for one innocent dance. *A simple peasant just like the other men in this ridiculous town.*

Ay, Gloria, you can be so unkind at times, Cecilia would tell her, her heart hurting for the young man who continued to arrive every Tuesday at the doors of the hotel, hope brewing eternally in his insect-mad mind.

Gloria had other plans for her future. Harboured visions of a glorious man from a large city, perhaps Seville or Madrid. Sophisticated. Tall. Worthy of someone with her kind of intelligence, her large yellow eyes, and her furious dark hair. *No peasant bumpkin for me. No awkward bug man, courting me with borrowed words and wool suits made by tailors who know nothing of this world, have never been to Paris, are confined to the narrowness of Canteira's provincial streets.*

Eventually Carlos stopped appearing, resigned himself to the fact that he would never win Gloria's love, and left for Valencia, where he would eventually become one of the most renowned scientists of the day. But he smarted for years from the memory of being dismissed by his one true love, the beautiful Gloria, who laughed at Cecilia's heated assertions that this was surely her prince, and who sent him home the way she had all those who came before him, clutching flowers, trinkets, turbid poems written during a moment of passion, the lunacy that accompanies all unrequited love. Carlos Ferreira would carry a torch for the Encarna girl until late in his years, would now and then stop to ponder how life would have been with her, a woman who, once he left Canteira, he never heard from nor saw again.

Years later it was Cecilia who would remember Carlos Ferreira the most. Mention his name along with all the other *if onlys*, all the regrets at decisions not taken, roads abandoned for other paths that later soured. Gloria herself would never look back. Would forget Carlos Ferreira more quickly than she would most of the guests who passed fleetingly through the hotel's doors. So deep would be her forgetting that many years later, when Cecilia lamented all the good men who had left unnoticed, all the good men who had come calling for Gloria only to be directed ungraciously to the door, Gloria would find it difficult to recall him, would search her mind furiously for a picture of this Carlos Ferreira, the man who Cecilia maintained unequivocally could have saved Gloria from making the biggest mistake of her life.

That year, the cold of winter was exceedingly bitter, the season unbearably long. People huddled inside kitchens during that period of confinement, and as the famous depressions grew noticeably more severe, two suicides occurred for every one that had taken place the year before. The coughs were worse that winter as well and so too the fevers, from typhus and tubercular meningitis and a host of other illnesses, each worse than the next. The diseases ate away at the people, who were debilitated already from years of insufficient food and a lack of hope.

In the Encarna household, it was Asunción who coughed the loudest, who seemed on the verge of retching out lungs and intestines both. She had been forgetting to eat regularly for some time so that her body, already frail and withered from all her mind's deliriums, seemed now to be in an even more precarious state. The women tried to get her to sit down, especially Cecilia, who always fretted over illnesses that could come calling from a lack of food, but Asunción would not appear at mealtimes, disappeared sometimes for days into her room, emerging only for the odd bit of bread, a bowl or two of milk. In Asunción's wretched coughing, her wheezing, and her pale face, which had become a sheer wall of sweat, the women watched and heard Cecilia's fears materialize, watched as an infection took over the already weakened body and wore it down even more.

So it was that Don Gerardo appeared at their doors once more, moustache still brilliantly upturned, the air of sophistication from his years spent inside the famed Madrid hospitals of San Carlos and Provincial still evident in the confidence with which he plied his trade, with his easy use of complicated medical terminology. *No talk of disembodied spirits from him, no, no,* María would tell the neighbours later, *no remedies dreamed by crazy people to ward off the effects of witch's curse and evil eye. No, Don Gerardo is a man of science. Don Gerardo knows all the tricks of the modern world, all the secrets of the trade being practised in London and New York by those of his kind. And those are civilized places, don't forget. None of our silly witch doctors there—no belief that short necks lead to brain hemorrhages, no foolishness like that. A man of science he is.*

The man of science did not, however, offer much hope. *It is tuberculosis and a very serious case of it at that,* he told the women after taking his first look into Asunción's vacant eyes, and listening to the irregular murmuring of her heart. Later, he berated María in his stern man-of-science voice. *How could you not have called me before, señora? Do you not hear her cough? That is not the cough of a little cold, a harmless winter flu. That is the sound of an infection, a serious infection that can kill, señora, can kill in the flash of an eye.*

What was María to respond? Was she to say, *Haven't you heard the stories, you fool—excuse me, you may be a man of science but it seems you can still be as dumb as a peasant from down south—haven't you heard about Manuel and all the talk that has regularly circulated in this town? Can't you see she is not well, that her head has migrated to another place and time, and that she won't let me near her, that it took all of my cunning to bring you to her now?*

Of course she said none of these things, remembered only to call him a horse's behind in her mind, not only then, but at various intervals later when she woke up from her fitful sleep at night. Instead—*No reproaches, señor, por favor,* she told him in no uncertain terms. *You know this house is still in mourning for Carmen the Holy One and coughs are a common plague in this land, coughs and colds and such complaints. The important thing is curing the cough, what we must do is make Asunción well again.*

But there was not much that could be done, Don Gerardo informed her in his detached voice, a voice that no longer pleased María *la Reina* one bit. *Didn't they tell you in your fancy medical school in our godforsaken capital how to deliver bad news, Don Doctor cabrón? Didn't they tell you how to talk to mothers especially? Mothers are especially sensitive beings and need to be approached gently and not with all the subtlety of a charging bull, a cow in heat*—and after a bitter interchange of heated insults on her part, clipped defences and entreaties to *Calm yourself, please* on his, María finally put an end to the warring by asking what was being done about this deplorable illness in the glorious Londons, in the fancy Madrids.

There is something he said. A drug, a substance whose very name made María suspicious at first, something about fungus and things growing in glass dishes inside the dark laboratories of strange countries up north. But it was a magical medicine he assured her, though Asunción's case was serious, eh? They couldn't forget just how serious it was.

No matter. *We must get that medication pronto, if that is what is being done in other countries. If that is what is needed to get rid of the cough,* María told the good doctor, relieved that a cure was possible at least.

Not so fast, señora. The drug is available, sí, but not to us, not to a country that has chosen—the doctor placed such emphasis on the word *chosen* that María realized immediately this was no supporter of the current regime—*a dictator. We are not considered worthy of a drug such as this.*

So it was that María learned of the insidious nature of the Dictator's land, of how people continued to die in Barcelona and Santiago de Compostela, screaming for remedies readily available in other lands. This was the punishment the country had to endure for being ruled by that little man, himself protected by his own personal amulet, the hand of the mystic Santa Teresa de Jesús, whose words, Carmen the Holy One had been fond of saying, were sweet music, her life a celebration of the mysterious, the sacred, of the power that lay at the heart of the mystical path.

No, it is not as easy as snapping your fingers, señora. Were it so, I would have cured all the infections in the land.

That very night, María summoned her network of contacts to her side, the Ramons and the Eduardos who had made a comfortable living from smuggling contraband into the coast. *We are in need of something called streptomycin,* she told them, spelling out this last word, placing all of her hopes in the hands of these men who had helped build the hotel—peripherally, at least, with all their lugging of whiskey, all of their peddling of sugar, wolfram, American tobacco, and flour—and who surely would know a way to find this mysterious drug. *There is a lot of money to be had from this drug, señores. I tell you, family fortunes can be made from this type of contraband.*

That same night, as the numerous clocks clanged and tick-tocked through the minutes and the hours in the parlour, Asunción's cough adopted a more wretched tone, a tone more evil than ever before. *Another stab at my heart,* María thought, awake in her room next door as she listened to her daughter's fits of retching and pain, as Matilde, Cecilia, and then Gloria, entered Asunción's room with bowls of boiling water and bay leaves to help her breathe again, as they mopped her brow and shushed her back to sleep, María listened, her heart beating loudly from fear and guilt. *Sí*, this was surely one more way her daughter has chosen to get back at her, to punish her for a crime she did not commit. She focused her strength on summoning God to her side, asking for a dosage of that miracle streptomycin, that strange remedy being administered liberally by other doctors in other lands. That night, she dreamed of two bridges and then a third, only to be woken by another of Asunción's violent coughing fits, punctuated by the clanging of one of her wretched clocks, the one with the porcelain flowers, María thought, the ugliest of the lot.

The following morning, Asunción's illness took a turn for the worse. María thought she heard the bells tolling already, another Encarna death, one she would surely not survive. Asunción was but a child to her, so much anger was still left to be assuaged. And so the week passed with Matilde and Cecilia tending to the patient with all the devotion that María wished desperately to give but her daughter would never accept; even at death's door, there would be no forgiveness, no love given or received. María had to content herself with talking to an increasingly worried Don Gerardo, who appeared regularly at the Encarna house, stopping always to take a good look at the beautiful Gloria, but discreetly, out of the corner of one eye, and asking in hushed tones about the streptomycin, *Listen, señora, has the medicina arrived?*

A week later, the cold lifted and the sky, which had been grey and pregnant with rain for almost a month, opened finally to reveal an unbearably beautiful sun, so beautiful it seemed to María a sign from the Lord himself, a promise that a change for the better was at hand. She was out in the orchard marvelling at the majesty and the calm of the sight when Cecilia came running, her fat jiggling and shaking in the sun. *Hermana*, she screamed at María, breathless, her hand on her heart. *Come quickly, hermana, it is Asunción. She is asking for you, she is asking for her mamá.*

María did not have time to consider the shock, that her daughter Asunción was asking for her, after all these years, all this time of not one look, one kind word, no fleeting touch, not even a kiss delivered into the air for appearance's sake—now, on the threshold of death, her daughter finally spoke her name. Amidst the elation of that thought, as she limped hurriedly back to the house, María was suddenly gripped by an ancient, instinctual fear.

So it is that she arrived at her daughter's bedroom door and was not surprised to find Matilde crying over Asunción's calm, outstretched body. Dead. No more coughs would now disturb the night.

She called to you, Matilde told her, *her last words, her last call for help was for her mamá.*

Bueno, she thought, so pained she could barely breathe. She would be able to exist in this unbearable long joke of a life if she could remember her dying daughter's words at least, if she could remind herself, on all the long and painful nights that lay before her still, that on the verge of facing death all on her own, Asunción thought of her mamá, called out for the one who had delivered her into this world, into this farce that had been her life.

That night as the bells tolled once again for the Encarna household, as a coffin was ordered and preparations were made for the funeral, María thought of her recent dream—the two bridges that were Carmen and Asunción. Then remembered the third, and in remembering, was once again tormented by a fear that broke though her grief. Later, Eduardo Moreira, a *contrabandista* from Lugo arrived—a package of streptomycin in hand.

Gracias, she told him sombrely, for another infection was sure to arrive and then they could rid themselves of it with the contents of this beautiful English vial, the mysterious remedy that, for all its magical properties, would never mend the hole in her bitter heart.

PART THREE

1947–1958

For her mother Gloria shed not one tear, not a single drop emerged from her cat-like eyes. She showed no other signs of lamentation either, no draping herself over the coffin, no monotonous wailing or emotional vigils by candle-light. Not at the wake did she shed a tear, certainly not at the funeral, and not even as Asunción's coffin disappeard into the grave—not one tear shed if only for appearance's sake. María *la Reina* was determined to get her granddaughter to cry, to shed some tears—*Privately, if you like, but what kind of monster refuses to shed tears for her own mother? What kind of coldness is this?* She confronted Gloria repeatedly as her own desperation, the thousand lines of pain etched onto her face, provoked endless commentaries at the funeral. *That is what death does to you,* the people whispered. *Those are the signs that guilt leaves in its wake.*

Gloria would not cry, in spite of her grandmother's demands and her aunts' many laments, despite all the exhortations, the recriminations, all the questions of *What kind of a daughter are you?* Not even after María had slapped her hard about the face; not then, not ever. *Look,* she told her aunt Matilde, *I simply feel no need for tears, no need for rage. I did not know her really, I never saw her look upon me with anything other than her vacant, horrifying stare, and I will not walk behind her coffin, weeping into thin air. I have no reason to lament what has disappeared when that which has disappeared was never really there in the first place. No, Matilde, I will not cry,* she told her aunt, who was worried less about the lack of tears than about the antagonism that was growing between Gloria and María. She feared that the anger worn like a cloak by her sister had been passed on from mother to daughter like a family canker, an heirloom of resentment and hate.

It was María *la Reina*, above all, who worried Matilde the most. The loss of a child was the most unimaginable nightmare, much worse for those who have not been granted the opportunity to forgive and forget. After Asunción's funeral, the townspeople—who loved a good story and rarely shied from an occasion to peddle the miseries of others, especially the hardships visited upon the rich—were as silent as the sepulchre that housed María's husband Arturo, encased there long ago with his cryptic rhymes and dislocated neck. That night no tales were told of Manuel and the disgorged eye, no questions asked of the wealth that had allowed for fifty beds and countless white bidets, no furious titters about clocks and contraband drugs, no dredging up of Civil War rapes. That night, the town was silent because a dead child was a punishment from God Himself, a scar as deep as a crater, destined to grow deeper with each passing day, and nothing, *nada,* could compare with this inversion of the natural order. *No reason to invite the black luck of the meigas our way,* they whispered instead—black as the night, vicious as those Moors talked about in all the officially sanctioned history books.

María shed copious tears, and at night, amidst the endless ticking and tocking of Asunción's clocks, she moaned her daughter's name. One day, weeks after the funeral—a barely remembered occasion, a day that passed in a rapid, indistinguishable haze—one day María *la Reina* suddenly stopped crying and descended instead into a silent, uncommunicative rage. Nothing now mattered; she stopped combing her hair, washing body or face, didn't bother with the ivory dentures fitted by a dentist in Orense just the previous May that had restored some of the beauty to her battered face. And no earnest cajoling from Matilde, no amount of Cecilia's pleas, would convince her otherwise. After all, she thought, what does one need teeth for? To what God must one bow with a scrubbed face?

In the mornings, once the others had departed for the hotel—the front door of which sported a wooden cross announcing to all the tragedy that had come calling at the Encarna house, a large ebony cross so macabre that it scared more than one client away—once Matilde, Cecilia, and Gloria had left, María emerged from her room and wandered to the verandah where she sat, hour upon hour, staring silently into space. It was a cold year; the rain had fallen undisturbed for weeks and the chill had left its mark on the cabbage patches and the fruit trees, but María felt no chill, did not move as the raindrops ticktocked like Asunción's clocks and rolled relentlessly down her face.

The neighbourhood children—seven and eight years old, too young to know of María *la Reina*'s once famous beauty, too young to care much in any case—came by the house in groups of eight and ten, hoping to catch a glimpse of the *bruja*'s face. There on the verandah they found this spectacle of pain—the long hair tangled, left eye gouged out, toothless mouth bending inwards, her black mourner's robes dishevelled and dirty, her battered hands resting on her shiny walking stick—and, seeing her, shrieked and ran around nervously. *It's the witch of Canteira, run for your lives,* they laughingly said. One or two of the boys—Eduardo and Ramón, brothers, well on their way to assuming their future roles as schoolyard bullies—threw things at the mad woman, potato peels taken from the hog's slop, bits of cabbage and *jamón,* and then, finding that she did not react at all, bigger things—apples, pears, unripe figs, and, once or twice, even a stone.

It was some time before the other women discovered what was happening while they tended to business at the hotel. Weeks went by as they whispered among themselves—*What is she doing to get all these bumps and bruises, dear God? And did you see that bit of ripped skin on her knee? Mamá, what are you doing to yourself?* Matilde asked her as she tried to run a comb through María's hair, as she wiped the blood from her mother's face and bathed her feet in warm saltwater, sponging down the bits of body that María would allow her to touch.

One morning, Matilde hid in the parlour, determined to figure this mystery out, and then, God, the things she saw—*Oh mamaciña, put your hands up, mamaciña, shield your face from the bits of rotten fruit, the stones thrown at your legs!* She rushed onto the verandah, long stick in hand, threatening the group of aspiring thugs, slapping an apple core from little Eduardo's hand, until the children dispersed, yelling, laughing—*Run for your lives, amigos, the witch's daughter has arrived!* They could never have dreamed up such fun, they were simply having the time of their lives. Afterwards, Matilde took her mother into the house and sat her in the kitchen, where María continued to stare at the wall silently, catatonic, not batting an eyelid as Matilde wrapped her arms around her, sobbed gently at her feet.

From then on, one of the women stayed behind with María, watching so that she ate her liquid diet of soaked bread and milk, her strained broth, her bits of fried fish. Watching so that she did not wander out onto the verandah in search of penance at the hands of the cold, relentless rain, the taunts of neighbourhood children, the sounds the sky made as it thundered and clanged its way into spring.

On those days when it was Gloria's turn to stay behind, to take care of her aged grandmother—*this bit of craziness,* she thought—on those occasions, María always managed to escape once more to the verandah, managed somehow to end up with bits of vegetable on her face. For this Gloria could only plead her million excuses—*I was tending to the chickens, I was talking with Edelmira, the sardine woman, and wait till you see them, Matilde, these sardines are as large as Moroccan silver hake.* Yes, there was always an excuse at hand, always a reason why María was left out on the verandah just long enough to be pelted with bits of vegetables, rotten fruit, and apple cores. Upstairs, from the window of her bedroom, Gloria stared at the verandah, watched the predictable scene unfold without a bat of her yellow eyes, watched and waited just long enough so that María *la Reina* was pelted with a fig, sometimes a rock, waited one minute longer than she should to rescue her grandmother, her heart unforgiving, her mind as cool as rain.

By 1954, the town of Canteira—once only a refuge for illegal commerce, the resting place for the endless stream of *contrabandistas* who stopped here on the way to retrieve their goods from the craggy edges of Galicia's beautiful coasts—by then the town had grown into something almost unrecognizable, fuelled by money made by those who had emigrated and returned and used to build grey concrete apartment buildings, slowly, one floor at a time, until Canteira boasted ten thousand inhabitants and the future loomed on the horizon, promising even greater things.

The town, surrounded by the most spectacular natural scenery in all of Spanish Galicia—this green, luscious region that poets have eulogized and many more have loved—had become an unfortunate dark monstrosity, a concrete garden with little visual respite. The aesthetic sensibility of their ancestors—those who had built the magic into the granite city of Santiago de Compostela, into Lugo's Roman wall—was now only a distant, barely remembered dream. Those who came from all over Spain to take the waters at Canteira's *balneario* could not help but comment on it—*The seafood is marvellous and the waters hot hot, but the town itself is hideous, the town is unbelievably dull.* But then, this was a different Spain altogether—Goya, Velázquez, even Gaudí had receded into the background, lay dormant, their art as quiet as the grave, worried lest they should offend all the men in three-cornered hats, whose efforts focused on silencing dissenting voices in this new, oh-so-Catholic Spain. *A good thing too,* a bureaucrat somewhere says, lisp in tongue, nose turned up to the sky. *Those so-called artistas of old were nothing but amoral rats.* Beauty—ah beauty, there was once so much of it, so much that the country could boast, could prance around like an insistent peacock, pointing to all the art, the architecture, all the words so powerfully organized upon the page. *Look here*, people could say. *An empire has died, no colonies, not even a Cuba left, but look, look here at how much beauty we've produced.* Now this no longer mattered—art and beauty were concerns of the past. What mattered now was modernity, ridding the buses of chickens and goats, appeasing the *Americanos* with their naval bases, the

English with their cheap hotels in the Iberian south. In small towns and bigger cities throughout the land, people peered nervously out the windows of their stacked, concrete dwellings that loomed high above the ground.

The Encarna and Hope Hotel continued to thrive, continued to bulge with the hundreds who arrived there during the summer months, hoping to cure themselves of their rheumatism and their arthritis, hoping to find relief in the waters of Canteira's *balneario* and magical spa. In the winter, once the rain began to fall and depressions intensified—because the curative powers of the *balneario*'s waters did not extend to illnesses of the mind, could not cure those afflicted with catastrophic thoughts—bedrooms were shut, and the hotel opened only for town celebrations: baptisms, confirmations, first communions, the odd wedding celebrated to accommodate a pregnant bride.

On the threshold of her thirty-fifth birthday, Gloria busied herself with canvassing the women around her for their notions of love. Canteira abounded with talk of Gloria's marriage-less state—*After all, she is no longer young. A beauty, though not like la Reina, nothing as stunning as that. But getting older, every day she is harder to unload on one of Canteira's young men.*

Hard to unload, my foot, Cecilia grunted when this gossip was shared with her over sweets and *café liquor. What Canteira's young men wouldn't do for a marriage with Gloria, with all her wealth, all her beauty, her intelligence—why she is smarter than Matilde even, more poetic than her dead grandfather, may he rest in peace.*

Still, Cecilia wondered privately about her great-niece's lack of interest in marriage, speculated about Gloria's habit of teasing the men who passed through the hotel until they were pathetic, nervous heaps. Pondered how it was that with all the

Canteira men falling at her feet, eager to get their hands on all the white bidets, to run their fingers along her niece's ivory skin, how it was that Gloria remained so disdainful, as haughty as her grandmother was once, in those days when she still possessed a stunning face and withering wit.

Why did you never marry, Cecilia? Gloria asked her one day, as the cook was instructed on the preparations of yet another elaborate four-course two o'clock meal.

One was too fat, one too short; one had nose hairs a metre long. One spoke with a lisp and who, dear God, can stomach the thought of a life spent with a man who talks like that? One came from a questionable family—the father was a drunk, the mother a social outcast of the very worst. Let me see now: another left for Uruguay before we could be married, where he died of typhus or the yellow fever, no one really knows. And then suddenly Cecilia had dissolved once more into a feast of tears for all the trials that had come visiting during her life, now almost seven decades long. For all those people she could barely remember, and those, like Carmen the Holy One, whose absence tormented her still. For all the children she wanted but was forever denied. She shed no tears more deeply, however, than those shed for the memory of her dead brother-in-law, the poet Arturo, the only man she had ever truly loved. But this she did not tell Gloria—of course not, not a word of this would ever leave her mouth. Her heart was an impenetrable wall of silence, harbouring only the memory of Arturo's dead body swinging ominously by the hams.

The rice needs more paprika, she told the hotel's cook Teresa. *More salt should be added to the caldo gallego and to the fruit salad perhaps a little wine.*

And why did you never escape with Don Miguel to the town

Checkout Receipt

Main Library
04/30/09 05:51PM

****

PATRON: CAMACHO, LINDA M.

The bitter taste of time : a novel
f
CALL NO: GONZALEZ
33206006791770 05/14/09

The goddesses of Kitchen Avenue /
f
CALL NO: SAMUEL
33206005384189 05/14/09

No place like home /
F
CALL NO: SAMUEL
33206004673343 05/14/09

TOTAL: 3

Heritage Faire, May 9, 11-3
Free entertainment! Free fun for kids! Main Library Plaza
577-3971

Checkout Receipt

Main Library
04/30/09 05:51PM

****

PATRON: CAMACHO, LINDA M.

The bitter taste of time : a
novel
f
CALL NO: GONZALEZ
33206006791770 05/14/09

The goddesses of Kitchen
Avenue /
f
CALL NO: SAMUEL
33206005384189 05/14/09

No place like home /
F
CALL NO: SAMUEL
33206004673343 05/14/09

TOTAL: 3

Heritage Faire, May 9, 11-3
Free entertainment! Free fun
for kids! Main Library Plaza
577-3971

of Aguas Verdes? Gloria asked her aunt Matilde one day as they tended to the cows near the prettiest spot in all of Canteira, which lay unchanged, as enchanting as it had been since Don Miguel first came to town.

He came calling for me at the wrong time, was Matilde's brief response, and no amount of cajoling from Gloria, no *what kind of answer is that?* would make Matilde say much more than this: *It is all there inside, Gloria. What is inside is all you need.*

Of her mother's love for her father, she needed no further elaboration. That mad, everlasting love, so potent it withered away only in death, so devastating it had turned her mother's heart into a pump of misery, her mind into a bottomless well. *Who needs that*? Gloria asked herself determined, above all, to avoid a similar fate. That love was a form of madness, a heady *locura* from which only the very few could hope to emerge unscathed, and Gloria was a survivor, just like her grandmother María *la Reina*, who sat in the kitchen shattered but still breathing—even after all the misery she had withstood, there she was, staring pensively into the wall, trying desperately to put herself back together again. And had she loved well and truly, like her own daughter, Asunción? Surely, the answer to that was no, Gloria thought, for a cold concrete slab like her *abuela* would have found it impossible to love anything that was not money, anything that did not pay in pesetas or with a promissory note.

On the eve of turning thirty-five—*An impossible age,* her neighbour Juliana told her, *from now on sagging breasts and a rotting womb are all that awaits you hija*—Gloria could still make the odd heart skip, more than one man weak about the knees. And she was wealthy too—never forget all those hotel rooms, that cavernous yellow dining room. Many men in town came calling, with songs and earnest pleas—why there in the corner, for example, was Javier, the tailor's son, staring at her with his big, fishy eyes, composing rhyming verse because Javier was a poet at heart, *sí*, a *poeta* just like her very own grandfather Arturo, writing verses well into the late hours of the night. But you know what insanity lies there, what fate awaits those in love with love, what thoughts of self-destruction can come from ruminations like these. What Gloria wanted, desperately and fiercely, was not poetry but sophistication, a respite from all of the loud voices and the rough manners of Canteira's eligible men. Here, the only sophistication to be had arrived with the odd visitor to town, leather valise in tow, hope engraved onto sleeves that a cure for his ills was finally at hand inside the waters of the *balneario*, in a town where time ticked only to the rhythm of the Encarna and Hope Hotel's splendid multi-course meals. *That Cecilia*, they would say, patting their stomachs, *is the real cure for all our arthritic and rheumatic ills.*

Gloria had not inherited her mother's penchant for tragedy, and could not find the love inside herself, the one Matilde was forever speaking of. She was no bride of Christ, smiled at the memory of Carmen's many sermons delivered atop the kitchen stool. What she had inherited was the propensity for smelling through to the heart of things, just like her great-aunt Cecilia—a sense of smell so powerful that with one whiff she could determine that Javier would never do, that he smelled faintly of bobbins and thread, of mother's fears, and countless never-to-be-realized dreams. And so it was with the other Canteira men who had come calling—Don Gerardo, the town doctor, straight from the famed sanitariums of Madrid and smelling of city arrogance, of mild antiseptic underneath all the expensive German toiletries. Worse, much worse, Don Gerardo smelled of death, of the desperation of others, which was worse than the desperation of the self because there was no way to contain it, no way to ease the pain that lay in other minds. No, Don Gerardo with his upturned moustache, his wicked eyes, and educated man's gait would simply not do, not with the smell of hospitals and disease lingering so near his flesh. Marriage to Don Gerardo would mean a life spent battling the pungent aroma of the newly dead.

So she resigned herself to a life of hotels and books, a life lived through others' eyes, others' dreams. Her friend Carmelita Pereira, all grown up now, had recently married a prominent Canteira shopkeeper and was given, in her newfound state of glory, to hinting at all the pleasures a marriage brought. Not that Gloria could understand—to her, Carmelita's husband smelled of gasoline and camphor, and what excitement, dear God, could possibly be found with that?—but she listened patiently to Carmelita's rapture, her friend had been married one short year and her rapture was destined to change soon into an everlasting distaste, she thought, so let her have her small pleasures, let her trick herself into believing that this mad love is all there is. Yet just as Gloria had resigned herself to living the rest of her life inside the world of women she had always known, Alberto Masip arrived at the hotel—a navy man, dressed up to his eyes in white and gold, tall as an oak, as sophisticated as a Spanish *hidalgo* from ancient times, no dirt hidden in the ridges of his fingernails, no shouting for his breakfast when the morning is announced by the rising sun.

And his smell! He smelled of distant countries, of sea-salt and a longing for inexplicable things, of those historic men in white shawls who appeared every so often on the screen of Canteira's new movie theatre, with its wooden chairs and fresh smell of paint. He smelled of excitement, of exotic happenings in places far, far away. More than this, better yet, Alberto smelled of pure intelligence—why he could recite entire verses of Machado, Bécquer, and Blake!

Don Alberto, dressed in crisp pants and an impeccable white shirt, occupied himself with the business of reading inside the hotel's large parlour. He was soon smitten with this lovestruck woman, this Señorita Gloria—for who could resist such overt devotion, such earnest appeals to the vanity that lurks inside every heart? And so it was with Don Alberto, who walked with greater confidence now, found his opinions growing more emphatic whenever the señorita stopped by to hear his tales of foreign lands peppered pompously with the words of whatever poet came to mind.

You know, señor, Teresa the hotel cook told him one day in hush-hush tones, sensing a great love was at hand, *Señorita Gloria is the most sought-after woman in all the town.*

María *la Reina* was coaxed out of the house in the mornings and placed in the kitchen of the hotel where she frightened many a late-rising guest, wandering there in search of some food on those days when they had luxuriated in their beds well past the hour when a breakfast of bread and *café* was served. There in the kitchen they found themselves suddenly staring into María's violated face—a socket where an eye should be, no teeth of any kind, a web of tangled hair falling furiously down her back—a sight that instantly banished all thoughts of hunger, their urgent need for a drop of coffee and a bit of bread.

María *la Reina* hardly spoke any more, was still wallowing in the pain of her daughter's death, but her powers of observation had not dulled one bit, and she had managed, somehow, to notice her granddaughter's desire for this man of white and gold, had observed every meeting, every batting of an eyelid, every inappropriate hint of cleavage, every quivering of lip. Frightened by the spectre of another great love descending upon the Encarnas like a cloud of hail and wind, she chose to break her silence one morning, after Don Alberto had, with one of his crooked smiles and a shake of his superior head, left Gloria yet again in tatters of nervous desire.

Niña, María told her granddaughter, her face immobile, her voice rough and unfamiliar from such a long period of disuse, *that señorito of the sea is a horse's ass.*

Those in the kitchen fell immediately into an uproar upon hearing María's voice. *Thank you, oh Lord, thank you,* Cecilia shouted at the ceiling, running to grab her sister, to deliver a relieved congratulatory hug, for now surely the worst was over, now surely María would be herself at last. And Matilde too, there in the kitchen to discuss the purchasing of foodstuffs for the midday meal, turned around in glee, delighted to see her mother back inside the realm of the living—back wearing her well-worn mantle of cynicism to be sure, but that was proof, at least, that all was still right with her head—and she too ran to embrace María about the feet, to thank God for the miracle that had befallen them on an inconspicuous day such as that.

As all this happened Gloria turned to stare into the still-immobile face of her grandmother, and looking at her listless eye, her lips sunken and pursed, her hair a tangled morass of black and white, decided right there and then to wed the horse's ass no matter how impossible the task.

It would turn out to be a difficult task indeed for Don Alberto, although flattered by Gloria's obvious interest, had grown accustomed to a life of travel and freedom long ago. There was also the issue of Don Alberto Masip's current marriage to a woman in

Barcelona, but this was something no one really needed to know, he reasoned, something he himself banished to the back of his mind, so that he was almost surprised, weeks later, to find himself standing in front of this wife—the improbably named Dulcinea, given this name by her father, a *Don Quijote* fanatic—and staring at this face, was depressed immediately by the sight, for this plain woman, his wife of almost two decades now, was the only thing standing between him and the beautiful Gloria, waiting for him patiently on the other side of Spain.

In Canteira, where Don Alberto had become a frequent visitor, as frequent as his career—not in the navy as he bragged to Gloria, but in the considerably less glamorous merchant marine—would allow, Gloria waited expectantly for the moment when he would prostrate himself before her and beg for her hand. *I am too old to wait forever,* she told him during one of his trips, worrying suddenly that the moment of truth would never arrive and that María *la Reina* would live to see her opinion vindicated that this man was nothing but a horse's behind—not to mention all the other coarse criticisms (assessments, she called them) of this man's character that her grandmother had issued regularly since recovering her voice miraculously months ago.

In fact, this recovery had become a serious problem for the women, who found that nothing would now shut María up, that she had an opinion on everything in life, every person who made his way through the hotel doors. And these were not simple little utterances, these words that tumbled from María's disturbed mind, issued from her throne atop the kitchen chair—no talk of weather, children, or other niceties emerged from *la Reina*'s lips. Instead what tumbled out were vats of venom, spittoons of spite, carefully chosen, well-formulated harangues of hate uttered without regard for propriety or the reputation of the victim to whom the words were aimed.

Who do you think you are, Señorita Madrid? she asked a young guest, who wandered into the kitchen in the morning, an hour past the official breakfast hour. *Coming in here looking for milk at such a late hour. If you had risen in the morning with the sun, like the rest of us you would have drunk your share. Now the only milk to be had is your mother's milk—if she's not as dry as she looks, that is. No other milk to be had at eleven in the morning, señorita-from-the-big-capital, señorita-I'm-from-the-uppity-Madrid.*

Go tell your stories to the priest out there! she screamed at Don Eduardo, one of the regulars at the hotel, when he strolled into the parlour looking for some company during the period between the siesta hour and the card games organized by Matilde for older guests such as him. *The priest will listen to your stories because he has to. Because he was ordained just so he could listen to the miserable outpourings of the likes of you. No, don't come running in here telling me your history and your dreams unless you're willing to pay for it with pesetas, señor, then maybe we can talk about your boring, miserable things.*

Beyond insulting and cursing the paying guests, María *la Reina* had also begun creating havoc by setting the hotel staff on each other. *Do you know what that miserable housekeeper, Marinita, is saying about you?* She told Teresa the cook one day in a secretive tone. *That the paella is full of the salt of your tears, because your husband is doing the cha-cha-cha with Domicilia of Ribadeo. Sí, I tell you, Teresa, that's what she says behind your back. That's what she tells the other staff.*

To Marinita, María whispered what Teresa had been saying

with respect to nasty toilet rings and dusty corners—*You know what that tower of fat the cook is saying about you? You will never believe what she is telling the staff.* In that tranquil period between the siesta and the preparations for the nine o'clock evening meal, María plodded through the hours setting waiter upon waiter, the head cleaner upon the kitchen staff, until everyone was angry with everyone else, and there was more tension brewing inside the Encarna and Hope Hotel than there was in all of the now-silenced, political parties hiding in the shadows of the Dictator's land.

About Don Alberto, Gloria's newfound love, María was especially vicious—for him she reserved the sharpest lashes of the tongue. *There is a rat in the land dressed in white and gold,* she would say, whenever she stumbled upon Alberto and Gloria whispering to each other in a corner of the parlour or in the patio during long, languid afternoons.

María could still remember all the men who had made their way through their lives. The José Juans and the Paco Vilars who had come calling on that hot August night, and all the others too. The ones who claimed to love them: Arturo her husband, lost inside the madness of his mixed-up words and laboured rhymes, and Manuel Pousada, the fiend responsible for her disfigured face and her daughter's wasted life.

Men have raped, men have loved too much the women they could not have. Some have even killed themselves, because to them death was better than life with a woman of a certain kind. But none are worse than those who lie.

Enough, abuela, Gloria screamed at her, worrying that these hateful comments, these words of spite (delivered to me, Gloria thought, now that she can no longer destroy my mother's life) would drive Don Alberto away, and she would die if that happened, she was serious about this! So Matilde found a way to quiet her mother, to silence her barbs—with regard to Don Alberto, at least, for María continued to insult guests and workers, found a role for herself inside the hotel as María *la loca,* just like that ancient, crazy Spanish queen. And then, one day, improbably, strangely—it was difficult to know how things like this happened, how surprising were the winds of change!—María *la Reina*'s habit of attacking hotel staff and guests alike, of insulting her own family publicly, turned into one of the hotel's charms, was cited as a reason to stay at the Encarna and Hope Hotel for, *Amigo, a funnier, more entertaining spirit is unlikely to be found anywhere in the land.*

Finally one day, after keeping her waiting for almost a year, Don Alberto proposed to Gloria by the steps of the town hall, offered to unite his life with hers. *The bruja can say anything now,* Gloria exulted, *for now I too will walk down that heavenly aisle.* They married on a Saturday in one of the largest fiestas the town of Canteira had ever seen, the seven courses including crab, goose barnacles, and three types of meat, fireworks at midnight, and doves that materialized from beneath tables and landed at the guests' feet. Dancing went on until the early hours of the morning to the tune of a maríachi-style band, and bottles and bottles of *aguardiente* and *café liquor* were drunk until the newlyweds found themselves, finally, all alone in their marriage bed filled with sticks and stones, placed there by the hotel staff as a wedding night joke.

Diablos, María *la Reina* told herself that night. She had not participated in the wedding, had refused to leave her kitchen chair, and now the newlyweds lay just down the hall. Another man, she thought, another *cabrón,* had weaseled his way into her house. She did not sleep that night, tossed and turned worrying about problems for which solutions had already been found, waited for the morning to appear and the voices of the dead to cease their tyrannical braying with the rising of the sun.

Wedded bliss lasted but one week before duty came calling and Don Alberto was off again towards the coast.

What kind of work would take a man from his own honeymoon? Cecilia commented privately to Matilde once Gloria had returned to the hotel, dejected to have shared only a week of bliss with Alberto roaming the verdant expanses of the Río Douro and the surrounding, misty Portuguese hills.

Everybody gets at least a month off for weddings and deaths. Are we at war that a man must be called back to duty so soon after such an important event?

Alberto's hasty return to work did not go unnoticed by María, who sat in her usual kitchen chair, staring vacantly into the wall, hands resting on her shiny walking stick, mind busy churning out her countless opinions on everything in the land.

It must be 1588. Yes, 1588 and the great Armada is set to sail from those fish-laden waters in the harbour of La Coruña. Soon Spain will be defeated by those godless English and then, señoras, maybe that little navy thug can return to us.

Something is stinking in paradise, I tell you, and it is not fish. Cecilia, you with your great big nose should be able to figure this mystery out. I think Señor Alberto stinks of a disease well known to the Encarnas. I think he stinks of the wanting-to-leave disease.

Bueno, Mamá. Enough of your dark talk, eh? Matilde told her mother, worrying that Gloria will hear all this bantering at her expense, all this doubt centring on her new mysterious husband, whose behaviour, it is true, even Matilde found suspicious—after all, no member of his family had visited, no relative had even bothered to attend the wedding last month.

And who are we to say what his duties should or should not be? He is a navy man, a man of responsibility, at least.

And a Catalán, eh? Never forget that he is a Catalán, and Catalanes are a notoriously treacherous bunch, María said, shaking her walking stick about.

The women ignored this comment as well. Yesterday the evil resided in the Andalusians, like the one who had come calling for some mineral water after lunch, or the one who had arrived on the doorsteps of the old *pensión* so many years ago—what was his name? *Ah sí, that lunatic of a man, that Don Miguel.* The day before, it had been the Castilians who had horns on their heads, claws on their toes, and the week before that it was those rascals from the town of Lugo of course. No one was good enough in María's estimation, not even a local—why even the Dictator was now criticized during the odd evening talk. No one deserved the attention he received at the hotel, the four-course meals and the fresh Ribeiro wine, the clean sheets, the card games arranged to help the guests pass the time.

She doesn't seem to mind their pesetas, eh? Teresa the cook commented to one of the many young waiters, busy serving the midday meal inside the yellow dining room. *No, the Encarna women have always enjoyed the pesetas of others. That, my boy, is a well-known truth.*

At night, Gloria dreamed of her new husband, of the week spent with him inside one of the historic *pousadas*, a beautiful castle made of stone as old as the town itself, with its own private chapel and strange elderly host, who—drunk on the beauty of the surroundings and at least one bottle of wine—serenaded them in the evenings with *fados,* Portuguese songs of unrequited love.

But how soon he was gone! Not eight days had passed before she was back at the Encarna house and Alberto was dressed once again in his white and gold. So little time had passed before he was kissing her earnestly on the cheek, assuring her that *Niña, soon we'll be together again like this.* And then one last wave, one languid look, the promise of his return drifting over them as he boarded the train towards the coast.

A month later, Gloria was still waiting for a letter—*This postal system of ours is a national disgrace*, she told Matilde, who nodded vigorously because she, at least, was no supporter of the Dictator's Spain. María took this opportunity to deliver her usual cantankerous words. *Ta-pa-ra-pa,* she said sarcastically. *Our postal system is the envy of the world. What do you know of the tragedies and inefficiencies that afflict other lands? The things I've heard of those unwashed Frenchmen, those big Germans as graceless as a night of crime. If no letter comes, it is because no letter has been written, mark my words. You can't blame that on the Dictator or any postal system in the world. No, Gloria, listen to me, your mother also wasted precious days waiting for the letters of a man unworthy of her.*

When another month had passed and only a postcard had arrived—*from Tarragona, Matilde. I wonder what he is doing in that part of Spain?*—Gloria surprised herself with the realization that she did not miss him as much as she thought she would during the initial flush of wedded love. *But then I am not my mother,* she told herself defensively when a patron at the hotel, a cook in the kitchen, a Canteira resident passed by and lamented the hard luck that had arrived and left her without a husband so early in the game, in that phase when it really mattered. *No, I am no love-struck girl, lost to the insanity of love. I am a grown woman, made and straight.*

She understood better now Matilde's belief in the importance of timeliness in all matters big and small. Everything had its own place, its own time, and the insanity of love was a concern for only the very young; it was they who panted expectantly, they who saw their salvation in their lover's eyes. By her age, it seemed silly somehow, all the tears, all the poetry, all the love songs sung beneath silver verandahs, all the declarations that emerged from half-opened doors. Gloria was a grown woman, and a practical one at that; she had inherited her grandmother's propensity for management and the hotel accounts were a marvel by anyone's standards, a testament to the intelligence running right through the Encarna line. And in the end, what had love brought them? What disasters had afflicted the women due to the machinations of overwrought emotion, the insanity of adolescent desires? A dead mother, a broken grandmother, a father she had seen but once.

Finally, it was not a letter that arrived but Don Alberto Masip himself. *Sí, hombre,* there he was, dressed to the teeth in his gold and white, bearing gifts of perfume and books and telling tales of South African exotica and Indian monks. *And what is the Spanish navy doing in those parts good God?* Matilde asked Cecilia—thankful for the book he brought her, but not so pleased that she didn't stop to question the peculiarities of Don Alberto's worldly travels, the evasions of all his answers to questions of a military kind. *After all, señora,* he told her, *you know our government must be careful with its secrets during these dangerous times.* And then, soon enough—because Don Alberto's visits were short, he had to return to the government's affairs in the far extensions of the earth, and the day of his departure was upon them yet again—soon enough all questions seemed spurious, all suspicions and curiosities were banished so that Gloria could enjoy these few precious moments of bliss.

María *la Reina* was another thing. Nothing could silence the voice that told her something was rotten in Gibraltar, that the navy had never been near enough the shores of *la India* for the men to have glimpsed even one of her skinny monks.

This man has more legs and arms than he knows what to do with, she told Matilde one evening as her feet were being soaked. *This man may yet be the ruin of us all.*

Shush, Mamá, you are always so suspicious, so willing to see only the black, Matilde said, annoyed that the saltwater had not cured the bunions that had appeared on her mother's feet, annoyed that calluses continued to sprout everywhere with glee, annoyed too by the heat at such a late hour—what use were the hills if they could not ease the heat of late summer? What use were the forests if they could not calm all her irrational fears?

All too soon Alberto was once again waving to Gloria from the train, blowing kisses across the railway tracks and into the sky, adopting the shattered look appropriate to a lovesick man. From the platform, Gloria waved back, tugging at the black shawl that protected her from the chill that emanated from her very heart. From the platform she waved, but her mind was on other things: the official closing of the hotel for the winter season which would take place the following month, the accounts to be prepared, the odds and ends to be fixed, and—deep in her mind, buried amidst all the worries and concerns—the fervent hope that she was pregnant and could thus finally fulfil her most cherished dream.

The pains that ran down her arm and the palpitations that turned Cecilia's breathing into a hard impenetrable ball commenced as preparations were being made for the wedding feast of the mayor's daughter that was to be held in the hotel's dining room. Already, even before vows had been exchanged and the union sanctioned by the priest in his black robes—a Don Valentín, for Don José, the town priest of old had long since died—already the wedding seemed on the verge of careening into an unmitigated disaster as the families of bride and groom fought over everything from the details of the first course to the origin of the coffee that was to be served with dessert.

It's the bride's fault, as spoiled as a peacock she is, Teresa the cook whispered to Cecilia on the morning of the wedding as crabs were laid out, the *salpicón* garnished with parsley and red *pimientos* and as María *la Reina* waved a butcher's knife about, threatening to demonstrate to the head waiter all the virtues that could be derived from a quick stab to his private parts—*Just think, no children to support, no thoughts wasted on women you will never have.*

It was to be the wedding of the decade—at least according to the mayor himself, Don Rogelio Duarte, who had appeared at the hotel the month before dressed ominously in his hat and English gabardine, to give his instructions that the best *cigalas* were to be purchased, the best goose barnacles, the best salt ham, and *You know what that means, señoras*; *jamón only from Lalín.* And so on for almost an hour, the best this, the best that, a band dressed up to the nines, Asturian *cava*, salted cod from the North, cognac and *aguardiente* but only from the region of Lugo, for only they knew what good liquor was.

The commotion that was part of every grand affair at the hotel was even greater that day with all the dignitaries, who were expected to arrive—*dignitaries a bull's ass,* María scoffed—and the mayor's insistence that the tableware be buffed strenuously so that clear reflections would be visible in knives and spoons, and that the guests, each and every one of the honourable invitees, were made to feel as important *as the very king of Spain*—who had actually been exiled to Portugal by the current regime, but no other royal figure had come to the mayor's mind at that moment and so he withstood the raised eyebrows, the cynical smiles. *And please, señoras, can we have a little European class?*

Class, you say, class? María *la Reina* screamed out. *This little man is milking the town of its livelihood, bribing the generals in Madrid, bedding the young women of Canteira . . .* and then she said no more because Don Rogelio's mouth had opened up in outrage, his face had turned an apple red, and he desisted from spurting out a torrent of *How dare yous,* only because of Matilde's endless apologies, her soft entreaties to *Excuse my mother, Don Rogelio, please. All the death has made her a bit loose around the head. You who are giving your daughter in marriage today, Don Rogelio, can surely imagine what the death of a child can do.*

Into his hands she placed a bottle of water—*from Monforte's own well, Don Rogelio, come now drink*—as María was ushered out to the garden, where she continued to slander the Mayor's name, unperturbed in the least. But before the situation could deteriorate further and the hotel lose the opportunity to stage the decade's most important event—because the Mayor continued to articulate his discontent, no water from Monforte, no amount of imploring to forgive the lunacy of a woman in pain would do, he was simply burning around the collar. *How dare she? Does she know to whom she speaks?*—before the situation could deteriorate further and the morning had turned into a war of spit and rage, Cecilia fell dramatically to the floor, clutching tightly to her chest, tears of futility spilling down her face.

It was her heart, encrusted in all that fat. *How shall we ever find it in there, will you tell me that?* Don Gerardo, the town doctor asked the women in a huff, because it was a Saturday morning of a long week and he had been enjoying this day of rest and was annoyed by this summoning to the hotel, was wary of yet another medical emergency, but even more he was enraged by the sight of Señorita Gloria who stood in the background, a worried look upon her face—and why had she rejected a good town doctor for a man of the sea? he wondered, outraged at having been passed over for an ocean layabout, diminished, Don Gerardo was, by the thought that Gloria had chosen a life of eternal waiting for boats to dock. *Men in white and gold, bah! Women have no organs for rational thought.*

Medication was administered, fans were produced about Cecilia's head, her legs were lifted, her arm was waved, nervous tears rolled down many a face as the doctor continued to plead for sanity, continued to beg for space, and eventually, miraculously, Gloria thought, the colour returned to Cecilia's countenance and her breathing resumed at an even pace.

But it will not last. No, no, it will not last for sure, Don Gerardo warned the Encarna women—Gloria, Matilde, and María, who had wandered back into the kitchen and was silent suddenly, her one eye fixed upon her fat sister's face. *Doña Cecilia is huge, señoras, huge as a mountain, and she is not at an age when hearts can withstand such pressures. She must stop eating or face a quick descent into diabetes, and worse, much worse, a painful death.*

During the next few weeks, the women took turns monitoring every morsel that entered Cecilia's mouth, fed her dishes of kale and garbanzos without even a sliver of a sausage added, without a pinch of paprika or a dash of salt, but healthy, good for the heart. *Tía, with these dishes you can expect to live forever,* Matilde told her, placing another small portion of *caldo*—unspiced, defatted murky water—in front of her aunt, who looked at it distastefully and then began to cry. *Who wants to live forever,* she asked her niece, *when forever is littered with insipid, unpalatable dishes such us these? When forever means no sugar, no flan, no garlic sausage, no salted ham, no Cea bread even—that is what forever brings. Forever, Matilde, will surely be the end of me.* And with these words she descended into more tears, into loud, heart-wrenching sobs in honour of her once delicious past. And soon handkerchiefs were produced and passed to Cecilia, the sound of *tsts tsts* reverberated loudly among the staff, but no one offered her what she really wanted, no one shared with her the hotel's meal of fried calf's liver, sardine *empanada,* and kidneys cooked in vinegar and wine.

Now even the telling of a story, something Cecilia had enjoyed all of her life, seemed to be possible only over a dessert of apple tart and young Ribeiro wine—the very things she can no longer have—and instead of stories she focused her teary eyes on the floor, dreaming of meals long past. In the evenings, when cooks and family had disappeared for a well-needed rest, she stole into the kitchen like a common criminal and gobbled up the delicious offerings she could find, bites of *lacón,* bits of fried chicken, pushed into her mouth entire portions of flan and Santiago almond tart until someone inevitably arrived, found her ingesting food like a scavenger and then the scolding began, *Cecilia, is death what you want?*

To be young again, to be free to roam the kitchen cupboards, to taste the future as it leaves its sweet residue atop the tongue.

To be young so that flan and wine both can travel through the body's alleyways safely, padding the heart during their long, arduous course through the veins. Ah yes, that was the power of youth for you—unlined faces, straight backs, the headiness of as-yet-attainable dreams, and above all, the pumping of heart and stomach in regular, beautiful beats. Old age was an invention of sadists, a punishment inflicted by an inhospitable God. *Let me eat, Gloria, let me eat and then forever will be gone,* Cecilia pleaded, hungry, unhappy, her body rebelling against the lack of sugar, the sudden absence of animal fat.

And then: *There is nothing to live for,* she told Gloria dramatically one day inside the hotel kitchen, as Matilde sighed and María nodded almost imperceptibly from her kitchen throne.

Oh yes there is, Tía, Gloria said enthusiastically, a triumphant smile appearing on her face. *There is something to live for all right. I am pregnant, Tía. Sí, another Encarna woman is on her way.*

Oohs and *ahhs* of delight followed this announcement, tears of joy fell down Cecilia's face, all thoughts of food banished for the moment as she patted Gloria's stomach and hugged her about the waist, and then it was Matilde who was embracing Gloria, turning away from her only to order that bottles of the best *cava* be opened and lamb *empanadillas* be served to all the hotel staff, but frowning a very clear *no* at her aunt Cecilia when she too began to salivate.

A sonorous thump on the floor suddenly called the celebratory group to attention. All talk ceased, hugs and kisses were abandoned in midair. It was María, who had sat quietly as the world around her exploded into a feast of congratulation, a virgin's fiesta of glee; as corners of eyes were dabbed at with embroidered handkerchiefs and babies' names were rattled off in twos and threes. Now the room grew silent as everyone waited in trepidation for what was sure to be one of *la Reina*'s famous decrees.

Another Encarna girl? Bah! Another excuse to bring someone into a life of misery!

On that note, she rose from her throne and left the kitchen to cross the darkly lit hall, her cane tapping threats right until the moment when she entered the tranquillity of the hotel garden, and the *thumping* of her cane was swallowed by the softness of the grass.

In the afternoons, the contemplation of life.

During the siesta hour, as the hotel guests napped away the hours of hottest sun, their stomachs satiated by the glorious four-course meals and endless bottles of wine, as *la Reina* settled into a disturbed sleep in her chair in the kitchen, one hand still on her cane, the other propping up her damaged face as it descended, finally, into some semblance of calm, during the only hour when the world ground down to a perceptible halt, Matilde headed to the prettiest spot in all of Canteira—pretty still, because it had been spared the ravages of all the new construction, lying well outside of town—and tended to the two cows the Encarnas still kept *(after all,* María argued, *what will the neighbours think? That we are too important for cows now that the hotel thrives? No, no, we must continue to milk*). The cows were a source of comfort to Matilde, company during the afternoons as she sat by the rock with the alchemical symbols and read. Letters, three a week almost—*Whoever said the postal system was a disgrace should talk to me*—written in Don Miguel's clean, elegant style.

The letters had begun arriving once the worst of the war had passed and Don Miguel had resigned himself to a quiet life of contemplation in Aguas Verdes, the Andalusian village where he had spent his youth before setting out for the farthest extensions of the earth. *And thus the inevitable return,* he wrote, *to the place where all things began.*

At first the letters spoke of love, of how he could hear Matilde's voice emerging from butterflies and blue sky, how her face wandered into his heart with the pungent fragrance of olive trees and orange groves, of the time, when he was sure he had caught a glimpse of her as he walked through the marvellous Alhambra.

And yet how could that be, Matilde, with you so far away and me so alone? And the nights are the worst yet, Matilde, Andalusian nights are unbearably long, indescribably hot—tonight you can fry eggs on the streets, tonight the heat is so palpable that the moon has surely been scorched by the sun. In such heat, it is impossible not to think of you, so far away near those verdant hills, the only place on earth where it is possible to sleep, to dream away the chilly nights.

Miguel, Matilde wrote in her girlish hand, *I implore you to block out the sadness with the sound of the stars. With the look of the sky. Oh, I am sure that the Andalusian sky is a wonderful thing indeed. In that sky, Miguel, surely you can find peace.*

Matilde, Don Miguel responded, *I struggle and struggle but cannot make my way to that place you speak of. Is this what old age does? Does old age resign us to endings as beginnings, or am I just lost today inside the pit of my stomach, inside the darkness of the night?*

In Canteira, in her perfect spot, she closed her eyes and thought of her own private God. Here, Matilde thought, was the centre of the universe—the rock attesting to the presence of Druids in a time so distant, it seemed almost real. To the east, the river Miño—beautiful, resplendent, and to the north the hills, still majestic, resembling those mountains that appeared in the pictures of the Alps given to her by a guest once, and which now hung inside her bedroom, the last thing she saw before falling into sleep. *Ah, but those mountains are wondrous things, so unknowable, the only barrier between ourselves and the eyes of God.*

To live, she wrote, *is to be really at one with river, mountain, and stream.*

Eventually she dispensed with the books—she interpreted the weakness of her eyes as a sign that she needed to search inside for things—and spent her free time away from obligations of family and hotel, staring at the mountains (yes, they were mountains, hills could never be as imposing as these), dipping hands and feet into the river, watching mesmerized as massive cow tongues swept the grass from pastures and farmers planted in the afternoon heat.

By then, Don Miguel's letters had been arriving infrequently—writing had become excruciatingly painful for his arthritic hands—and it was Matilde's turn to send him letters, two and three a week for almost a decade, until the day a notary's letter arrived informing Matilde that Don Miguel had been dead for almost three years. *But then, where did all my letters go?* Matilde wondered, for the notary's dry tone surely indicated that he would not have been interested in all her heartfelt outpourings. Life for him was a sad song of a few clients, sparring children, and long afternoons of card games and glasses of *manzanilla* sherry inside the local bar.

A year after she stopped writing the letters, a young man of melancholic face arrived at the hotel. *Another Andalusian,* María told Cecilia in a tone of disparagement. *Those southerners suffer badly from diseased livers and other ills. One wonders what they are doing to deserve such things.* The man, younger than the average visitor to the hotel and desperately poor, dressed in well-worn trousers and an ill-fitting jacket of black wool, asked to see a Doña Matilde: *Por favor, is there a Doña Matilde about?*

Hombre, María l*a Reina* said from her chair, *it is bad enough that you hail from the land of the gypsies, those thieves, those thugs. But must you also stutter like the village idiot? Cecilia, come here, sister, you must really listen to this.*

The young man was flustered and red now—this could not be Doña Matilde, he thought, this was a horrendous old woman, a witch in the strictest sense of the word—and then, thankfully, the real Doña Matilde appeared, wiping her hands on a crisp, white apron, smiling a million apologies for her mother's behaviour as she touched her fingers to her head: *She is old now, young man, too old to be in full possession of her wits.*

Convinced that he had found the Doña Matilde he had been looking for, for her face was as luminous as the moon, her eyes so kind—he had never seen so much kindness in anyone's eyes, why, this woman was the goddess he had dreamed of—he took out a stack of letters from his burlap sack, wrapped carefully in his sister's red ribbon as a sign of respect, and he handed them to an astonished Matilde, who stared incomprehensibly at three years' worth of words intended for a man now dead.

I hope you don't mind, the young man stammered to Matilde, *the words were so beautiful and I so alone once Don Miguel passed away. He spoke of you so well. Why, you were the earth, the wind, and the olive trees to him. For him, nothing could ever compare with you. By the time he died I had grown so accustomed to your voice and found it difficult to say adiós . . . .*

He stuttered nervously as around him waiters ran to and fro preparing for the two o'clock meal, as María enraged the cook in the kitchen with her questions of how much salt she should be using in the *paella*, how much lemon juice should be sprinkled onto the fish—as the world rattled around them, the young Andalusian rambled, his words an outpouring of desire and raw nerves. And underneath it, a desperate plea left unspoken lay waiting to be heard—*For I did not choose this stutter, this twisted body, these rotten teeth. I did not say to God, Give me a dark face in a land of raven hair and alabaster skin. I am a descendant of gypsies, it is true, and the way people turn their noses up at me will forever remind me of that.* After all the stuttering and the silent entreaties, his mouth finally found a way to explain the reason for his visit, the stammer momentarily banished by the urgency in his words: *I want to be a poet, Doña Matilde. Please teach me how and I will work hard for you, clean and do odd jobs and the like. I am a carpenter and can work very very hard.*

But niño, I am not a poet, Matilde argued, *why I've never written a proper verse in my life. I cannot teach what I do not do.*

Sí, sí, you can, Doña Matilde. Don Miguel told me to come to you.

And then what could she say? For if Don Miguel had sent this young melancholic boy, so obviously distressed, so full to the brim with longing and sadness, then surely this was a message sent straight from the grave. She found a room for him at the hotel, offered him work doing odd jobs, much to María's chagrin. In her ire, she swore and cursed at the young man during his first long month of sweeping and cleaning at the hotel until the day the only curse left to her was *gypsy boy,* and *bueno,* he had long grown accustomed to that. And then, who could have foreseen it? The two, the hardened old woman and the young gypsy boy, grew to like each other and, unbelievably, María started looking forward to the mornings when he arrived with mop and broom, and he to her biting words, her rage, her often acid wit. But then in her tragic, disfigured face, he could see with poet's eyes the million lamentations, the pain, the guilt—a universe, he thought of rhyming, beautiful verse.

In the afternoons, during the siesta hour, Matilde took him to the prettiest spot in Canteira. There she taught him the only poetry she knew—of changing skies and the worlds to be seen in a single blade of grass, of cows as they licked their life's blood from the pastures and the way the river murmured its truths. There she traced with her fingers the outlines of the symbols that lay on the jutting rock—*Here Don Miguel and I first recognized each other*—and then refused to speak of him again. Instead, she revealed all the secrets offered by Medusa's head and the six-pointed stars, told him of the seven rooms in the castle and the need to explore, slowly, each one, listened as he read her the verses of poets alive and those long dead and gone, pointed to the river Miño and the hills that were mountains in her mind.

There is the most potent vision available to a poet's hands.

At night, she worried. The gypsy boy, with his melancholic eyes, his intense love of verse, had been given to her as a gift, of that she was sure—why, even her mother had grown close to him, even María now asked for the gypsy boy to sit by her side. Yet he was frail as the porcelain cups used at the hotel during wedding feasts. She could not help but feel, a sixth sense told her this, that something was seriously amiss, but before she could ascertain just what it was, the season was over and he had returned to his native Granada, back to the locus of his old life of pain—God only knew what lay in his past, what bits of degradation he had suffered during his short, rough life—and sure enough, not three months after his departure, as the winter in Canteira had murdered the sun for months on end and the famous depressions had begun to intensify, a letter arrived. From his sister, she of the red, red ribbon, the one that bound together all of Matilde's outpourings of old—but not written in her hand, of course, because she had not been taught to write, had had no Don Miguel to save her from her gypsy plight. The letter had been recited instead to a kind neighbour who had taken the time to inform Doña Matilde that the gypsy boy had killed himself, shot himself through the left eye. *These troubled youth of ours,* the anonymous person wrote, *these troubled youth will yet be the end of us all.*

Matilde did not tell María the news that had arrived on that cold January morning. *No use making her sad.* But she had not counted on her mother's endless curiosity, on her habit of going through Matilde's private things—*Privacy is an idea invented by those Americanos, a crazy, unruly bunch*—a habit that had kept María informed of the goings-on between Don Miguel and Matilde during their letter-writing days of old, and she now read, a magnifying glass held precariously before her right eye, of her gypsy boy's fate.

Later, in the kitchen, as she watched the evening meal being prepared by a now thinner Cecilia, who had shed her gaiety with the pounds and pounds of fat, María stared as the fire burned and crackled inside the large wood-burning stove, silent tears spilling sporadically from her right eye.

What is the matter, sister? Cecilia asked alarmed, watching as a giant, perfect drop made its way towards María's mouth.

It is nothing, Cecilia. Nothing. It is just that, today, I feel all the poetry has finally died.

Bueno, Cecilia said soothingly, relieved because she did not know of the gypsy boy's violent end and thus thought her sister was once again lamenting Arturo's death at his own hands. *Bueno,* she said, shedding a tear for him as well as she salted the *caldo* for the others more vigorously, her own meal a baked potato and a piece of boiled, desalted cod.

My penance, she told the others sadly, *though I do not know the sin.*

By the eighth month of the pregnancy, Gloria had experienced every possible inconvenience, every infirmity available to expectant mothers—high blood pressure and elephantine legs, violent nausea in the first trimester, rectal bleeding in the third, acne, backaches and just when she had thought it would end (for surely nothing was left in the catalogue of pregnancy despair), a thyroid dysfunction came calling, throwing body and mind into a chaotic state of disrepair. *But don't worry,* the town midwife told her when she saw her struggling down the street. *Difficult pregnancies mean beautiful, healthy children. Children like angels. Children handed to us by God Himself.*

Yet still, what pained her most of all was her husband's complete absence from Canteira since hearing of the news of the pregnancy six months before.

Can this be normal? Cecilia asked Matilde one day as Gloria tried to cope with her back pain, with the lightness in her head. *How can it be normal, leaving a wife to fend by herself? No letters written, no phone calls, no news of any kind. Surely we are not at war. Surely the prospect of a newborn child, a first child no less, should inspire more interest than this?*

Hmm, Matilde answered, shaking her head. She had long had her own suspicions, had long worried that something was seriously amiss. She knew little of the navy's ways—the women had been living in the interior for so long, and who could trust the newspapers when every word was pruned by censors' hands? But she knew that her country could not be involved in a war. Censors or no censors, important news had a way of making itself known. No, they were not at war, nor was it normal for even a navy man to be away so much from his home—why he'd been back only four times since the wedding almost three years ago.

In the meantime, it is Cecilia who dealt with the ailments that afflicted her great-niece, who grew increasingly large with each passing day. *That girl is turning into another Cecilia, growing as fat as an ox,* María told the hotel cook as preparations were made for yet another town wedding, one that featured a visibly pregnant bride as well. *Times are not what they used to be. No, no. It is good Carmen has passed on to another world, for she would have been shocked at the state of things.*

To relieve her pain, Gloria ate the sweets cooked especially for her by Cecilia who, condemned to a bland life of boiled cabbage and silver hake, found consolation, exhilaration even, in watching her great-niece enjoy the dishes that she could no longer eat. *Bombas,* sugar-coated cream creations, *cañas*, the ones she was famous for, small bouquets of pastry stuffed with sugar and cream, chocolate palm trees, fried milk, and of course, Cecilia's very own *crème caramel.* Six months of eating these treasures had padded Gloria tremendously around the face and legs, had distorted her features so severely that even Don Gerardo—stopping in to check now on Cecilia and Gloria both—could not help but feel a secret delight, could console himself with the thought that if Gloria had married him, he would be stuck now with this growing tower of fat.

As one of you loses, the other one gains, Don Gerardo said to them sternly, but not too sternly, eh? Let that navy rat return to the arms of the once beautiful Gloria Encarna and see her elephant legs and triple chins, the bad case of acne that had marred her alabaster skin, and her indifference, *sí,* nothing was as disturbing as this sudden lack of interest in anything but her next *bomba,* her next plate of food. By the sixth month, a case of diabetes had developed and Don Gerardo was forced to prohibit Gloria from eating Cecilia's sweet creations, *the only thing,* she argued, crying hysterically, *that keeps my spirits high*—the massive doses of sugar keeping her doubts over her husband's considerable absences at bay.

Still, there were other dishes to be eaten, other food to help one pass the time, and so Cecilia applied herself once again with fervour to her cooking, found a way to keep her niece content despite the torments that plagued her mind. Fresh pork liver, kidneys in onions and brine, veal boiled in garlic sauce and paprika—and the seafood! Every day, Cecilia ordered the very best seafood from the coast—*for appetizers, of course*—oysters, scallops, spider crabs, and clams. As a second course, Cecilia's own potato omelette made with mushrooms, onions, peppers, and rock salt. The third course, tripe with chickpeas—*after all, Don Gerardo did say to add some chickpeas and greens*—followed by sardine *empanada* and roast lamb with rice and an enormous salad on the side. For dessert, sliced fruit and homemade cheese. *We must remember to heed the doctor's orders like this.*

Are we feeding an army? Has that rat of a man come back with the entire Spanish navy in tow? María asked Cecilia.

Hombre, hermana, you have enough food here to feed our hotel guests for two years or more.

Bueno, Cecilia told María, waving her comments aside, *let me take care of the niña. She is motherless, after all.* And with this, Cecilia dabbed at the corner of her eyes, wiping the emotion that surfaced when speaking Asunción's name. In the parlour, the clock with the porcelain flowers clanged its way into a new hour, signalling that the time for another four-course meal was at hand.

By the time news arrived from Alberto Masip, it was not in Alberto's hand, nor was it with his presence. Instead, a distinguished-looking older man, carrying a dark valise and sporting a sombre face, came calling nine months into Gloria's pregnancy. The seriousness of the man's visit was clear in his visage—dark jowls, small eyes under which dark bags flowed down to his knees—and his smell, a mixture of sweet cologne and stale air. It was his smell, above all, that alerted Gloria to the fact that something was seriously amiss.

Cecilia, Matilde, and Gloria were soon joined by María, who came hobbling in, her cane announcing her way along the cold tiles of the hall and then into the kitchen, where she stopped suddenly, seeing this man. *Who is this señor?* she asked no one in particular, for she could feel the tension brewing, could sense that this man in his expensive suit had arrived bearing serious news, and *God, have they finally come calling for my contraband past?* she thought, for she guessed that this man was a government type. This thought filled her with a surge of terror, an emotion she had not felt since the death of her beloved child—with the death of a child, who had space left for feelings other than grief?—but now that queasy emotion was back and she began to tremble until she heard the man say, *I am here on a matter pertaining to Don Alberto Masip.* And then relief, waves upon waves of it washed over her body as she took a seat.

What news do you bring of Don Alberto Masip? Gloria asked, alarmed, attempting to get up from her chair, but it was simply impossible—her legs were so inflated that to get up was to begin life anew. *I am his wife, señor. Is he dead? As his wife, I must know.*

No, Don Alberto is not dead. No, this is something much worse, the man responded in a sober tone, a tone which had been announcing tragedy since the time of Hermes—and already the women could hear the hand of the ancient messenger knocking at their door, in tune with one of Asunción's parlour clocks. *Is he injured? Has he been shot and cannot talk?* Questions came tumbling from Cecilia's and Gloria's hysterical minds, interrupted only by María's insolent query as to whether Alberto had dared become a Protestant in the Dictator's Catholic land.

Señoras, please calm yourselves. Don Alberto is perfectly fine, though he does not deserve such a title of respect as I'm sure you'll all soon agree. He looked sadly into Gloria's eyes, affecting all the concern taught to him by his superiors long ago.

He is not dead and you are not his wife, he told her gently.

What? Whatever do you mean? Guffaws of disbelief followed this pronouncement. Why, of course she was his wife, who was this man to come strolling into their house issuing insults like this? *Look, here is my wedding band and upstairs is the paperwork from our marriage three years ago. I fear you have come here to insult me, señor.*

Señora, Alberto Masip was already married when he married

you, to a Dulcinea Torres from Barcelona twenty years and three children ago. Your husband is a bigamist, señora, has made it a habit of wedding women, if two can be considered a habit and in my mind a habit it is. This he said with a shake of the head though secretly he was enjoying this part, this divulging of shocking news to such outraged ears. Later, he would share the moment with his wife, would luxuriate in telling this sordid tale inside his neighbourhood tavern for close to a year. But now—

How? Are you sure of what you say? It cannot be! Commotion erupted, taking over kitchen and house. Meanwhile, María *la Reina,* sitting like stone upon her kitchen throne stared unemotionally into the black wood-burning stove. Only one question came to her mind: *Dulcinea,* she said, *what kind of a silly name is that?*

And then before the jowl-faced man with bags down to his knees could furnish further information, Gloria's waters had burst onto the floorboards of the kitchen spraying feet and tile with their urgent warning that a new life was set to begin. The uproar began almost immediately—*twelve hours to go, she'll be here in twelve hours more or less*—Cecilia screamed, as she ran around in circles, ordering water to be boiled, rooms to be heated, and the midwife to be called *pronto* to the house.

So it was that Alberto Masip was forgotten—momentarily, at least—as Matilde guided Gloria gently to the large bedroom in the corner where there was space for babies' births, where Gloria herself had been born almost forty years before except that it was a different house then, no marble on the staircase, no varnished floors, no foreign clocks. As Gloria climbed up the stairs towards the bedroom and Cecilia put cauldrons of water and bay leaves upon the stove, María *la Reina* hung on to her cane with increasing desperation, contemplating nothing now, lost in the circles of existence that had been forming from the very first. And as preparations were made inside the house, the jowl-faced man found himself crossing the streets of Canteira in search of the midwife and a certain Don Gerardo, a doctor, he was told by Cecilia, trained in the better hospitals of Madrid.

Despite all assurances to the contrary—*difficult pregnancies, easy birth*—labour stretched out for hours and screams of horror filled the house. *Oh-eh, you'd think she was the first woman with her legs in the air,* María told the neighbours who had come calling with food and wine in hopes that a celebration would soon be at hand. Inside the kitchen was Don Gerardo, waiting in case something should go wrong—after all, children's births were women's affairs, not to be intruded upon unless a moment of disaster should visit during the final push. For all of her sarcasm, though, María's fear was greater than she had ever felt before, and she issued her quips in a nervous, high-pitched chirp.

The townspeople shared gossip and jokes amidst the endless ticking of Asunción's clocks, a noise which grew steadily louder with each passing minute, each tolling of the hour, until it was three in the morning and María's head was bursting from the endless interplay of ticking, clanging, and screaming and the neighbours' gossip had been extinguished by the late hour and they had all departed, promising that they would return in the morning. María's mind was filled suddenly with fears of twisted baby's feet, of death in the cradle, and of other horrors even greater than this—so that she felt nauseated from all the worries, all her ponderous irrational fears. *There is only one thing left to do in the world*, she thought.

After almost eight years of wilful denial, María placed palm against palm and began to recite barely remembered childhood prayers. And then nothing seemed enough for her: out came her catechism, her rosary, even Carmen the Holy One's ebony cross upon which Jesus twisted, blood pouring from gaping wounds, head cocked to one side, a look of sad resignation upon his face—out came all of the paraphernalia of worship that she had abandoned with the death of her daughter. And then fifty *Ave Marías,* one hundred *Padre Nuestros,* a thousand other mumbled-jumbled prayers barely remembered, but uttered just in case.

Finally, at nearly four in the morning a baby's cry was heard, and then, shortly after, the midwife's confirmation that the baby was a perfect specimen and in outstanding good health—but what was this? Had she heard correctly? Did the midwife really say it was a boy? And what, dear God, María thought, were they going to do with a boy, when no boy had been born to the family since her own mother gave birth to three successive boys, all dead, wrapped in linen blankets, placed in white coffins—*angelitos,* they called them—even today, a dead baby was a little angel for those forced to bury one in a very different womb.

But then Matilde appeared, telling her mother, *Sí, can you believe it? You heard correctly Mamá, it is a boy.* And the thought occurred to her—of course it did—that a boy was a good thing indeed, a boy would never be abandoned by bigamists, suicides or lecherous fools, would never be exposed to the violence of others on a hot summer eve.

Let it be a boy then, she told Matilde, suddenly relieved.

Ay, Mamá. Matilde smiled at her. *As if our words could change anything.*

By the third day, Gloria was once more on her feet, more vibrant, more alive than she had ever been. *I have two things to say,* she told the women during the two o'clock meal. *First, I want never to hear Alberto Masip's name in this house or in the hotel.*

Understood? For me, he is already dead. Second, the baby will be named Arturo for my dear grandfather whom I never met.

Over my dead body this child will be called Arturo, María shouted. *No, no, never, do you hear? In a thousand years, he will not be called that*—she ground her cane into the floor. *Or were you looking to be saddled with another weeping weakling? Are you resigned to another death by the hams?*

Mamá, Matilde said, trying to calm her mother's cane-wielding hand, *those are stories of village minds. A borrowed name does not mean a borrowed fate. A name, Mamá, is after all just a name.*

And what do you know of these things? You, who wander the forest like the village idiot, humming in the woods. That's what those village gossips tell me. That's what the people say.

But before *la Reina* could tear into the others—could begin to berate Cecilia for her late night secret feasts of gammon and cheese, could embark upon a rambling critique of the errors to be found of late in the management of the hotel—Gloria had stood up and had begun screaming at her hysterical grandmother. *I decide, vieja, what name my child will have, and if you are so opposed to Arturo, then Arturo it is.*

There was no more talk, that day at least. Gloria barricaded herself in the bedroom with her newborn child—thought of her grandmother only fleetingly, and then turned her thoughts upon that *cabrón* of a husband of hers, Alberto the two-timing Masip, cursing him silently: *You will never get near to this child, that you can count on.* For Gloria was determined to instil so great a love of Canteira in this child that he would never be burdened with the desire to explore the world, the world that Gloria had so desperately wanted and which had arrived, finally, inside the treacherous uniform of a bigamist rat. No, this child would be taught to see the beauty in what was around him, in Matilde's forests and jutting stones, in the way the sun fell upon the Ribeiro Valley, turning grapes into jewels—would grow to love the way the winds in the winter moaned. This child, she thought, would revel in the fortunes of the hotel and would be a giant in the community, celebrated in Canteira and beyond.

Downstairs in the kitchen, María continued to complain until, defeated, it was not her screams that filled the house but her sad, raucous sobs.

PART FOUR

1958–1984

WHAT LAY IN A NAME INDEED? WHAT LAY IN A NAME WAS the difference between night and day, between heaven and hell and all the tortured souls trapped in purgatory in between. What lay in a name was the difference between a dictatorship, with its three-cornered hats and its antiquated ideas—because in a dictatorship only old men flourish and even they not very well—and democracy, *la democracia*. Ah, but how beautiful that word was, how mysterious and promising, like all those bare-legged blond *americanos* with their big teeth and their loud voices and their innocence—Lord weren't they innocent just? What lay in a name, above all, was the endless torture of memory—faces, feelings, and words that María thought forgotten had all, with the baptism of one child, appeared at the door once more. And it was no use ignoring them, no use trying to banish them with other feelings, other thoughts. No, they barged their way through and inhabited the rooms of her mind until the only space left was the three inches kept open for the various diseases that came for a visit as well, and why not? Once the floodgates were opened the water roared, tumbled, crashed into every nook and cranny until there was nothing but breath left—but ah, that at least, my friends, that at least, meant life was still about. A small consolation, perhaps, but one imbibed gratefully during these wounded times.

So it was that Arturo came calling for María, appearing more alive in death than he had when he walked the earth and lay not six feet under, ashes in a stone sepulchre beneath Carmen the Holy One and Asunción, his daughter also lost to the world. The memories surprised her, for she had long thought them buried by layer upon layer of daily life, the rituals of walking and talking and eating the same meals without a thought given to the reason for this or that. *Why eggs on a Tuesday and broiled chicken every second Saturday? Why, Cecilia, will you tell me that? And why now, Arturo, why is it that you have chosen to come back now when you have been gone for fifty years, and that is a long time, eh? Sí, empires have fallen, entire lives have been lived in fewer years than that.* But suddenly there he was again, standing before her in the verandah, in the bedroom, in the hotel kitchen where she thought she saw him sprinkling salt into the soup, pouring wine over the lamb.

With the birth of her great-grandchild Arturo Masip (or maybe not Masip; that question would involve a legal battle that was never fully resolved) suddenly and curiously the only memories available to her were those told with words from her dead husband's lips. All María could do now was think about him. The way he smiled, the verses he recited, his irritating habit of disappearing for hours, later days, in the Canteira hills. Now the only presence she felt in the deepest hours of the night—the hour, especially, between two and three, for it was then that the wolves howled most intensely in the not-so-distant hills, and it was then also that the dead spoke the loudest, according to the town *meiga* at least—was that of Arturo, obliterating even the spectre of their dead child, for so long the exclusive occupant of her weary heart. In the deepest hours of the night, Arturo appeared for a dance on the verandah, a twinkle in his eye. In the morning, he visited her inside the hotel gardens in a butterfly's guise.

By little Arturo's seventh birthday, María *la Reina* had been plagued by more ailments than anyone in the area had ever been known to survive. It was the talk of the town, María's inability to die. Why in the last seven years a stroke, cancer, and a heart attack had all appeared to batter María on the back of the head, searing holes through her insides, making impossible the easiest tasks, and yet there she was still, a ruinous tower of ills, talking to butterflies. Her days of chasing waiters and insulting guests were now only anecdotes told inside Canteira's casino, the preferred meeting place for the town's Latin American expatriate *nouveau riche*.

The ailments had begun afflicting her almost immediately after the birth of little Arturo—Arturito to the hotel staff, who took turns smothering him with kisses and attention, for he was an astoundingly beautiful child, even María had to admit that, though at times she thought she saw the eyes of Manuel staring back at her, a sight that chilled her bones and heart. Yes, it was not long after Arturo's birth that her dead husband and the various illnesses that would plague her for the rest of her life had begun making their rounds, a stroke days before the baby's baptism which had left her partially paralysed, arthritis so severe that she soon found herself being spoon-fed by Arturo's side, and after his third birthday an infection—*You know, Doña María, the immune system of the old is no better than that of a small child,* Don Gerardo told her as he attended to a bad bout of pneumonia. By Arturo's sixth birthday, she had a case of cancer—none of the doctors could tell her specifically what kind, but there was something wrong with her blood, that they knew without a doubt. She insisted that these *matadors* in white—that's how she referred to them, for her tongue was as wicked as ever, if used more sparingly now—these big-city doctors not touch her, not hover over her for too long so that they found it impossible to determine the specifics of the disease, but the word cancer was given, since cancer was a powerful and all-inclusive name for illness then.

Because she was on the verge of death for seven years, the townspeople soon grew accustomed to the stories told by Matilde and Gloria about María's daily, never-ending woes. *And how is la Reina today?* they would ask at the market, at the hotel, at the fiestas that grew larger and more unruly each year, until the town was fully shut down for five days every July, just so the saint could be celebrated properly and the people could dance till dawn. *A bit better* was the inevitable response. As the years passed and María's illnesses grew more theatrical with the passing of time, the people began to associate the tolling of the church bells which announced each town death exclusively with María, and when they tolled, someone in Canteira inevitably commented, *There it is, the moment of truth for la Reina has finally arrived.* Seven years passed like this, with cancer and gall bladder irritations and kidney disease—and yet, despite earnest prognostications from town pundits and scientific pronouncements from the doctors in Madrid, María *la Reina,* she of the unbearable beauty once, survived to become Canteira's official Queen of Disease.

In the kitchen she sat with her sister Cecilia, almost as immobile as herself, fat again due to all the secret eating, all the dipping into *caldo* and cream desserts. She had tried to hide her fat at first under layer and layer of clothing, until she seemed to be wearing a large matador's cape. And then, enough—out came her clothes of old, *your giant death shrouds,* María told her, worried about her sister's courting of disease, but growing silent eventually, as she accepted the futility of staving off death. For *Hermana, truly, do we really want to live much longer than this, you with your food angst, me only with my memories of the dead? Eat, hermana, eat. Go happily into the other world at least.*

They were a curious pair, two sisters side by side in their giant kitchen chairs, padded with Portuguese cushions on all sides, ebony canes in one hand, and silent—long past the days now of gossip and insult, of veiled threats and manipulative tears. It was almost as if they had made their peace with death and each had one foot already placed gingerly in the grave.

Have to secure my place, María would say. *With Cecilia's fat, there won't be room left for even one of my fingers, I'll bet.*

Between visitations by her dead husband and debilities arising from her various illnesses, María raged inside against the indignity of old age. And she was not the only one. No, one had only to look at Canteira's verandahs, at the sidewalks where old people were wheeled out during the summer to be roasted by the sun, wrapped head to toe in their funereal black, talking rubbish, some of them, for not all could lay claim to clear heads and sane minds. Yes, old people were everywhere, and not the old of before, not the sixty- and seventy-year-old specimens; those were youngsters compared with this lot. These were members of the newly formed century club—widowed, immobile, as toothless as their great-grandchildren not yet one year old.

If María was immobile and sick, Cecilia, who had begun to eat once again with abandon, ignoring doctors' warnings and family guilt, found that her beloved dishes, both savoury and sweet, did not taste the same any longer, did not sit well upon the tongue any more. Did the palate grow old with the mind, *señor*? Was nothing sacred in this long hard tumble towards decrepitude and decay? Of course, the palate grew old, the ravages of time spared nothing, not even Asunción's clocks, most of which had long ago grown rusty and unbalanced with their endless ticktock.

As María and Cecilia grew old in their kitchen chairs, their companionable silence interrupted with moments of despair, and little Arturito grew older, stronger, taller than most of the boys his age—*and beautiful too,* the talk in Canteira went, *why it is almost as if he is a perfect blend of the once-beautiful María la Reina and the long-lost Manuel*—as women grew old and young men grew tall, Gloria dedicated herself heart and soul to the task of erecting new businesses right across town. The Encarna name was soon plastered on a movie theatre (bought at a bargain from a family on the brink of bankruptcy), on the town's only driving academy—*After all, Matilde, every new car must have a driver, sometimes two*—on Canteira's first proper supermarket, not all that large really, but equipped with impressive black adding machines and young men who bagged groceries and gawked at the girls arriving there in search of milk. And, of course, the hotel continued to prosper, continued to attract the summer hordes with its four-course meals and the on-going assurances of *balneario* relief.

Just as promised, Canteira had grown with all this activity, with emigrant remittances and investments in other parts of the land, until it was not just another town in the Galician interior, but a towering, gleaming grown-up *pueblo* with a church that resembled a miniature cathedral—but not too ornate, for it had been built during recent times, and recent times were barren of spires, ideas, and things of that kind. It had also a casino and cinema and over a dozen cafés run by those who had returned from emigrant lands, so that there was not one Café Buenos Aires but two, as well as a Café Montevideo and a Café Swiss Alps. So many cafés littered the town, in fact, that it was almost impossible for any one of them to sell more than a Coca-Cola and three *cafés con leche* on any given day—six or seven perhaps on a holiday when people were more generous with their pesetas and time.

In this town of miniature cathedral and cafés this-and-thats, the Encarna name was revered, for the women had become the town's wealthiest citizens and not to be toyed with—*Sí, señor, the Encarna women are as strong and smart as a thousand dictators lined up side by side*. The origins of the wealth that had laid the foundations for the showpiece of the women's fortune, the Encarna and Hope Hotel, were no longer a topic of discussion—not when stranger fortunes had been made with prostitution in the Caribbean and the bribery of policemen in Mexico and Brazil. Compared to these dubious activities, how serious could a little peddling of contraband have been? Especially, it is true, as it had all occurred during such distant, depressing times.

As the family wealth grew larger and the old grew older and the young more beautiful, Matilde, humming in woods and pastures just as in times of old, was occupying herself with instilling a love of the land so strong in little Arturo that it would be responsible, strangely enough, for eventually blowing him up.

And then, on the eve of Arturo's seventeenth birthday—*un milagro*, a miracle, for on that day Canteira's church bells tolled but not for María *la Reina*, still maintaining her old woman's vigil from her kitchen chair, nor for her sister Cecilia, still fat but not as in the old days, for it was simply impossible to be as fat with an aged body such as hers. No, on that day—a cold November day, rainy as usual and hardly auspicious in any other way—the bells of Canteira's church tolled for Spain. The Dictator, that little man in his curious hat, lately Alzheimer-mad, had finally and officially died. Oh, they could hardly believe it! Confusion, surprise and then fear flooded the streets of Canteira immediately after the death. Long faces and nervous looks were exchanged, because what was to happen now, Dear God? The old were not so old that they could not recall the debacle that had descended upon them almost forty years before. And the young, the young were lost in the emptiness of youth, the wine, the American music, the dancing until dawn.

As champagne corks popped in Catalonia, and Basque intellectuals danced in the streets of San Sebastián, the people in Canteira waited for time to pass, for emotions to cool, for their futures to be assured by the sombre men in dark suits who occupied the seats of power in the very distant Madrid. When the nation finally arose from the death, after many tears had been shed and jubilant cries uttered inexhaustibly in all the soon-to-be autonomous regions of Spain, the world looked disappointingly similar to the one that had been lost. There were no moving slogans yet, no words of communist fury, no discernible evidence that something momentous had occurred, that a world that had been lying so long at the periphery of freedom had finally been unshackled by the last choking breaths of the man at the top. For days, people simply stared at their bulky black-and-white television sets, watching as old women crept by the casket weeping and praying over his remains. And what were they weeping about, Dear God? Why all the sorrow? Can't you see—yes, you, the woman dressed in black, so ancient you could have been his mother—can't you see that this is the modern world, that we have finally been set free?

And then another king appeared on the scene, except that this one had some legitimacy, cousin of the English Queen, in fact, a tall man who sounded foreign, not Spanish at all. *Let there be democracy,* he declared. *Let the people choose who they will for their own reasons. It is time to join Europe again.* Well, it was true they had not been a part of Europe. It is true that for forty years they had just been this abutment hanging down like a bad dream trying to touch Africa. It is true that the world had forgotten by now about Cervantes, Quevedo, and Velázquez. For the Europeans, Picasso was a Frenchman, Dalí a derelict, and all of the art in the Prado could not make Spain look like anything other than a collection of backwardness strolling in the rain with its cows and its Catholicism.

In Canteira, the signs of *la democracia* were few at first. The hotel continued with its business, comforting liver ills with sulphuric waters and four-course meals. *La democracia* did little to cure the people of degenerative diseases, did little to change the rhythm of life. It was the same cycle with winter rain and dark unbearable thoughts, followed by spring and the beginning of hope, and finally the joyfulness of summer, a time for fiestas, for dancing, for forgetting the misery that knocked at the door from the lack of reasonable pensions, the uncertainty of the future for the nation's young.

The priests were the only truly nervous ones, the priests and the old people like María and Cecilia, afraid of change at such an inopportune moment of their lives, just when they were ready to die and wanted to do so in familiar surroundings. The priests were giving different sermons now, more impassioned, more political, smacking of their concern for the future of Spain and for their own welfare.

Don't go voting for the communists now. Don't go making decisions that will end with all of us in the infierno, Don Valentín, Canteira's priest, would rail week after week from the pulpit of the miniature cathedral. *You know, señores, if Spain is going to survive, we must be prudent. We must take care to be moderate or we'll all end up in hell, a hell on earth like the kind we've seen before, back in the days of war and discontentment.*

The old people would nod in agreement at Don Valentín's words, their fears for the future evinced on their well-lined faces and their mud-caked working galoshes. They had seen things, had lived long lives of upheaval and uncertainty, and had enjoyed the last forty years of blessed steadiness.

So change came slowly at first because everyone was afraid, was mindful, knew change was upsetting and you don't want to upset things, *señora*, not yet, not with the ancestors newly buried and not yet forgotten. Take your time, what are you hurrying for? Why all the impatience when the fiestas still boom, and the stars hover overhead like wasps, and if you press your ear to the ground and listen intently, you still hear those voices, the wailing, the endless humming of a lonely earth abandoned like an orphan, pining, in despair, in abject loneliness, in Celtic longing. *Madre de la tierra, come back to us*. But she will not come back, for she too has been lost to emigration.

At school, Arturo was one of the best students in his grade—diligent with work like his mother, but hoping for change because he was of a new generation, after all, and desired change above everything—but the curriculum remained the same as always, the same history books, the same maps, the same hour of religious instruction day after day. And what did God think of the change? The old Spain had been very good to God. The old Spain had made him the centrepiece, along with the Dictator, of course. It had made God the star. Church attendance had been up, priests were respected after almost a century of ongoing distrust, and nuns taught boys and girls about holiness. In universities, law faculties had concerned themselves with the laws of the angels, the laws of the heavens, *which are more important than our laws down here below, eh?* A priest at the faculty would tell his students, *If you should doubt this, try testing our Lord and see the disaster that will ensue from such behaviour, see the punishments that are in store for you.* What would happen to the laws of the angels with *la democracia*? Would these laws disappear, taking God with them?

A new priest, a Don Alberto, had appeared on the scene, eager to discuss these pressing issues with teenagers like Arturo. *Get them while they're still young I tell you, get them before the corruption sets in.* But Don Alberto was less concerned with the fate of God than with the more pressing issues of sex and hashish. *If you're going to do something unholy*, he would say to his students, *something against the rules of the Lord, then you'd better think of protecting yourself, about ensuring that no baby comes your way until marriage.* Don Alberto was a young priest and proud of his progressive views in this new age. Later, he would leave the priesthood and take up residence with a woman from Calais, but now he spoke in his most righteous tone, a dark figure in black, his white collar rubbing nervously against an adam's apple imploding with unexpressed desire.

María *la Reina,* forgotten in the chair in the kitchen for years now, plagued by visits from a dead husband and an assortment of never-ending ills was jolted awake by the changes that were occurring, even if subtly, in all corners of the land.

This is not good, she told Cecilia. *The world is already full of idiots wanting to rip you apart with all those ideas they've inherited but don't understand. A collection of donkeys is what they are, Cecilia. Sí, this is anarchy pure and simple. All those magazines with the rude language, the bare breasts. What kind of freedom is this?*

In the early evenings, when the school day was over, Arturo headed to Canteira's prettiest spot, still unchanged, the only place that had withstood the pressures of pesetas and time and there he breathed in the landscape that Matilde had taught him to love, encouraged by Gloria—*We must make him obsessed with this land.* And obsessed he was; why he loved this spot more than anything, and it was here that he came with young Ana Martínez, the daughter of a local farmer and more beautiful, he thought, than the whole of the world. Here they held hands and traded wet kisses and exchanged caresses in the open air, oblivious to his family's disapproval—gossip about the two had come to land in Cecilia's ears and a family meeting had been called, where his mother had railed and cried, arguing that he was too young for such things and, even worse, that Ana Martínez, with her peasant stock and her family's two skinny cows, was simply not good enough for the heir to the Encarna empire, not even if this was merely a passing, youthful affair.

Little Arturo, not so little anymore, almost fully grown by now but respectful still and eager to assuage his mother's tears, said, *All right, I will stop seeing her, of course, if that will make you happy,* meaning not one word of it, intending to continue seeing Ana at all costs.

In the corners of Canteira's discotheque, as lights bounced off stools and young people groped each other in the dark, Arturo laughed at his family, recreated the melodrama of the kitchen meeting for Ana's enjoyment as well. As to concerns over family wealth, *God aren't they funny*, they would say to each other. *Such drama, such typical small-town snobbery*—but these ideas were just the ditties of old people, of *that generation*, of the pitiable participants of forty years of nothing happening, and their warnings were unbelievable, their worries ridiculous. *Joder*, you would say, *can you believe the viejos, the old people, say such idiotic things? That is what a dictatorship does to you, no? Long live la democracia! Sí, hombre, la democracia must live.*

As he grew older, Arturo also began acquiring other ideas introduced into his head by one of his favourite teachers, and then learned from others, inside the Café Buenos Aires number one and then inside the Café Paris, a *vino tinto* in a white bowl in front of him, the contentious Ana Martínez by his side. It was this teacher—known as Pedro to his students—no Don this or Señor that, *por favor*, for these are modern times—it was Pedro who had appointed himself guardian of Arturo's political maturation, for *Arturo, my boy, ideas are men's concerns. Hotels and what you can and cannot do, you can learn from all those women who loom by your side. But how to change the world—ah, amigo, that, you see, is a concern for men.*

Pedro had been building a following for quite some time. Long before the democracy, as if smelling the coming death of the Dictator with his long, powerful nose, Pedro had been busy building the underground of Galician separatism, preparing the forces that would emerge with the changing tide to beckon the new age in, the age of choice, the age of freedom, the age—damn it all—when ancient insults would finally be redressed in the corridors of power, political and financial, with the publication of long-silenced poets and in the echoes, even, of bombs placed by terrorists to clear the way for not only a new order, but the vindication of a people, so done in, so exploited, so abused, *Dios mío*, that there was nothing left but violence in this small unhappy world.

It was Pedro who led the official wing of the Separatist Party of Galicia, one of seventeen regions soon to be declared autonomous so that the country would, eventually, come to resemble a quilt made of patches of historical grievance and regional pride. One of the first to be recruited was the young Encarna boy—*for every party needs its rich, though only because the rich have access to the powerful, those bastards, given so much just by virtue of birth*. Arturo grew to feel embarrassed by his mother's habit of accumulating wealth when his real allegiance was to this group of men, and these men were not wealthy, were not looking for pesetas or foreign cars. They were the reformers, the ideologues, the ones who painted political slogans onto town walls and on farmer's hogs. They did other things as well, organized demonstrations, sang traditional folk songs, attended town meetings where they booed down the officials in their patent-leather shoes and navy blue ties. Above all, dressed in their startling long V-necked sweaters and with their unruly beards, they scared the priests and the old people, who balked at the thought of such radical ideas and feared most of all the men's youth. Youth was a dangerous thing, they told each other. The young had done much of the killing during that *guerra*. What, pray God, would the young do now?

Pedro the Leader was a man of palpable charisma, son of a dirt-poor labourer but smarter and quicker than a million lawyers of the state, and the people, Arturo included, could not help but listen to him, would appear at the odd demonstration just to hear him speak his fine *gallego*—*for ours is the language of the people, banished and silenced by a Dictatorship which lasted forty years too long. Ours is the language of the pueblo, of those who labour and toil; the language of all those poets and dreamers exiled and murdered long ago. Ours is the language of lamentation, but soon it will save us all.*

The stories he told would be remembered for a long time, would inspire the burgeoning poet to write more than one beautiful, haunting line. And the way he sang! His voice boomed, crashed, and roared over the crowds, supported by the gentle strumming of a guitar, which did not sound quite right—but the bagpipes, the *gaita,* he played majestically, made them sound like the fine rain that falls in a constant drizzle on this melancholy land so mistreated by history and abandoned by emigration. People would congregate at the *Mesón Pepe* to discuss ideas and strategies, to hear him sing and talk, and to eat the *jamón serrano* and the *chorizo—the blessed fruits,* Pedro would say, *of our beautiful land.*

Alone with Ana and his newfound passion in life, this philosophy that was his guiding force, Arturo knew that no hotel or movie theatre could be as important as this—*because Ana, it is for ideas that men live.* Now they met secretly—*no use getting my family all worked up*—in darkened discotheques where they confessed their love; and beneath the bridges of Canteira where ancient vendettas had been played out during that war, they would meet and laugh at the ancestors, at the stories peddled by Arturo's mother as family lore, at a world so foreign it was like India, when all that mattered was being there on such a beautiful night like that *chica,* with the stars so bright and the air as smooth as silk and the eyes of God resting on their stomachs in such holy approbation.

But of course the Encarna women learned of it. In a town as small as Canteira—with ears propped everywhere in the expectation of a story and eyes opened as wide as the sky—it was impossible to keep anything a secret for any decent period of time. And soon enough, Arturo found himself being lectured by his mother in the kitchen once again, the other women sitting silently by her side. This time, though, there were no preambles, no lengthy expositions of motherly love. This time, his mother's words were a little more desperate, her threats worthy of a *telenovela*, where beautiful women are forever discovering that they are, in fact, the long-lost daughters of the richest men in the world.

If you wish to persist with this madness, she told him coldly, *you'd better think of finding somewhere else to live, other pesetas to use in your Café Buenos Aires, your Café Madrid. Sí, Arturo, listen well, I did not spend my life toiling so that you could squander it all on a nothing like her.*

Arturo bit his lip, hung his head, assumed the well-rehearsed pose of contrition, thinking of the many errands he would have to run for Pedro later that afternoon.

Arturo, listen. Do you know what it's like to live without money, without the means to buy yourself a coffee or a pack of your beloved cigarettes? Ah, of course you don't, you wretch. Not when you've had me to waste my life on work, just so you could have a future. Just so nothing would ever be denied to you. Ah, the things we mothers suffer. The agony that is inflicted upon us by ungrateful children, unconcerned in the slightest with the pain felt by those who have brought them into this world.

And then there were more threats, that she would leave him as destitute as a farmer's daughter, as poor as his *querida Ana*, she of the long face and the two skinny cows. And again he said *Sí, Mamá, sí*, not meaning a word of it, but he did not want to hurt her really, no matter how antiquated her ideas, how ridiculous, or how unfair her small-town mind. After all, these were women trapped inside the barriers of a more traditional time, and this was the modern age, modernity had finally arrived. But now he listened gravely as his mother threatened him with anything she could think up, *señor,* to keep him locked up in the kitchen and in barns, to deprive him of his considerable inheritance, to prevent the world from moving in its cyclical way, round and round it goes, till the last kiss is delivered, the last moan uttered and the world is world no more.

Later, after speeches had been given and warnings issued inside the kitchen of the family home—a mansion now really, with three bathrooms, Italian furniture, and all of his dead grandmother's strange clocks—after he had emerged from the oppression of women's worries inside the overheated kitchen which now sported a gas stove next to the wood-burning specimen of old, Arturo crossed over to Café Buenos Aires number one to meet with Ana and there, hand in hand, talked of future plans and the saving of their land, just as they had yesterday, just as they would *mañana* and on and on and on.

For ten years Matilde had been taking him there, to the prettiest spot in Canteira, to the top of the known world. For ten years, the increasingly ailing Matilde, cane in hand, had walked with little Arturo to where the rock with the alchemical symbols stood as erect as ever, unperturbed in the slightest by the changes that had taken over this part of the world, with the death of dictators, the demise of the old order, the arrival of democracy and kings, unaltered it stood, as industrial angst took over the country and created an entirely different set of *nouveau riche*. What lay here was unmovable, impervious to the goings-on of a country spinning out of control.

But Arturo was not a little boy anymore. Could not accept Matilde's simplistic renditions of such a complicated world. Look here, he had heard men speaking, had been won over by Pedro's convincing words. And if this corner was beautiful, that was because it lay in Galicia. This abandoned piece of the world. This aggrieved chunk of land where a famous saint had once appeared, dead on a platform of stone.

Matilde, we must become independent. We must learn to stand all on our own. Galicia is its own nation, has its own people, its own language, its own future separate from the rest of Spain.

These ideas he shared only with Matilde, for he knew the other women would never understand his newfound urgency. A *locura,* they would call it. Evidence that their youth had gone mad with the arrival of *la democracia*; that the pestilence that had taken over the country had made madmen of them all.

But the youth of *la democracia* were no different from the youth of old. New ideas, maybe, but ideas all the same. Matilde could remember the ideas that had taken over the land fifty years before; the consequences of those ideas were not hard to recall.

She tried to reason with him. *There are no nations, no regions left in such a large, splendid world,* but she could see that he had been hijacked, had been seduced by new minds that loomed all around resplendent, that offered up intellectual anodynes to Arturo and those of his kind. What, in any case, could she do? She had done her own bit of learning, had been left to make sense of the world on her own, and it was his turn now, his turn to lay down the tracks on which others would travel for fifty years or more.

In this world, communism still brewed. Socialism loomed ahead. As the parties of the left battled with the parties of the right, nationalism hovered in the shadows, waiting for its chance to set things to rights. Soon there would be many nations inside many countries. Long-forgotten symbols would be revived. Maps would be redrawn. Wars would be fought to right the grievances of old. The dead, who once rose from their graves to move the stones that separated small patches of land from other equally small patches of land, would rise in answer to the call of much larger work.

Arturo could not stop thinking about the new world about to unfold, inhaled it with every drag of his *Ducados*, a dark made-in-Spain tobacco. A harsh reminder of the work still left to be done.

Matilde, lost in her own world now more than ever, now that time had conferred on her the sort of peace granted only to the very old, failed to notice the spark in Arturo's fervent gaze. Failed to notice that for Arturo, talk of separation was not idle chat. It filled him with spirit, empowered him, gave his days their smattering of fervent joy. For Arturo, talk of separation had become his reason for living; the contributions he hoped to make were all wrapped up in the white and blue flag of a nation waiting to be fully born. Matilde, happy Matilde, much loved by all who stumbled upon this pure spirit, this fountain of joy in a world devoid of much hope, failed to see the embers that brewed furiously in her nephew's eyes. Soon they would all see how the fire raged. How the smoke billowed. How the dust settled first and then blew magically off.

The first to die was Cecilia, in her sleep, dreaming, it was supposed, of five-course feasts and celebrations of saint days and virgin births. By then, she had already deteriorated into a formless heap, her stomach a series of flabby waves, her nose bereft for years of its famous sense of smell.

It was Gloria who found her in the morning, her body cold, her face now fully relaxed, and how she cried, Gloria! She shed more tears for Cecilia than she had spared for her own mother, Asunción, gone so many years ago. The priest was summoned and found that no words of condolence seemed strong enough for the misery of the Encarna women—for now it was not only Gloria who cried but Matilde and even María shed tears, if less desperately than the rest, because after all it would be her turn next and she needed to conserve her energy in order to assure herself of an easy death. *But Mujeres,* the priest Don Valentín said, *she was a good person and is guaranteed a place in Heaven next to the angels and the saints. And her death was an easy one, for it arrived in her sleep. Proof, señoras, proof of a life well lived.*

That morning, when the bells of the church tolled for the Encarna household, the people assumed that *la Reina* had finally succumbed to one of her mysterious diseases, but then death, *amigos,* death waits for no one, not even a formidable personage such as her. But it did not take them long to learn of the real Encarna victim and then—*Not Cecilia, that Cecilia was always the best of the lot. None of her sister's harshness, none of Gloria's enormous hankering for wealth.*

Though younger than María, Cecilia was almost old enough to lay claim to full membership in the ever-expanding century club, and it was this fact, ultimately, that checked the people's tears the most, for the old were meant for dying, the old lived merely to ward off death. And because this was a small town and she was so old, no autopsy was ever conducted, no examination was made to determine the ultimate cause. But María knew already—knew that Cecilia had died from the bitter taste of time.

She asked to dress the corpse, though she could hardly walk, could stand for only short periods at a time and then only with the help of her brass-tipped walking stick. But to María belonged the privilege of dressing the corpse, for it was she who had been with her sister every day since she had come into the world. Locked in the parlour with Cecilia's calm, ivory flesh, flowing and spreading around the dining room table from all the sag and decay of old age, María busied herself with the task of sponging down her sister's skin and dressing her in one of her better matador's capes. As she sponged and dressed, she told the story of Cecilia's life, year by year, one blessed step at a time, so that her sister would remember, could take the lessons with her to *el cielo*—for heaven was where peace could finally be found. And the words that Cecilia had so longed to hear finally tumbled from her sister's mouth: *Cecilia, all the love I've had for you, all the tears we've shared in this long, unbearable life. How the world weighs now, how bleak the future seems. All your cooking, all your silly stories, how I will miss them, Cecilia. How I long already for a taste of your famous caldo, a bit of your empanada doused in all those mysterious herbs.* Hours passed like this, with Matilde waiting patiently outside lest she should be needed by her mother, and with Gloria making the final preparations for the funeral that was to occur the following day.

More people arrived than had appeared for the funerals of Carmen the Holy One and Asunción both. The line of mourners coiled around fields and streets, disappearing finally into the edges of the town. So many people arrived, in fact, that not all were able to enter the house to pay their final respects. Some came for the usual reason—a visit to one of your dead for a visit to one of mine later on. Others came out of curiosity, for the Encarnas were one of the most powerful families in town, and their beautiful house had attained legendary dimensions in the mouths of gossips, many of whom could gain access to the parlour with its marble and clocks only on such an occasion—after all, who was going to turn you away when you'd come armed to the hilt with prayers and tears? *Ah,* someone whispered somewhere in the line, *remember José Juan? La Reina had no qualms about throwing him out.* And then, one by one, the stories about the Encarnas suddenly surfaced, told by the very old and the not-so-old, of Civil War rapes and disgorged eyes and *Have you heard what the young Arturo is up to? That fool has become a communist now. A communist, when his own family is the wealthiest in town!*

Whispers and more whispers. The shushes and titters were heard as far as the parlour inside where María sat by the coffin, walking stick in hand. *Make them stop*, she told Matilde, *make the gossip stop whatever way you can.*

Bueno, Mamá, talk is talk is talk. Who cares about all that now?

I want to see her being placed in the grave, want to make sure there is space left for me.

Don't be ridiculous, Mamá. You are too weak to be there, there is no need for you to see.

But sí, I want to, I tell you. Sí, I do.

It was no use. Matilde could say nothing to dissuade María from going to the cemetery. She simply had to do what she had to do and was ready to put up a fight by her sister's coffin, no matter the lack of propriety, no matter the lack of respect. After all, grief-spent bodies have thrown themselves tragically over coffins, wails have risen like a banshee's cries from the houses of the dead. *La democracia* could cure the country of mediocre poetry, could allow all the once prohibited languages out into the open air, but it could not alter the way the people mourned. Or not yet. Eventually, though, after years and years of *la democracia*, people would begin to die in hospitals, in crisp, white surroundings, away from family eyes. Mothers would stop nursing children and feed them milk from boxes, canned vegetables, bottled fruit, and powdered meals. And only dignified tears would be shed at funerals, no matter how tragic the death. But these were the early years of *la democracia* and there is, as the man at the top says, much still to be learned. So much, in fact, that melodramatic funeral scenes continued to be common enough to not merit even the batting of an eye, the wrinkling of a brow, or a silent *por favor!*

As María stood before the grave, propped up by Gloria and Matilde on either side, and said a *Padre Nuestro* for Cecilia and for all the others long lost to the world, as she stared at the beautiful church with its tinted glass and ancient stone and felt the sun on her back, the touch and strength of family arms, as she heard the drone of the priest drifting through her own *who art in heavens* and *give us this days*, she decided, there on that hill, after years of disappearing inside memories of the dead, to fight and claw her way back into life.

No tumbling into decay for me—my beauty left me long ago. No latch, no key, no desperate hanging on to anything that is not breath. No despair, no despair, no despair. Instead repair. Repair, the golden echo shouts, across fields of grass and varnished corn.

Into Gloria's hands the task fell of making sense of her grandmother's newfound zest for life.

I would like to go to the hotel in the mornings. Just like before, just like in the days of old, María told her one day, not two weeks after Cecilia's funeral. Surely, too little time had passed for a proper mourning period.

Mourn? María scoffed at the suggestion. *I have no time to mourn. God only knows how much time I have left, and you want me to mourn?*

The other arguments she countered easily. *I am not so lame I can't move. And anyway, there are sophisticated chairs with wheels now, Gloria. I can do things at the hotel—sí, sí, watch over that tower of a cook of yours, make sure she's not stealing from the hotel pantry. Those people, you know, Gloria, those people are a wretched lot.*

After almost two decades of withering, María *la Reina*, survivor of countless diseases and an unimaginable war, was back in splendid form, insulting the kitchen staff, making life miserable for Matilde—old now herself and plagued by weak hips and degenerate knees, which forced her to lean on a cane, forced her to peruse the ground before catching a glimpse of the infinite, beautiful sky. And now this new twist, her mother's restored zeal for life, which would require issuing more apologies on María's behalf—because she was back, *sí, señor,* she was definitely back, passing judgements on the guests and creating the havoc she was once famous for, once before her many illnesses had reduced her to staring at the floor. Yes, she was back indeed, but this time it was even worse because *la democracia* had arrived and with it bare breasts in magazines, pornographic movies galore, and the language! Oh Lord the language was as nasty, as brutish, as rude as a thousand peasants during harvest time. Once upon a time long ago, when the world was supposedly young and decent people dressed always in black, María *la Reina* had a sharp tongue and even sharper bite. Now, her sharp tongue was sharpened by an even ruder axe and she enhanced all pronouncements with *coños, carajos, cabrones,* and words of the like.

Eh, señora, she screamed at one of the Castilian matrons at the hotel, with her large freshwater pearls and hair coiffed and teased up to the sky. *It must be fine to have the time to point your fat ass at the sun, to lie on the riverbed with those sagging breasts and those flaccid stumps by your side.*

And it did not stop there. Matrons were only one of her targets. Priests, and young men with their brains between their legs, and that ageing skinny runt of a banker, *what is his name? Ah sí. José Miguel,* son of the famous sadistic rapist from the ruinous village of Lazar. Ah, what fun, what glorious fun it was to be alive.

Gloria had enough problems already. Look here, her head was filled to the brim with problems. Too many businesses to run, too many accounts to keep in order, too many political challenges now, hands to bribe had become many hands: blue for parties on the right, scarlet red for Felipe's socialists, and a million other little fingers poking their way through the growing tower of wants. And in the midst of her worries, the rumours of her own son's political leanings. *After all the work done, erecting empires, building dreams, this is how he repays me, by turning red, by pushing separation for this pathetic piece of the world!* And Ana Martínez, that skinny indistinguishable runt, no money, no education, not even pretty, not one thing to commend her to a man like him, and yet there he went, her son, meeting the girl privately in bars and in empty fields. *As if I didn't know. As if there weren't a thousand gossips willing and happy to regale me with news of this kind. And the look on their faces when they do!* The enjoyment, the gleeful satisfaction. Why they didn't even bother to conceal their delight. But then, rich people were never liked and probably never would be, for that was the proven way of the world.

Now her grandmother, the crazy, eternally ailing María, sat again in her hotel kitchen chair, insulting the guests with such vituperative spite that they were sure to leave and never come back. After all her work, all those years of toil, years spent banishing memories of lost fathers and two-timing, treacherous navy thugs, years of forgetting but not forgiving (ah, that would be wholly impossible), after so much wealth had been accumulated and a semblance of security had been achieved, now the generations were closing in. On one side, her grandmother, shutting Gloria's business down with her tongue, and on the other, her son Arturo—who is Arturo no more. Just yesterday he ceased being Arturo, had charged into the house announcing his own demise.

My name is Artur from now on. Not Arturo, Mamá. Arturo is a Castilian name and I am a Gallego, just like you and all your ancestors, right back to the first of the wretched line. You may not have spoken to me in my own language, you may have deprived me of my most important birthright, but you will not rip the roots from my name. From now on, I am Artur, Mamá. From now on, I will refuse to respond to any other name.

Out of the corner of her eye, Gloria caught her grandmother smirking at this declaration by Arturo—henceforth to be known as Artur for the rest of his short, eventful life—caught the glee that entered María *la Reina*'s cloudy single eye.

I told you; I told you, she seemed to be saying, although, for once, she uttered not a single word.

The demonstration had been planned for months. Inside the makeshift headquarters of the Separatist Party of Galicia—at the back of Café Buenos Aires number one, by the pinball machines, which punctuated all serious talk of political change with obnoxious pings and dings—signs had been drawn, megaphones secured, and evacuation plans devised in case the batons of the *Guardia Civil* descended upon the crowd with the same vicious fervour as was their custom years ago.

Almost ten years had passed since the arrival of *la democracia*. Ten years in which the face of Spain had changed—some, those who clung to the notion of a "glorious past," argued that the change was surely for the worse. Political slogans peppered the walls in towns. Women with bare breasts had become commonplace now; on the beaches of Galicia's beautiful jagged coasts, men and women sunbathed calmly in the nude. On the eve of joining Europe's economic union, and agreeing to unified standards and things of the kind, Spain had become official, acceptable, exciting even, the place to be, until this title was appropriated, five years later, by the city of Prague. In Madrid, a group of avant-garde artists would start *la movida*; fashion designers were popping up in all corners of the land. Once considered a poor and backward pit, Spain was rising to the democratic challenge with flying colours. By 1984, Spain had become a bona fide worldwide hit.

For Artur the changes were not enough. In some ways, they had made the country worse. They had made the rich richer—he had only to look at his own mother to see the truth of this. And as his mother grew richer, Artur's embarrassment grew greater, his need to appease the Party faithful increasingly strong.

For Galicia must be set free.
For our people have been oppressed for too long, our language stolen from us by those in the seats of power, by the ignorance of old.
For remember, señores, that it is better to die on your feet than to live on your knees.

Inside the regional parliament, no one was dying. Inside the regional parliament, the few extremists elected to power banged their shoes against tables made of noble oak, wore pastel colours to draw attention to the regional plight, gave lengthy discourses on the oppression of the Galician people, waxed poetic inside political corridors and in cafés of old. A bunch of *locos,* they were considered. A bunch of hooligans hovering on the periphery of modern Spain.

The demonstration had been planned to demand independence from the central powers of Spain. In truth, few people wanted independence for Galicia except those who belonged to the Separatist Party itself—those like Artur, who spent their time devising strategies and writing slogans, dreaming of a new world waiting to unfold. But a demonstration was a chance to come together and chant, a chance to eye the women, a chance to gossip about the neighbours, to express collective anger at the whole world if you liked.

Due to an extraordinary mix-up, a confusion that would confound the mayor of Canteira for years and years afterwards, the nuns of the nearby Convent of Santa Clara had heard of the demonstration and, cloistered as they were from the rest of the world, had understood it to be a demonstration in opposition to opening stores on Sunday. To protest this—a blasphemous outrage, an insult aimed at the Lord—they too had prepared some signs, they too planned to appear and chant with the rest of the holy ones—though in truth, they could not fathom why the Separatists, godless communists the lot of them, were suddenly taking the way of the Lord. *But the Lord is a mysterious agent, eh?* Sister Inés, an aged nun with a tremendous lisp told the others—*The Lord is forever fashioning miracles and this surely, sisters, is just one example more.*

On the day of the demonstration, a bright sunny day—unusual for that time of year—it was not only the Separatists who had appeared in front of the town hall with their incendiary signs, their call to rebellion, their bugles, bagpipes, and righteous might, but twenty-five nuns from the Convent of Santa Clara and the nearby Convent of Cluny who showed up to offer their support, and made their way pushing and kicking through the throng that had congregated there to the surprise of Pedro the Leader and the whole cadre of Separatists. Caught unawares in the midst of their political rant, they balked at the sight of this pugnacious army of nuns in their black and white garb, who with their chants of *Hail Mary, Our Father,* and *Commerce No, God Sí,* put an end to the political speeches, put an end to all talk of separation and the rise of a new nation on the periphery of Spain.

Those who had appeared that day to whittle time away, to gossip and eye the *señoritas* up and down, could not believe their luck. A confrontation! Between the godless radicals and the agents of God—oh, this was simply too much! One ran to tell another, sons called their mothers to the scene, and one by one the people of Canteira appeared at the town hall, hoping to catch a glimpse of the impending disaster before the police finally intervened.

It took hours to sort out the confusion, to placate the Separatists and silence the nuns, who would not be silenced so easily, would not be dismissed so soon. They had travelled from a very different world, a world filled with God, and out here, with the fiends who rejected all talk of the Lord, the nuns felt empowered as they had never felt before. Pedro the Leader and his group of Separatists, Artur as noticeably agitated as the rest, attempted to put the pieces of their demonstration back together again, attempted to keep the people there with more speeches, with impassioned chanting of their own, but it was too late. The morning had degenerated into a tale told by a circus clown, and nothing in the world could restore dignity to the event planned by this group of earnest young men. *The Lord has spoken, eh, señores?* Sister Inés told them with her own brand of passion and her stupendous lisp. *The Lord has spoken and He will not rest until he infiltrates the hearts of the likes of you.*

By two o'clock everyone had dispersed, had left to tell and retell the story during the afternoon meal and, later, during the café hour at quarter-past six. The square at the front of the town hall lay in tatters, littered with signs, confetti, and cigarette butts accumulated during that morning's commotion, a commotion that would metamorphose into the story most often told in the months ahead.

At the headquarters of the Separatist Party of Galicia at the back of Café Buenos Aires number one, heads shook, threats were issued, one blamed the other for the fracas that had taken place that morning, until the heat subsided and the earnest demonstrators tried to make sense of the affair. Where had the nuns come from, *joder?* How could the sisters have imagined that the Separatists had gathered there to keep the stores from opening up on Sundays, to keep people from decent work? *Eh,* wait a minute, another one shouted, *maybe those nuns are right! Maybe stores opening on Sunday means the exploitation of the workers, just like in the days of old. Ay, sí,* of course it would be so. Out came the guitar, the wine, the lamentations for a people so sorely trod upon. Tomorrow new plans would be developed, new battles would be fought.

At the Convent of Santa Clara, confusion reigned as well. Sister Inés, still lisping, still impassioned by the morning's events, argued with the others about the importance of keeping the fires raging against the heathens who dared to disturb the day of the Lord. That afternoon, a visitor arrived to see the nuns, a visitor who had been spending many an afternoon with these women of late: María *la Reina,* the matriarch of the powerful Encarna clan, a woman who has felt the need to be in the presence of such holy ones during the waning years of her life. The very same woman who informed the nuns that the purpose of the demonstration was to rail against the opening of stores on God's holiest day. *Ah, so sorry,* she told them now, her gnarled fingers gripping her cane. *You know how it is to be so old, your hearing is a disaster, your mind befuddled by the simplest things in the world.*

Inside she was laughing. María *la Reina* had pulled off yet another one of her mischievous tricks, had struck back mightily at one of her greatest fears. Those men, those vermin, who had trapped her great-grandson Artur, who had made a pudding of his mind, a joke of all the promise his future once held. She had heard of the demonstration, knew of all their plans. María *la Reina* would not be toyed with. She could still remember the young men who had come calling on that distant hot August night, and she remained suspicious, thought that no good could come of all this talk of political change.

And lovely Artur, as dejected as the rest, but surely there will be another opportunity, he thought, another chance to inform the people of the struggle—ignorant of his great-grandmother's shenanigans, unaware of who has been visiting the nuns of Santa Clara, inciting them to their own demonstrations, provoking them to chant passionately, loudly, black and white women emboldened by the power of the Word.

It's because they don't know he thought. Because they don't hear the whimpering of tortured skies and wounded trees. It's because they're old, most of them, too old to hear the wind in the heather and the animals screeching as the fire rips and rages and burns. It's because they never learned to fight the good fight, to oppose the tyrannical rulers of their own oppressed unhappy land. But most of all, it's because they can't hear the leaves—the agony of a world driven to its knees.

Even within the passionate cadre of people that made up the Separatist Party of Galicia, Artur was considered particularly passionate, at times, even somewhat strange. It is because he loves this land, Pedro the Leader told them. Pedro the Leader wanted Artur to continue to fight the fight, particularly as he was the sole heir to a vast and desperate wealth. *Not that I care for money. But the Party, the Party needs funding to plaster every town wall with posters, every television screen with our names. That is my interest in money, amigos. Money as a means to an end.*

Artur cared little for money as well, was a strange duck in a land recently inhabited by youth dressed in clever copies of Givenchy and Dior. Every pair of jeans bore a label, a mark of distinction shot at the world. His own labels lay covered under oversized white shirts and V-necked sweaters, the unofficial garb of modern-day revolutionaries, of those obsessed like him with changing the world.

He loved his women desperately. María *la Reina,* his strange great-grandmother, this legend from whom he had received so very much: courage, determination, and, above all, the tenacity that arose from guilt. Much lamented fat Cecilia, now gone, but he had loved her too. How could he not have loved such a puddle of pure goodness, such well-told stories, such appreciation of good food?

And, of course, his own mother. So passionate, so intelligent, working herself into the ground. It was true, she had sacrificed much for him. It is true that she had done the work of many men, building monuments of wealth all around town, obliterating the talk of nasty gossips, talk of the abandonment she suffered at the hands of a father Artur had never seen once.

But it was Matilde he loved the best. Romantic, poetic Matilde, forever engaged in the naming of things. It was Matilde who introduced him to the power of the land he loved so much, who forced him to appreciate the green of the pastures and the peace to be found in the bubbling brook. It was Matilde who had told him the really important stories, who had told him how it was that dragons were slain, how to find meanings in the study of the heavens, the role that each planet played in the unfolding of destiny.

But even Matilde, with all her love of the earth, all her reverie for the spirits that appeared in those few moments between the waking hour and the dead of sleep, even Matilde couldn't hear those voices, the eternal whispering that kept him awake for hours and days and weeks.

It may have started happening after he began smoking the hashish that was all the rage among the youth of Canteira, straight from Morocco and known as *chocolate* to those who smoke it openly inside certain pubs. Maybe it happened after his first hit of acid, given to him by Pedro after a trip to the Netherlands, almost a year before.

Regardless. It did not matter how or when or why. The point is that he heard them, was tortured by voices moaning and pleading throughout the night. It began one hot summer night, when a great fire raged inside the forest that framed Canteira, a fire so powerful it seemed on the verge of consuming the town whole. On a night of alarms and trucks and the hauling of water until the early hours of the dawn, a night when entire families were forced outside, their cherished heirlooms in hand, on a night like this, as fire raged and fire burned, Artur was awoken by a thousand gentle voices, the voices of the forest which for the first time called to him in fear, in despair, for the forest was burning and with it the memories of untold generations who had lived, fought, and died in its caring hands. They wailed inhumanly as they told a hundred stories, of the Celts building stone fortresses and the Romans destroying them; of Jews driven from their homes and those who had stayed, renouncing their faith and adopting the names of fruit trees instead; of women who toiled in the fields, their backs broken, their men in distant lands that they themselves would never glimpse, of the wailing of the ocean, the bitter, beautiful seductive call of the sea that swallowed people whole, keeping their bodies for eternity. On and on the voices went, recounting so many stories and so many tragedies that night that Artur thought he would go mad.

And in amazement, he realized that these voices came from the leaves of the trees, from the mouths of animals, and even from the pine cones that lay on the ground—they had all converged there, at the foot of his bed, on the sorriest night of the year, a night when the church bells tolled and people sobbed and animals died, scorched alive by the anger of human hands, and all Artur could do was to cover his ears in agony, until finally, after hours and hours of storytelling and despair, the forest grew quiet and silence reigned once more.

From then on, with every fire, no matter how small and inconsequential, how far or how near, Artur was visited by the voices of the forest, voices that told their stories desperately, speaking in the language of times past, in the spirit of his ancestors, giving Artur no peace until he began to investigate their origins, their truths, reading the ancient elegies to this mystical land and recognizing, in wonder, his own connection to the earth, to *la madre verdadera*, who waited patiently for him to rescue her from her misery, from all the exploitation and neglect, just so she could sing this mournful but beautiful tune. Mother Earth, the greatest mother in this world full of mothers, in this world of women's pain and mother's laments.

On the night of the great fire, they whispered their truths and sobbed inconsolably in his ear until the early hours of the morning, when they said one final word. *Cuidado,* they said. *Be careful*, and then they said no more.

I hear voices, he tells Pedro as they share a *porro* made from the wondrous Moroccan hashish.

I hear voices and they come from the ground. From the ground, Pedro, do you understand what I'm saying? I'm telling you I can hear the trees speaking and the wind moaning for help.

Home, amigo, Pedro the Leader answers, a smirk upon his face. *Perhaps it's time to give up this shit. Shit like this can make you totally insane.*

It's not that, Pedro. I hear voices I tell you. I think we should focus our efforts more on the land. The land, Pedro, is the basis for all our demands. Remember? All the talk of the mother earth, the great mother. Why doesn't the Party focus on our origins, on saving the forests and caring for the land?

Pedro has heard this before. Artur of late has become obsessed with the land. It's all right, he thinks. Let the boy have his obsessions. Everyone feels the need to voice their own particular ills. But it's the Party that counts. In the end, what matters is the allegiance to those of his kind. Now he talks gently but firmly. Like a father. Like the father Artur never had.

I think this living with women has made you sentimental, my friend. Has made you a bit loose about the head. It's all right, though. In the future, when the people have enough to eat, then we'll focus on saving the land. Then we'll have a Green Party just like those Germans. For now, Artur, the people are what matters. The people are for whom we fight.

The response does not satisfy Artur. Pedro can see this, can see the worried look still engraved upon the young man's face. Perhaps it is best he stop sharing his *chocolate* with him. Pedro has read somewhere about the things it has done to some people's heads. How some have gone completely *locos,* their minds so broken that no one can find a way to put them back together again. Later, he will meet with other Party members and laugh at Artur's expense. *This is what living with women does to you eh, señores? Turns you into a weeping handkerchief, a lamentable piece of pulp.*

Ehh, careful, muchachos! scream the women in the Party, long-haired passionate women dressed in jeans and V-necked sweaters of their own. *This Party is for women too, don't forget. Don't forget that it was women who saved us during that war, who farmed the land and broke their backs when you men left to seek your fortunes far and wide.*

Well, all right. The Separatist Party of Galicia is a progressive group, a shining, glorious example of the virtues of free thought, free speech, and free love in the new democratic age. More joking follows, more gossip about Artur and the famous Encarna women, who are rumoured not to be women at all but a bunch of men in disguise, selling contraband, starting businesses, giving rise to gossip that rages across the land.

Ehh, the women shout again, laughing. *Be careful with the things you say about those women. Those women are our mentors, the ones who have paved the way for all of us.*

And then more laughter, more drinking, the sweet smell of hashish, mingling with freedom on this languorous night. Not another word about Artur and his voices, his rather poetic concern for their glorious land. Out comes a guitar and then a song, a sad song of abandonment by that popular group *Fuxan os Ventos,* sung gloriously by their own Pedro the Leader, lately known as Pedro the Great.

Outside, Artur sits with little Ana Martínez by his side. She knows about the voices, has heard his stories and torments patiently since the very first. *Listen, Artur, I have something that will silence the voices, something that will take your worries away.*

I'm pregnant, Artur. Soon enough a child will come to take away your pain.

Dios, Artur thinks, shocked, not shocked, confused by this bit of news that merges with the rhythmic pelting of the pouring rain. *Dios,* he thinks again. How to tell his mother? How will things ever be the same?

But that night he would have no opportunity to divulge this bit of news. Hours before, as rain pelted the dark streets and people laughed at the voices that spoke within a young man's head, María *la Reina* fell ill once again, except that this time it was serious enough to warrant the intervention of greater powers than Doctor Gerardo's, who had, in any case, returned years ago to Madrid. María was rushed to the hospital in Santiago de Compostela, such a famous hospital in such a venerable town, so visited and admired by generation upon generation of English and German pilgrims alike—look here, the most *bonita* in all of Galicia. But María just kept cursing at the world.

Take me from here, cabrones, she screamed, kicking her scrawny legs into the air. *They will kill me, I know it! This collection of grim reapers, these doctors with saws and hammers in their hands; they will kill me, because only then will I die. I warn you now, that is the only way I'll die.* And then silence finally—her energy had been spent.

Coño, she thought, *life is no good without strength.*

And then she fell asleep, exhausted from issuing insults and threats, still holding onto her cane in case the doctors appeared and she had to fight them off, or worse, fight off death, which had come calling on so many occasions, only to be denied entry—and you know death, it does not have unlimited patience, the patience of popes. One day, death would come marching in, and María was not ready for it yet.

The doctor took Gloria and Matilde aside and warned them of the seriousness of María's condition. It was the cancer acting up again, acting like a *loco,* and he would have to cut her stomach up to get at it, to rid her body of that invader that was trying to spread until she was nothing but sagging skin and rotting bones. The doctor was not very encouraging. *She is an old woman and has been through so much. Chances are that she will not live through such an operation. I'm sorry to have to say this. Take a seat, señoras, and someone will be along pronto to console you both.*

At night, they slept by María's side, woke with her every half hour, calmed her down as she continued to scream and issue threats. As the day of the operation approached and preparations were made to bring the parish priest and the important locals to the hospital just in case the unthinkable happened and the world, which had changed so much of late, would take it upon itself to wrench away the last remnants of the old order—as all the preparations were made, María grew more and more cantankerous, more venomous, began to terrorize the nurse assigned to her, a man of effeminate character and vicious tongue who would not let *la Reina* intimidate him. *Doña María*, he would say, *por favor, keep quiet. You're waking the dead people in the morgue and they need their rest, poor old people, having to recover from such long lives*. And then he would walk out of the room, her chamber pot in hand, whistling the unrecognizable tune that drove María crazy.

María would try to get up from her bed and run after him, but her legs were as weak as the chamomile tea the hospital was serving to calm her nerves, so she would scream after him instead: *Maricón, you are a maricón! Whoever heard of putting a poof by my side? This hospital is trying to kill me. I told them and told them and no one would believe me and now here I am, all alone, with an effeminate cabrón by my side with the eyes of a stranger. They scare me those eyes*. And then she would ring her bell interminably until there were two, three, or more nurses, two doctors and a hospital administrator by her side trying to calm her down, but she was simply *furiosa*, she would not calm down, until one of them—no one ever knew for sure who—was able to turn her on her stomach and jab a long sharp needle into her skinny white behind. After this she would finally fall into sleep, mumbling curses still, but less threatening now that she had been sedated.

The morning of the operation dawned as rainy and dark as a long winter's day. Already a large group had congregated in the narrow hallway that served as a waiting room, to comfort the family and await the outcome of the surgery. Waiting there were the priest, the baker, the hotel cook and head cleaner, and an assortment of distant and almost-forgotten relatives, all dressed up in their black and navy blue, waiting for the end to finally arrive for this remarkable woman who, just moments earlier, had screamed brazenly at all of them as she was being wheeled into the operating chamber, warning, *Ya veraís. Sí, ya veraís, you'll all see, you'll all rot before I'm through with you, cabrones and maricones, that's what you are, that's what you'll always be and you will pay!* until 5, 4, 3, 2, 1, the anesthesia took its toll, leaving the hospital quiet and the doctors harried, for this was an important woman they had on their table and not a peasant without name or pesetas. They would have to be careful all right.

Two hours passed and then three, during which Gloria held onto Matilde and Artur stared listlessly at his feet. The feeling in the hallway was funereal already, the air of melancholy so strong that it could be cut like *empanada*, and all they could do was wait for those doctors and their news and the grace of God who hovered over them, watching from the heavens in his easy, dispassionate way.

At four in the afternoon, the doctor finally appeared, with tired eyes and a defeated gait. *Doña María is alive but slowly fading. I am sorry, but she is so old. Her body is tired and I think it wants rest, which is understandable really.* Shaking his head in condolence, he informed them that she would be brought to her room where the priest could administer the last rites and Matilde could cry for her mother and all could say their final farewells. As the afternoon grew heavier until it became evening, the people walked into the room, one by one, where they sombrely said their good-byes. Afterwards, they huddled in the hallway waiting for the moment of death to arrive. But suddenly, and unbelievably, in the midst of the sorrow and the tears, a bloodcurdling scream emerged from María's room.

The maricón! María was screaming. *Where is my maricón? I need water and food, my stomach is an endless well and there is no water, nothing, not even a drop of aguardiente to soothe my ailing heart. Nada. Only insults and bad smells and where in the hell is that maricón of a nurse of mine?*

And then she was quiet—but not dead. How could she die when she had so much yet to do? She lounged in her bed for a week like that, keeping everyone guessing, doctors and family alike, keeping everybody ready, until the priest had no patience left and went home. The others, thinking this to be one of María *la Reina*'s better circus feats hurried back to tell the news to the amazed townspeople of Canteira, who retold the stories of all her accumulated tragedies, all her successful efforts at warding off death. A week later she was on her feet, partly at least, hanging on to her walking stick, smacking it against the irritated knees of the effeminate nurse who tried to control her with the threat of many enemas, and a month later she was back home, issuing her loud complaints there but not before shoving 10,000 pesetas into the surprised hands of her favourite *maricón* and telling him, *Get yourself a woman in the name of God and his funny angels, get yourself a woman with the money and you'll be all right,* and patting his legs once more, except this time with affection, with a half-smile and a glow in her one eye, her one eye that still, at that age, saw everything.

Back home, Artur fretted as Ana grew bigger with each passing day. *We'll tell them next week, Ana. Let my great-grandmother fully recover before I scare her half to death.*

Back home, the days grew longer with the arrival of spring. Soon it would be summer. A good time, he thought, for a marriage, a child, and finally some peace.

As Ana grew larger and María *la Reina* recuperated fully and miraculously from the operation the doctors thought would be the end of her, Artur's worries increased until he could think of nothing else. The voices were back, louder than ever, and Pedro the Leader was growing increasingly impatient with him. Encarna or no Encarna name behind him, Artur was becoming too difficult for the Party to keep. Lately, as the voices had grown louder and Ana's stomach had expanded inside her small frame, Artur had started keeping company with some questionable types, three long-haired layabouts from the wrong side of town. It was Pedro's fault, really. He had instructed those in the Party not to supply *chocolate* to Artur anymore, worried that the drugs were wreaking havoc in the young man's head. In truth, he had asked the Party to stop with the drugs entirely. The ports of Galicia, to which *contrabandistas* once travelled from all corners of the land to retrieve American tobacco, French perfume, and Bavarian clocks, had become a hotbed of anarchy. Increasingly, the jagged coastline, so beautiful that it could make grown men weep, so secretive that in its nooks and crannies many illegitimate children had been conceived, had now become the ideal hiding place for the illegal drugs arriving from Colombia and Morocco to be shipped to the streets of Madrid.

With Pedro's newly imposed ban on such things, Artur

sought out the long-haired trio, who had already been arrested more than once for a series of petty crimes. His ideas were, in any case, increasingly shunned at official Party levels, where moderation of thought and spirit was slowly taking over the once strident, revolutionary tone. *We are growing older, wiser, more at peace with ourselves,* Pedro the Leader would say, patting an increasingly disconsolate Artur on the back.

It was because the voices were growing louder and his sense of futility greater that Artur resorted to the drugs. Then there was the problem of Ana's growing bulk—he had to tell his family. Everything, lately, had been getting out of hand. No amount of studying had improved his grades nor helped him pass the selectivity test needed to get into any university in the land. His mother was busy plugging in her connections, making sure that he would make it to Santiago, no matter how much was paid or who was bribed. That was what wealth was for, that was why she had worked so hard.

Artur appears before the women on a rather sleepy evening in early June. Behind him, so scared she can hardly stand, is Ana Martínez, one hand on her protruding stomach, the other one hanging on to Artur's arm for dear life. He tells them quickly, without preamble or apologies. Ana is six months pregnant and he intends to marry her and start a family life.

Gloria begins screaming immediately. *No, you cannot be serious, Arturo, you cannot destroy us like this.*

And then she is thinking, *what to do, what to do*, questions are flooding the cavities of her mind.

There is London, she says. *In London, they can fix this in a minute, in a private clinic and with little risk. Sí,* she has heard much of these things from the people who stay at the hotel. After all, the country has gone crazy lately with *la democracia*, democracy has produced sexual liberation and its consequences, girls like Ana patting their stomachs in regret.

What are you saying? Matilde asks astounded. She is shocked by what she hears. *These are not solutions, Gloria. These are the answers of angry minds.* She turns her attention towards Ana, quiet, mousy Ana, she of the long face and quivering lip. *What do you want, my dear? It is up to you decide what must happen in your life.*

That is easy, of course. Oh, how relieved Ana is to look into this calm woman's face. She has heard much of Matilde. Why, once Matilde even taught her for a year—the poetry of Antonio Machado, the lyricism of Rosalía de Castro, the beauty to be found in all those complicated words.

I want to marry Artur and have his baby, that's all.

Of course you do, of course, Gloria screams. *Who wouldn't want to marry my Artur with all his wealth, with his future so assured?* Now she turns to Ana Martínez, considers her for the first time with cynical, suspicious eyes.

You can have the child and give it up for adoption. There are many good families that would take a child in. I, of course, could arrange the adoption for you and make sure you are paid handsomely for it. That your family benefits greatly from your plight. Her mind is going ti-ca-ti-ca-ta, rolling over options, considering this and that. How fortunate she has all that business experience to count on, how fortunate she has built mountains from tiny mounds before. It will be all right, she tells herself, trying to calm down. It will be all right.

But it will not be all right for Artur, her son, can simply not believe what he is hearing. His mamá, abandoned herself by a man, left to cope with a child and an empty life, and her own mother before her, left as well by her husband to a life of ticktocks, and finally, María *la Reina,* the mother of them all, sitting there with a tragic look upon her face, as tragic as on the day she lost her Arturo to the illness that had crucified his mind. And let's not forget sweet Mother Earth, our own sacred land, abandoned in recent times by the man she spewed out and who grew up to be Dictator, only to forget her also, his roots, the very place that gave him birth.

And with this illustrious history of abandonment, Mother, you too would have me leave my own child?

And then he is gone, taking a teary Ana with him, dragging her away from the cold marble of the house. *And we will not return, dear Ana. You will never be exposed to her venom again.*

Artur takes Ana back to her home—to her parents and their two skinny cows. That night, he stays with one of the three long-haired men in the darkest part of town. That night, the voices grow louder, his heart more restless, his anxiety greater than it has ever been. The following day, the three men convince him that the only way to get attention is with a little action, with a small explosion struck at the right nerve in town.

No deaths, no casualties of any kind. Just a small bomb placed on the steps of the town hall at midnight, once everyone has gone home. And then a message to save the forests—save the forests now. Only then, Artur, will they stand up and listen. Only then will things start changing for the better.

It is an excellent plan, he thinks. He thinks the voices will approve. He has been so passive lately, so willing to listen to the directives of people from above, just because they're older. Just because they have more power than he does. But they can't hear the voices, can't hear the screaming of the trees. It's all right. The three long-haired men have their own connections. They will make sure the bomb is made. *Your job, Artur, is to place it at the foot of the hall in the middle of the night. Your job is to get the message home. Sí*, in Artur's abandoned, desperate state, this solution seems like nectar from the gods. Perhaps then, perhaps only then, the voices will see and the voices will stop.

The bomb is handed to him in a small package the very next week. *Carry it to the steps of the town hall. Place it there quietly and get the hell away from it quick. Don't worry, the timer has been set and the bomb will blow up only at two in the morning. It will be a quiet night, a Tuesday of a very uneventful week. No bars lie anywhere near the town hall, no discotheques are even within sight. The whole thing will take minutes, Artur. Don't panic though. Calm is what you need.*

Artur has been living with one of the three young men now for almost a week. His mother has not tried to find him or talk to him since their kitchen meeting, a meeting that seems to him a lifetime ago. A wall of silence has been erected between mother and son, a barrier of pride and guilt. Let him see, she thinks. Let him see what life is like without the support of his family, without the money he has taken for granted for so long. No, she will not budge this time. María *la Reina* has tried to intervene, has pleaded with her granddaughter for the very first time, and Matilde has tried time upon time to reason with her, but Gloria will not change her mind. *That child inside Ana Martínez will never enter this house. I did not work as hard, did not toil every waking moment, just to see these sacrifices inherited by an unworthy, unwashed village wretch. Lord, the trials that come calling in the name of children everywhere.* She knows. She's heard them all before at the hotel.

By nine o'clock, Artur is restless, has paced the room back

and forth, back and forth, imagining the package he has and the silent tick-tock-tick-tock-tick. His palms are sweaty, his mind cloudy from one too many *porros* smoked, from being alone with the voices for much too long. Ana has been left with her parents, knows nothing of what is to take place later on. His three friends have things to do, errands to run. *We'll see you later, amigo, we'll meet up once the town hall has exploded and the time of judgement is upon us all.* Laughter. They are all nervous, Artur most of all.

Across town, the long-haired men meet with another plan in mind. The Encarna house. Empty, they know, except for *la vieja*—well, in truth, all the Encarna women are old, *but the really old one, that María whatever, about one hundred years old.* Gloria and Matilde will be at the hotel they know. It is a June night and dinner is served until midnight in the cavernous yellow dining hall. They know this because they have been listening to Artur, to his tales of family life, to his declarations of love for Ana Martínez and their unborn child, and the voices! *Joder, can you believe that idiot hears voices? What a crazy, unbelievable lout!* But rich. Never forget how rich. Inside that house, there must be a million valuables, thousands of pesetas hidden in cupboards and beneath mattresses. *You know these old people, hiding money everywhere but in banks.*

Laughter. The three men are dressed in black. Black jeans, black shirts, black farmer's caps. They will enter the house at eleven o'clock. The *vieja,* they think, will most definitely be asleep by then.

Across town Artur inhales one last time from a half-smoked cigarette and then walks to the door. It is a hot night. Very hot. It is unusual this heat, especially so early in June. The sweat is falling from his brow, falling onto his oversized blue shirt.

Underneath, his arms shake, his heart pounds and roars. Must get out. Must get out before the voices start to wail. To the discotheque. The Good Fun Discotheque, oh Lord, another one of those silly English names! It will be almost empty, he thinks, it is a Tuesday, so only the odd couple will be there, the odd couple engaged in an illicit affair. Cecilia would have sniffed them out, would have caught them with her powerful nose and glorious sense of smell.

Crash. Across the verandah and through the kitchen door. *These women have barricaded themselves, joder! These women know how to defend themselves from the likes of us*. Nervous giggles. They are too close to their object of desire to blow it now. *Be careful. Shush*, they signal to each other. Silence on an already intensely silent night.

Inside the house, María *la Reina* is awake in her bed. Her hearing is not what it used to be, has grown extremely weak, yet another insult of old age, yet another sign of the body's defeat. Her heart lurches into her mouth when she is confronted by the sight of the three young men, dressed in their criminal's black. Black used to be the colour of mourning once, she laments, used to be what one donned for the shedding of tears, and now look what *la democracia* has wrought—black worn for criminal acts. *Hombre,* her one eye is weak, but she thinks she knows the three who have traipsed quietly into her room, thinks she recognizes these long-haired drug-addicted blurs. Javier, Ricardo, and Vicente. The three monsters who took in her great-grandson last week. One of them, Vicente, is the son of a distinguished lawyer, a descendant of one of the more important town names. Lord, and what is he doing with these thugs, what is her own Artur doing with this collection of miscreants, these nobodies, these intensely angry young men? María has heard of how drugs are poisoning the young minds and hearts in town. Freedom—freedom to inhale funny things, brandish bare breasts, break into the homes of the very old.

Hombre, she says now, her voice rough from the confusion and the late hour of the night, a voice that scares the three young men half to death. They thought she was asleep. What is she doing awake?

Vicente, my boy, she asks sadly, *how did you ever come to be mixed up in this?*

Across town Artur has made it to the Good Fun Discotheque, package in hand. A few couples lie spread out here and there, whispering and embracing in the dark. Good. Just as he thought. *I will sit here by the speakers, and let the sound wash away my fear.* Silly boy, he tells himself, the only thing to fear is the voices, and they are no longer whispering in his ear. They are happy that he is finally taking action and not wasting his life on to be's and not to be's. He waves at the disc jockey, Pablo—he thinks that's the man's name—and he lights another cigarette, his legs still shaking, his mind racing like the wind.

Shut up, vieja! Vicente screams. *Mierda,* he thinks. What do we do with the old woman now? She has seen them, has recognized them, and that is a serious thing. Back they will go into the hands of the *Guardia Civil.* But no, no, he will not be sacrificed like this. Not for a woman a million years old. Especially not this one—God, the stories the old people tell about this witch! A quick strike to the head and she will be silenced, no matter the many ailments that have surrendered before in defeat.

He raises the baton he is carrying.

Inside the discotheque, the beat of the music is shaking the room and moving Artur's feet. One hour to go. One hour till the package is dropped off at the steps of the town hall and he has taken the first step towards his plan. With some surprise, he realizes now that he doesn't know what the actual plan is. No matter. It will come to him later. He raises the *cuba libre* he is drinking to his lips. Moments later, the world explodes, falls and crashes around his head, as the vibrations from the music detonate the cheap bomb that lies in the package by his feet.

I don't want to die, not yet. Oh Lord, how is it that I have not yet grown tired of life, when life has delivered to me a fate such as this? No, *I don't want to die. I want to dance one more dance, with Arturo, if he will allow me the pleasure that is. I want to insult one more tourist, one more Andaluz who dares to pass by my side. I want to live a thousand years more. After all, I am not yet a century old.*

Ah, the heart is willing, cariño, but the flesh, I fear, will not go on.

And then Vicente's baton descends, striking her once, twice, three times on the head.

God, he jokes nervously, *you'd think her head would be even harder than this.*

And then she is dead—oh, they are sure of this. They have placed their hands on her heart and listened for her breath. And there is no movement, not a breath or a sigh. Yes, she is dead. *Beaten to death by a stick,* as the old saying goes, *for in no other way would she die.*

It is just as well that she has died. For across town, amidst a raging fire, lies her great-grandson, the young, haunted Artur, his body ripped into a thousand bits by the explosion that shakes Canteira on a sultry Tuesday night.

EPILOGUE

1994

ONE MINUTE BEFORE THE TOLLING OF THE HOUR ON THE porcelain clock, the one with the flowers that her mother loved so very long ago and that is repaired now, can ding and dong with the precision of old. One minute before a new day in an empty house, in an unforgiving world, for eyes that think they have seen everything. And maybe not.

Ten years have passed since the debacle that took her son and grandmother both. Ten years of replaying the memory: the telephone call, *run, run*, fire everywhere and her son in bits, no body to hold, no body to mourn. Ten years have passed since she was taken hysterical to her home and then carried away from it again, for *la Reina*'s body lies upstairs in bed, blood spilling from the white crocheted bedspread onto the floor. *Dios!* The pounding in her head. Still today, Gloria's head hurts from the insanity of that Tuesday night. *Tuesday.* It used to be on Fridays that tragedies arrived.

During the last ten years, the family home has wilted, has fallen into a state of pathetic disrepair. Rooms have been shut, the parlour abandoned, clocks have been allowed to grind to a halt, except for the one with the porcelain flowers—strangely enough, Gloria has grown attached to it with the passing of time. At back, the garden is overgrown, the verandah is starting to crumble, and the rats have taken over basement and attic both. The walls, though, are the worst. The eternal humidity, the rain that never stops, has left its imprint on the blue walls in the kitchen, the green walls in the hall, giant stains, patches of black spreading unevenly throughout the once palatial house.

And Matilde has died. Over six years ago, but hers at least was a quiet death, a natural stopping of the heart. Since then, Gloria has lived in the kitchen, spends her time sitting in María *la Reina*'s Portuguese chair. There is little left for her to do now. The Encarna and Hope Hotel was shut down years ago, another victim of modernity, of the changes that have transformed the country, that have turned it into just another piece of Europe, the Europe they had once longed so fervently to join.

Outside, the town of Canteira, once a vibrant bustling place, is now only a shadow of its former self. Long past are the days when *contrabandistas* travelled through peddling their wares on the way to the coast, stopping only to tell their colourful stories of demons and wars inside the kitchen of the old *pensión*. Long forgotten also are the faces of the innumerable guests, dressed in their black wool and imported silks, who arrived in search of a cure for all their diseases of the liver and the skin inside the waters of the town's *balneario* and hot springs. Today, Canteira is a relic full of old people left behind by the urgent dreams of their children. Time, which has always moved slowly here, moves more slowly now that the world around the town speeds along like a top spinning. Now time crawls, plods on quietly, almost imperceptibly, adjusting itself ever more to the weight of a single heartbeat. At night, when the hands of the clock grind down even more and all of the sounds in the world are uttered in the darkness, the visions are even clearer still—Gloria in her yellow frock, waiting for the father who never came because when he did he was not what she wanted and she therefore dismissed forever the memory of him.

It is nine and a half years since the last Encarna woman came into the world. Ana's child, a child Ana insisted on naming María Cecilia Carmen Asunción Matilde Gloria de la Tierra. The priest had voiced some grave objections to *de la Tierra*—the world of late was growing increasingly batty with people naming their children all manner of strange things—Breogan, Guadalquiviria, and a host of unchristian and unpronounceable American names. *But de la Tierra? This child already has six names*, he told her. *And de la Tierra is not even a name. We are all from the earth in the end.* But Ana Martínez held firm. If her child was going to be baptized by the Church, the Church would have to accept all the names. That was how Artur would have wanted it, that was what he would have demanded, had he been there today. *Bueno,* Don Valentín, the aged parish priest, finally said. Enough tragedy had already come this young girl's way.

Gloria smiles—not at the long list of names given to her granddaughter or even the *de la Tierra* bit, but at Ana's determination, worthy of the Encarnas themselves. Perhaps it was this quality that Artur had seen in the girl.

Gloria had begun to visit her granddaughter only six months before. After almost ten years, she had donned her mourner's black, a dress that stretched to the floor, one that had belonged to *la Reina* once, and had appeared at the house of Ana Martínez for the first time, requesting to see her granddaughter *por favor.* Ana Martínez had refused all the pesetas thrown her way by Gloria, offered to her through lawyers and friends. Instead she had chosen to raise the child her way. With the new help offered by the state, the grants for this and the grants for that, Ana had educated herself slowly, become an administrative secretary, found a solid position in the Canteira town hall.

What do I call her? Gloria asked, when the rather serious child appeared before her—for although she had heard the story of the baptism from many a Canteira gossip's mouth, no one had bothered to tell her what name the girl is known by—this grandchild of hers who stood gravely before her now, a white ribbon tied smartly on her head, brown eyes settled fixedly on the ground.

María, Ana whispered softly and then disappeared quickly into the dark corners of her parents' house.

María. Of course, María. María whom she never fully forgave until her head had been smashed to bits. María, who had founded the line, weathered more storms than a million ships. María, once beautiful, then disfigured, and in her later years, Canteira's reigning Queen of Disease. María, founder of *pensións* and hotels, briber of *contrabandistas*, and lover of life to the very end, because she had wanted to live, had so much wanted to continue breathing for another five centuries, ten if God was feeling especially generous with her.

And then Gloria was crying, holding on to this other María, this granddaughter, too young to know what the tears were all about, but kind enough to wrap her arm instinctively around this crumbling heap, her *abuela* according to her mother, a woman she had seen today for the very first time.

After that the visits became regular, less awkward than the first, and she now strolled with her granddaughter proudly all over town.

Ay, Doña Gloria, the people say, *so glad to see you finally about.*

And then it is midnight. The porcelain clock begins to chime; the others join in later, each in their own time, each in their own way, a cacophony of disorder, a wayward shower of ticking minutes and endless days.

Acknowledgements

Although all the characters, situations, and relationships in this book are fictional, the narrative dealing with the region of Galicia and the history of twentieth-century Spain has been greatly informed by the work of many writers and scholars. The most important of these include Amando de Miguel, *La España de nuestros abuelos;* Manuel Rivas, *Galicia: El Bonsai Atlántico;* Ana Liste, *Galicia: Brujerías, superstición y mística;* X. Rolf Carballo, *Mito e Realidade da terra nai;* Xavier Costa Clavell, *Los Gallegos;* Nicolás Tenorio, *La Aldea Gallega;* Xosé Ramón Mariño Ferro, *La Medicina Popular Interpretada;* Álvaro Cunqueiro, *Fábulas y Leyendas de la Mar;* Jesús Rodríguez López, *Supersticiones de Galicia;* Ramón Villares, *Historia de Galicia*; Hugh Thomas, *The Spanish Civil War;* Paul Preston, *The Spanish Civil War;* Gabriel Jackson, *A Concise History of the Spanish Civil War;* Phillip Toynbee (ed.) *The Distant Drum;* David Mitchell, *The Spanish Civil War;* and Ian Gibson, *Fire in the Blood.*

I would like to thank Teresa Fernández Ulloa and Felix González Madrinán, two angels who provided shelter, food, and untold support during my research period in beautiful Santiago de Compostela, Spain, and Sela Bernárdez Gil and her husband Octavio Santamarina for doing the same in Vigo. Thanks also to the others who took the time to help, including Pastora, Pepe, Elba, Antón, Umberto, and Loli. Dr. Manuel Fernández Fermoso, besides being a valued family friend, provided instrumental guidance in the areas of Spanish history, medical issues, and the Knights Templar. And thank you to the beautiful Viguesa (by way of Brazil) Rosa, for relating the story of the grandmother who lost an eye and providing me with the seed to begin telling my own version. *Muchísimas gracias a todos.*

I am extremely grateful also to the first readers of this novel who provided invaluable feedback and encouragement when it was most needed: Chechi Stewart, John O'Callaghan, Mark Ely, Robert Castle, Jeff Miller, Linda Fleming, Jackie McKeown, Denise Coombs, Anita Herrmann, Julia Zipresz, and Giovanna Asaro. A great big thanks also to Martha Watson who believed from the first and who ensured that the book landed in the right hands at the right time.

This book would have been impossible to write were it not for the support provided over the years by two special men: the very wise Mohanlal P. Mehta (Bapuji) and his son, the very generous Chand Mehta who gave me work, a computer, and an office full of wonderful people where the novel was written. I thank also the Canada Council for providing the financial support that allowed me to dedicate myself to the task of writing for one glorious year.

I owe a very great debt to my family, Mamá, Papá, Andre, Mary, and Chechi and the new generation, David, Jackson, Daniel, and Maxwell, and to my husband Andrew Graham, editor extraordinaire and constant source of inspiration, love, and light.

And finally, a very earnest thank you to the fabulous group at HarperCollins, most especially Karen Hanson, for her wisdom and encouragement, and Iris Tupholme, a vibrant, positive spirit who has taught me much and has been instrumental in making this experience an extraordinary one.